Praise for the Novels of
Elizabeth Thornton

"Thornton skillfully combines Regency-style suspense, a roguish hero with a good heart, a heroine ahead of her time, a psychic curse, an evil stepmother, a budding book industry, and a truly twisted villain to make an unforgettable tale."
—*Booklist*

"Only an author of Thornton's talent could pull off a story as tangled with plotlines, as filled with memorable characters, as tingled with paranormal touches as her latest... One of the best books of the season. It's lush, rich, exciting, passionate, and humorous. What more could you want?"
—*Romantic Times*

"[A] fun, fast read. Ms. Thornton is one of the best storytellers in the historical romance genre. All of her characters are wonderfully written and her attention to detail is second to none."
—*A Romance Review*

"As multilayered as a wedding cake and just as delectable... [Thornton] excels at creating likable characters who play well off of each other... A memorable start to a new trilogy and a fine introduction to Thornton's work."
—*Publishers Weekly*

"Exhilarating Regency romantic suspense... Fans will gain plenty of pleasure from this fine historical."
—*The Best Reviews*

The Runaway McBride

Elizabeth Thornton

BERKLEY SENSATION, NEW YORK

THE BERKLEY PUBLISHING GROUP
Published by the Penguin Group
Penguin Group (USA) Inc.
375 Hudson Street, New York, New York 10014, USA
Penguin Group (Canada), 90 Eglinton Avenue East, Suite 700, Toronto, Ontario M4P 2Y3, Canada
(a division of Pearson Penguin Canada Inc.)
Penguin Books Ltd., 80 Strand, London WC2R 0RL, England
Penguin Group Ireland, 25 St. Stephen's Green, Dublin 2, Ireland
(a division of Penguin Books Ltd.)
Penguin Group (Australia), 250 Camberwell Road, Camberwell, Victoria 3124, Australia
(a division of Pearson Australia Group Pty. Ltd.)
Penguin Books India Pvt. Ltd., 11 Community Centre, Panchsheel Park, New Delhi—110 017, India
Penguin Group (NZ), 67 Apollo Drive, Rosedale, North Shore 0632, New Zealand
(a division of Pearson New Zealand Ltd.)
Penguin Books (South Africa) (Pty.) Ltd., 24 Sturdee Avenue, Rosebank, Johannesburg 2196,
South Africa

Penguin Books Ltd., Registered Offices: 80 Strand, London WC2R 0RL, England

This is a work of fiction. Names, characters, places, and incidents either are the product of the author's imagination or are used fictitiously, and any resemblance to actual persons, living or dead, business establishments, events, or locales is entirely coincidental. The publisher does not have any control over and does not assume any responsibility for author or third-party websites or their content.

THE RUNAWAY MCBRIDE

A Berkley Sensation Book / published by arrangement with the author

PRINTING HISTORY
Berkley Sensation mass-market edition / February 2009

Copyright © 2009 by Mary George.
Cover illustration by Jim Griffin.
Cover design by Diana Kolsky.
Interior text design by Kristin del Rosario.

ISBN: 978-0-425-22634-6

BERKLEY® SENSATION
Berkley Sensation Books are published by The Berkley Publishing Group,
a division of Penguin Group (USA) Inc.,
375 Hudson Street, New York, New York 10014.
BERKLEY® SENSATION and the "B" design are trademarks of Penguin Group (USA) Inc.

PRINTED IN THE UNITED STATES OF AMERICA

10 9 8 7 6 5 4 3 2 1

*This is for my family, past, present,
and the next generation.
And they know why.*

Chapter 1

DRUMORE CASTLE, SCOTLAND, 1885

*It was February, the coldest, most miserable February in Scot-*tish memory. Out on the North Sea a tempest raged, and fishermen had long since drawn in their nets and steered their boats to the safety of the harbor. Gusts of raging wind and torrential rains blasted the coastline, driving everyone to find shelter.

John Sievewright, the landlord of the local tavern, dried off a tankard as he glanced out the window at the overcast sky. "It's the witch's doing," he said. "Lady Valeria McEcheran," he added respectfully for the benefit of the stranger who had taken shelter from the storm and was nursing a whiskey in a dark corner.

The few locals in the bar bobbed their heads. They were well aware of the name of the celebrated witch who had come to live at the castle when she became a widow.

"Drumore Castle is her son-in-law's place," Sievewright felt obliged to add. He was a businessman first and foremost, and he made a point of making strangers feel welcome, especially strangers who ordered the best whiskey the house had to offer.

One of the locals took up the story. "When the storm dies, it will be all over for Lady Valeria."

"Aye," said another. "The witch will be gone, and another will take her place."

The landlord's wife straightened from the table she had been scouring. "What superstitious nonsense!" she declared. "No one believes in witches these days. We're living in the nineteenth century, for heaven's sake."

No one contradicted her. She was a newcomer to the area, having married Sievewright a scant ten years before. Besides, she was English. One had to make allowances for *furreigners*.

Mrs. Sievewright sucked in a breath when a sudden shriek came from outside.

"It's only the wind," her husband soothed.

An ancient graybeard spoke to his tankard of ale. "Could be a banshee," he offered. "They only comes out when someone is near death, someone like a witch. She's calling her own."

Mrs. Sievewright shivered. Her voice wasn't nearly as confident as before. "That's only a fairy tale. She can't be a witch. She is a great lady, isn't she?"

Another sudden shriek had the landlord's wife scurrying to the back of the bar counter. There were subdued chuckles, but not from the landlord. He looked at each customer with a steely eye. Few could withstand that hard stare, and they looked away.

"Dinna fash yersel, m'dear," Sievewright said, then, remembering that his wife was English, translated from the vernacular. "Don't upset yourself, my dear. It's not the storm that tells us her ladyship is not long for this world. The family is gathering. Her three grown grandsons are already there. They wouldna travel in this kind of weather unless they were sent for."

"What of the rest of the family?" There was a quaver in her voice. "I don't trust those trains. What if the wind has blown their train over? There have been accidents before now."

Her husband gave a reassuring laugh. "There will be no trains out in this weather." He spoke with as much confidence as he could muster. In fact, he'd never been on a train and wouldn't travel on one even if someone paid him. "Take my word for it, Esther. They'll be holed up in some comfortable inn at the border, waiting for the storm to pass."

The wind had lost some of its bluster, and the shrieks had died to a moaning lament.

"That would be the fairy bagpipes calling the witch home to her own," a voice piped up.

Someone coughed into his hand. Another slurped his beer.

Mrs. Sievewright knew when she was being mocked. She lit a candle from an oil lamp on the counter. "I'm going upstairs to see to the little ones," she said, her chin jutting aggressively.

"Aye," said her husband, "you do that, lass."

She pushed through the door to the vestibule and quickly mounted the stairs. The Sievewrights had three boys, only a year or two apart, and the hurricane-like storm had made no impression on them. They were snuggled together in the big bed, sleeping blissfully.

Her own three boys made her think of Lady Valeria's grandsons. They were very affectionate, by all accounts, and very attentive to their grandmother. That covered a multitude of sins in her eyes, and if the gossip that was rampant was to be believed, there were quite a few sins to cover.

Two were brothers, Alex and Gavin Hepburn. The

eldest, James Burnett, was their cousin, and one day he would be the Laird o' Drumore. James was viewed as a tragic figure who had turned to drink for solace when his wife died. He could drink anyone under the table, an admirable virtue in Scotland, though her own chapel folk would consider him the devil's disciple. Gavin was known as "the randy dandy," and that was viewed with a tolerant eye as well. Alex was a bit of a mystery. He kept to himself. What was known was that he was clever and worked at a government office in Whitehall.

She wondered how her own boys would fare when they, too, went into the world to make their way. She hoped they stayed close to home. Lady Valeria's grandsons all lived in London. It was nothing to them to hop on a train when they were needed at home. Money was no object. She shouldn't find fault with them. She'd left her mother and sisters in England when she'd come north to marry her John.

After setting her candle on a table, she walked to the window and drew back the lacy curtain. From this vantage point, she could see the lights of the castle, but only barely. There was a steep incline down to the rocky promontory on which the castle was built. With lights blazing, it was like a beacon to ships at sea, warning them away from the treacherous rocks. Tonight, it seemed to be calling the storm to itself.

She made a small sound of impatience. Wouldn't those old codgers in the bar laugh up their sleeves if they could read her mind? That was the thing about the Scots; she never knew when they were being serious and when they were not. Perhaps making fun of her was their way of saving face. What sane man wanted his neighbors to know that he believed in the old superstitions? Witches, sorcerers, banshees—those were old wives' tales.

Her thoughts shifted when her youngest son rolled out of bed onto the bare floorboards and began to howl.

In the four-poster bed in her chamber in the east tower, with its sweeping view of the North Sea, Lady Valeria smiled faintly. For the last hour or two, she had been drifting in and out of sleep. Occasionally, when the wind gave a sudden shriek, her eyes fluttered open, but the thick walls of the castle shut out the worst of the storm, and her dreams were barely disturbed. Her mind had drifted back in time to when she was a child. She could see quite clearly the faces of her brothers and sisters as they played their games in the extensive, overgrown gardens of their parents' home in Feughside.

Other faces flitted into her mind, other memories: Mungo McEcheran, in full Scottish regalia, the day they married; their daughters, Morag and Lucy, the mothers of her grandsons, taken from her before their time. Her soft smile faded. They were all gone, the people she loved best in the world, and it was more than time for her to join them. She wasn't afraid. She was an old, feeble woman, and frail age was a burden she no longer wished to endure. But before she made that final journey, she had a sacred duty to perform.

She turned her head on the pillow and focused her gaze on the three young men who lounged on the far side of the room, talking in whispers: her three grandsons.

Her heart sank. This was what her ancient line of Celtic diviners and seers had come to? Lady Valeria loved her grandsons dearly, but she could not deny that they lacked something essential for the heirs of the seers of Grampian. They seemed more English than Scot. She doubted there was one kilt among the lot of them. They knew no Gaelic worth mentioning, and the soft Scottish burr had been bred out of their accent by the years they'd spent in England.

A granddaughter would have given her some comfort. Females were more sensitive to what could not be grasped by sheer intellect. A man's intelligence was too easily corrupted by his carnal appetites.

She let out a little sigh. It did no good to torment herself like this. She had no say in the matter. The mantle would pass from her to the next generation, to one of her grandsons, and in spite of her ability to see into the future, she could not discern which one.

Her throat felt paper dry, and she swallowed. "What are the villagers saying?" she asked.

The muted conversation at the fireside died, and her grandsons filed over to her bed.

"Granny, you're awake."

That was Gavin, the youngest. Those sleepy, midnight-blue eyes shaded by sinfully long lashes made him too attractive for a woman's comfort. Her ladyship could well understand how he had gained his reputation with women. Nobody could resist his smile, not even she, who should know better.

"They're saying that the Witch of Drumore is on her deathbed." That was Alex, the scholar of the family, straight-faced and straight-spoken. It was hard to believe that as a child he'd been a tear-away, but that was before he'd discovered numbers. She wished he would discover girls.

"But they're verra respectful," Alex added, imbuing his voice with the accent of his youth.

His grandmother perceived that he had cracked a joke, and she let out a cackle of laughter. "There may be hope for you yet, Alex," she said.

Her gaze shifted to her eldest grandson, James. There was a glass in his hand, which he held out to her.

"If that," she said testily, "is Dr. Leiper's vile restorative, you can pour it away. I'll not depart this life with the stench of garlic on my breath."

"It's good Scotch whiskey," James replied, "distilled in Moray."

"In that case, I don't mind if I do."

As she took a minuscule sip, she gazed over the rim of her glass at the grandson who made her heart ache. James had been a widower now for four years, and those years had not been easy on him. Though he was the only son and his father's heir, he rarely came to Drumore. Some said that it was his genius for making money that absorbed all his time and energies. Others thought that he stayed away because the memories of his wife were too painful to be borne. Lady Valeria knew better. There was something else, something that even her finely tuned intuition could not discern.

They called her a witch, but really, her powers were limited. She could not read minds, or tell fortunes, or cast spells. Her gift was to see into the future. Sometimes she saw clearly, and at other times, as now, she saw through a glass darkly.

"Well, don't stand around like pallbearers," she said. "I'm not dead yet. Pull up chairs and sit ye down. I have something serious I want to say to you."

Her grandsons chuckled, but she was aware of the veiled glances they darted at each other as they did her bidding. They knew well enough what was on her mind. When they were children, they'd been enthralled by stories of the diviners and seers in her clan. They'd known that one from their own family would be chosen to carry on the tradition, but as they'd grown older, wiser, and more and more Anglified, they'd lost their innocence.

Without preamble, she said, "When I die, one or all of you—God help us—will inherit the gifts of your ancestors. You know what I'm talking about, so let's not bandy words."

Alex heaved a sigh, Gavin ran his finger under his collar, and James bolted his whiskey in a practiced movement that made her ladyship's brows snap together.

She gave each grandson a piercing look from narrowed eyes. "Don't look so worried. It's not in my power to choose my successor. With any luck, it may skip a generation, though I've never known that to happen. I console myself with the thought that sometimes the weakest vessels surprise us all."

Alex said, "I vote we go with skipping a generation. Granny, you'll not get much joy out of us. Well, look at us." He added helplessly, "We can't even speak Gaelic. We'd be no use as seers."

"What's a seer?" asked Gavin.

"Someone with second sight," replied James. He was looking around for the whiskey decanter. "Would someone mind telling me which of us is going to make the supreme sacrifice and produce the next generation of Grampian sorcerers?"

His question was met with stark silence.

"I thought as much," he said.

He found the decanter, topped up his glass, then took his chair again. "Go on, Granny. Tell us what's on your mind."

"It must be the air," her ladyship observed with a coy smile. "You're beginning to sound like Scotsmen again." She exhaled a long breath and went on, "I have a message for each of you, so listen well. I don't know what it means, and I doubt that you will, either. However, in the not too distant future, you would do well to remember my words and act accordingly. Gavin, take my glass away and give me your hand."

It looked as though Gavin would argue the point, but

when James kicked him surreptitiously on the ankle, he gave a pained smile, set his grandmother's glass aside, and extended his right hand. Lady Valeria held it loosely, but she did not look at it. She gazed into his eyes with an unnerving intensity. No one moved; not a sound was heard, not even the hiss of the gas lamps on the walls, only the frail rasp of an old woman's voice.

"Look to Macbeth. That's where your fate lies. You stand on the brink, Gavin. Fail Macbeth, and you will regret it to your dying day."

When she released his hand, Gavin gave an involuntary shudder.

"Alex?"

Alex meekly gave his grandmother his hand. "Calluses," she said, opening his fingers to stare at his palm. "Now, how would a man who works behind a desk come by these bumps?"

He shrugged indifferently. "I keep up with my fencing."

"Mmm," her ladyship intoned, searching his expression as though she doubted his words. There was nothing to read there. Of all her grandsons, Alex was the most adept at concealing what he was thinking and feeling.

She let out a sigh. "You will pass through fire," she said, "but it will not consume you if you trust your intuition. Logic will not help you. You will know what I mean when the time comes. Hold fast to what you feel, Alex. That's where you will find your salvation."

Gavin stifled a yawn and received another kick on the ankle from James.

"Thank you, Granny," Alex said. "You've given me a lot to think about."

Her ladyship gave a snort of derision. "Aye, you may thank me, but your gravity does not deceive me. There's none so blind as those who will not see, and you three are no better than those three wee blind mice in that cursed nursery rhyme. Disregard my words if you will, but you do so at your peril."

She ignored their feeble protests and looked at James. After setting aside his glass, he surprised her by taking her hand between his own and cradling it gently.

He spoke first. "You see how it is with us, Granny. You can't leave us, not yet. We're practically Sassenachs. Stay a while and tell us the old stories and teach us the old ways."

Her throat tightened. He'd had a harder row to hoe than his cousins. A shadow seemed to cling to him, as though all his dreams had faded away. She longed to help him, but her time was past. All she could do was point the way.

She spoke so softly that he had to put his ear to her lips and ask her to repeat herself. Inhaling a shallow breath, she whispered haltingly. "Your bride is in mortal danger, James. You must find her, or she will surely die. Don't despair. Your gift is to see into the future, and the future can be changed."

She saw the doubt in his eyes as he pulled back to stare at her. "I know, I know," she said querulously. "It doesn't make sense, not yet. Just remember my words, and in due course all will become clear to you."

James's cousins looked at him with raised brows. They had not heard their grandmother's message to him. He gave a slight shrug and lounged back in his chair.

Her ladyship seemed to be dozing, and Gavin turned to the others and said in an undertone, "Do you think we've been given a test, you know, whoever successfully completes his quest become the next"—he made a face— "grand master or whatever?"

James replied, "If it were that easy, all we'd need do is fail the test, then we would be free and clear."

Alex shook his head. "Sometimes I wonder about you

two. We're not living in the Dark Ages. This is the age of progress. Granny is a . . ." He had to search for the word. "A relic of a superstitious era. I no more believe in seers than I do in King Arthur and his knights of the round table."

Lady Valeria joined the conversation at this point. Without opening her eyes, she said, "Your trouble, Alex, is that you spend too much time with numbers." She opened her eyes. "Let me tell you that I have seen more of the world than you can possibly imagine. I was born at the turn of the century. I was in Brussels with my parents when Wellington met Napoleon at Waterloo. I've lived through other wars *and* the reigns of four monarchs as well as countless prime ministers. The changes I've seen—" She shook her head. "Trains from one end of the country to the other, gas to light our homes, water closets, and I don't know what all. I understand what is of this world as well as you. I'm asking you to pay attention to what is unworldly and unchanging."

"Granny," Alex hastily interrupted, "I did not mean—"

She waved him to silence. "I know what you meant. Make sure that you know what I mean." She looked at Gavin. "I don't know whether or not you are being tested, but those messages came from my heart. All I want is to see my grandsons happy. Promise me you won't forget my words."

They promised.

She beamed at them. "Now, make me happy by offering me a wee dram of *uisge beatha*."

It was one of the few Gaelic expressions they all understood.

"Slàinte Mhath!" said her ladyship.

"Slàinte Mhath!" her grandsons chorused as they knocked back their whiskey.

It was moment of complete harmony and happiness.

In the wee hours of the morning, with her three grandsons by her side, Granny McEcheran drew her last breath.

Chapter 2

This time, he wasn't dreaming. He was hallucinating. He, James Burnett, who had never demonstrated the slightest tendency to confuse imagination with reality, was slowly going out of his mind.

One heave sent the woman on top of him flying back on her bare rump. She squealed in fright and scrambled from the bed. Snatching up her chemise, she clutched it to her bosom as she backed away from him.

She was stunned. He was a regular customer. She thought she knew him, but this wild man with the fierce eyes looked like a savage who had just walked out of the jungle.

"One cry from me," she got out with a catch in her breath, "and big Andy will come crashing in here and break your frigging legs." He didn't move; he didn't say anything. He might have been a sleepwalker, and that emboldened her to say, "What got into you, Burnett? I've never seen you like this. Are you all right?"

James combed his fingers through his hair. Disoriented, he looked around him. Slowly, enlightenment dawned. He recognized the setting. He should. It was practically his second home, this superior brothel just around the corner from Crockford's on St. James's Street. This was how he spent most of his nights: an hour or two gambling in Crockford's, then seeking oblivion either in a bottle of whiskey or with a woman, sometimes with both.

"It was the mirror," he muttered, speaking to himself. "Who put that bloody mirror on the ceiling? It's... obscene."

He blinked rapidly, trying to dispel the grotesque picture of Granny McEcheran's reflection in the mirror peering down at him. He'd had too much to drink, he told himself. He was working too hard. His grandmother's death had affected him more deeply than he realized. No one had ever loved him as she had loved him, and now he felt bereft. She'd only been gone four or five months, but never a day went by when he did not think of her.

Hearing his own words, he winced. God in heaven, how much whiskey had he had to drink, anyway? If he went on in this vein, he'd soon be blubbering like a baby. He'd loved his granny well enough, he supposed, and she him, but not enough to explain how he'd lost his grip on reality.

Impatient with himself, oblivious of his nakedness, he reached for his clothes and began to dress.

Celeste—not her real name—edged onto a velvet upholstered chair and watched him warily. If it had been anyone but Burnett, she would have been out the door, but Burnett was openhanded. She could make more money in an hour with him than she could in a week with her other customers. And he wasn't demanding. A quick romp on the bed seemed to satisfy him. He spent more time drinking his whiskey than he did in pleasuring his body. In fact, it seemed to her that pleasure was the last thing on his mind. Nor did he care which girl he got, but they all made sure that they each had their turn with Burnett. And why not? It was easy money, and fair was fair.

That's how she thought of him now: easy money. Not so the first time she'd set eyes on him when she was the new girl. Her calloused heart had damn near melted. He was tall, broad-shouldered, with the harshly sculpted features that she'd seen in pictures of medieval knights. Someone had told her that he was a baron, and she could well believe it. As it turned out, he was one of those barons who had made his fortune in railroads, quite an achievement for a man in his early thirties. But his money didn't seem to bring him happiness. For all his wealth and good looks, he was still a dour-faced Scot.

An openhanded dour-faced Scot, she reminded herself, and if she wanted to earn her money, she had better do her job.

"You're not leaving already?" She edged off the chair and let her chemise slip to the floor. "You've only just got here."

He looked up with a distracted air. "What?"

She was beginning to lose her temper. She had her pride. She wasn't a common prostitute. She was a high-class lady of pleasure whose beauty and talents were much in demand by the well-heeled clients who patronized the Golden Fleece. A girl couldn't just walk in off the street and get a job here. Beauty was commonplace. She'd had to learn how to walk with an air, talk without an accent, dress and undress so that her clients would know they were paying for quality. Burnett paid more attention to the quality of the whiskey than he did to the girls.

She jiggled her shoulders and thrust out her breasts. "Look at me, Burnett."

He looked.

She hadn't met the man yet whom she couldn't bring to a quivering climax just by jiggling her well-endowed anatomy. This time, she jiggled her hips. That was better. Now she had his full attention. But just when she thought she had him, he took a step back.

He pressed a hand to his brow. "This isn't going to work." He gave her an apologetic smile. "It's not you. It's me."

She thought she understood. "Burnett," she chided, "don't you know that the best way to forget one woman is to lose yourself in another? I can help you forget."

He shrugged into his coat. "Tell that to my granny," he said.

She was puzzling over his words when he pulled a wad of notes from his pocket. After peeling off two, he slapped them into the silver salver on the dresser and left without another word.

It was only a five-minute walk to his house in St. James's Square, and he made straight for home like a fox going to ground. In the last little while, he'd been plagued by nightmares, but this was the first time he'd hallucinated when his eyes were wide open. He gave himself the same lame excuses—he was drinking too much; he was working too hard; he wasn't getting enough sleep—but deep down he feared the worst. Either he was going slowly out of his mind, or Granny McEcheran had sunk her teeth into him, and she would never let go.

He knew what Alex would say. His cousin would point out that this was the age of progress and that there had been amazing advances in every field of knowledge, including medicine. He should consult one of those new doctors who

called themselves psychiaters and who studied the workings of the mind.

He didn't need a psychiater to tell him what was
wrong with him. He'd been perfectly well until Granny
McEcheran had whispered her prophecy in his ear: *"Your
bride is in mortal danger. You must find her, or she will
surely die."*

He hadn't understood until the nightmares started. Not
his bride, but McBride, Faithless McBride, as he'd taken
to calling her in his own mind. She'd promised to wait for
him, but her promise turned out to be worthless. For the
last eight years, he'd deliberately suppressed all thoughts
of her, but that was before the nightmares started. Now he
couldn't get her out of his mind.

His butler opened the door before he had time to lift the
knocker. That was Hallam, always anticipating his master's
needs. He was in his sixties, short and rotund, with a ruddy
complexion and silver hair. The only fault that James could
find with his butler was that he talked too much.

"There's a fire burning in the library, sir, and—"

James waved him away. "Not tonight, Hallam. I think
I'll go straight to bed." He crossed the hall and made for
the stairs.

"Shall I bring you your usual nightcap, sir?"

James hesitated on the bottom step and rubbed the fur-
row from his brow. "Ah, no. Not tonight."

For once, Hallam was speechless.

As he climbed the stairs, James flung over his shoulder,
"Coffee, Hallam. And lots of it."

Upon reaching his chamber, James flung himself into a
chair. In spite of himself, his eyes were drawn to the cheval
mirror that was positioned to one side of the long window.
Gritting his teeth, he got up and ambled over to it. He hadn't

known how tense he was until he looked in the mirror and saw nothing more frightening than his own reflection.

He grinned sheepishly and shook his head. "The drink is getting to you, Burnett, m'lad," he said. "Go on the way you're doing, and you'll come to an early grave." He turned from the cheval glass, then turned back again. "By the way, Granny, just in case you're listening, if you want me to find the McBride, you're going to have to tell me where to look. She doesn't want to be found, not by me. She made that abundantly clear. So, please, no more nightmares and no more apparitions. You practically scared the hell out of me tonight when…ah, well, we won't go into that. A man is entitled to a little privacy, and—" He stopped and shook his head. "What am I saying? It was nothing but an alcohol-induced hallucination. From now on, I'm going to stick to milk and lemonade."

After a drinking a pot of coffee sans whiskey to flavor it, he was feeling quite virtuous and sober enough to attempt sleep, so he got into bed and closed his eyes. He tossed, he turned, and eventually he focused his thoughts on the delectable Celeste. A man would have to have one foot in the grave not to be affected by her luscious form. So what was his excuse? Demon drink? The spirit was willing, but the flesh was weak. But it was more than that. He craved something genuine, not something bought and paid for. There wasn't much difference between the women at the Golden Fleece and the debutantes who hoped to snare a husband before the season ended. All they wanted was to part him from his money. At least at the Golden Fleece he wouldn't be committing himself to a life sentence.

His thoughts drifted, and he slipped into an uneasy sleep.

The McBride. A mane of copper curls. White throat and shoulders. Eyes as deep and clear as a Scottish loch.

And a heart as black as sin.

One part of his mind knew what would happen next, and he tried to tear himself from his dream, but it was no use. Faith's image faded, and he was there again, standing outside the wrought-iron gates that barred his entrance to the grounds of a ruined stately mansion. As is the way of dreams, he passed through the gates without opening them and found himself in a marble foyer with a cantilevered staircase rising in a graceful sweep to the floors above. Faith was somewhere here, and she was not alone. A figure was waiting for her in the shadows, someone with hatred in his heart and murder on his mind.

Fear rose in James's throat, and he began to run. He wasn't in a house, he was in a labyrinth. He was shouting Faith's name, but all that came back to him was the panicked echo of his own voice. He knew that he was doing the wrong thing, that he should slow down and look inside his own mind. He had the gift of second sight, but he had never used it, had never wanted to until now.

A terrible scream pierced his mind, and he knew he was too late.

He wasn't too late. The future could be changed. Isn't that what Granny McEcheran tried to impress upon him? He could change the future.

Gasping, soaked with sweat, he dragged himself from his nightmare. Hunched over, he sucked air into his lungs in great, greedy gulps.

He wasn't drunk, and he wasn't hallucinating. He was stone-cold sober. For his own peace of mind, he knew what he had to do. He had to find Faith McBride if only to satisfy himself that she wasn't in harm's way.

As the minutes passed and the nightmare faded, he began to feel foolish. He debated whether he should do anything at all to find Faith. Their meeting was hardly likely to be cordial. Finally, he shrugged. He wasn't planning to climb the Matterhorn. All he wanted was a good night's sleep, and if that meant he had to renew his acquaintance with Faith McBride, so be it.

The following morning, James was at breakfast when his cousins came calling. Rising to his feet, he said, "This is a surprise. I was thinking of calling on *you*. Sit down, sit down. You'll join me for..."

His voice died away as his gaze shifted to Gavin. His cousin sported an ugly bruise on his left eye. "Brawling?" said James. "I thought you had outgrown that."

Gavin laughed. "All in a good cause. Macduff, say 'how do you do' to your cousin."

James's gaze dropped to the floor. A huge, shaggy sheepdog with smiling eyes offered him a paw.

Alex said, "Gavin found the dog in a lane off Covent Garden. Some young bucks thought it would be fun to beat him to death. Gavin disagreed."

"So did Macduff," said Gavin. He was at the sideboard, helping himself to a hearty breakfast.

"What were you doing in a lane behind Covent Garden? It's notorious for footpads and thugs."

"I was seeing a lady home." Gavin flashed James a grin. "I won't be doing it again. She didn't like Macduff any more than he liked her."

James sank back in his chair as both cousins filled their plates. He was reflecting that Alex and Gavin were more like brothers to him than cousins. They'd spent a good deal of time together when they were infants, as was to be expected when their mothers were sisters. They'd fought a lot; they'd laughed a lot; they'd grown up to be the best of friends. They were still the best of friends though not as easy and carefree as they once were. It was to be expected, he supposed, now that they were older and had followed different paths. Gavin had yet to find his way; he, James, was the man of commerce; and Alex . . . well . . . Alex was a bit of a mystery. He was too athletic to spend all his days behind a desk. Working for the government could mean many things. And there were those calluses on his fingers.

As Alex sat down at the table, Gavin shoved a heaping plate of sausages and kidneys under Macduff's nose. "Now mind your manners," said Gavin. "Remember you're a gentleman."

Macduff cocked his head to the side, then nibbled delicately on the end of a sausage, but as soon as Gavin's attention was diverted, he swallowed the sausage whole, then started on another.

"Some gentleman," said Alex.

"Macduff," said James musingly. "Didn't he kill Macbeth?" When Gavin looked at him blankly, he elaborated, "Shakespeare, Gavin, or haven't you read the play?"

"Of course I've read the play." He looked at the dog, then back at James. "I know what you're thinking. You're thinking of Granny's prophecy, and that is ridiculous. I pulled the name out of thin air. I could just as easily have called him . . ." He fumbled for a word. "Dog."

Alex sighed.

James rested his linked fingers on the flat of the table. "It has started, hasn't it?" he said. "Granny's prophecies? They're coming home to roost."

"You, too?" said Alex.

James nodded. "I have frightful dreams."

Gavin said glumly, "I have visions, premonitions. I didn't go into that lane by chance. I could see in my mind's eye poor Macduff cornered by those louts. I went into that lane with my cane swinging, determined to rescue him."

"It's the same for me," said Alex. "For the past few months, I've been trying to unmask someone who has been leaking information to the other side. I caught him in the act, but it wasn't my powers of deduction that unmasked him. I . . . sensed what he was up to and set a trap."

"Who knew," said James laconically, "that the War Office was so exciting?"

Alex turned his head and gave James a level look. "I didn't say I worked for the War Office. I work for the government in various capacities."

James smiled and nodded. "Well, we've all heard that one before, haven't we? Don't worry, your secret is safe with us." Before Alex could respond, he went on, "What about that new breed of doctors you mentioned? 'Psychiaters,' I believe you called them. Didn't you think of consulting one of them?"

Alex buttered a slice of toast. "I thought about it, but Granny's medicine was stronger. Anyway, how could I explain Granny McEcheran to a tribe of unbelievers? They wouldn't understand."

Gavin interrupted. "But what are we going to do?"

"Grin and bear it," said his brother stoically. "What else can we do?"

When the cousins got up to leave, Alex turned to James with a sheepish smile. "It probably means nothing," he said, "but if I were you, I'd start reading the newspapers from cover to cover. That may help your nightmares."

James lost no time in following his cousin's advice. As soon as they left the house, he had his butler bring him that morning's paper.

Chapter 3

❦

Faith felt a little buzz of excitement as she walked briskly along Woburn Walk to the bookshop and lending library on the corner of Woburn Place. She was on her way to collect the responses to the advertisement she had placed in all the London papers, and she had high hopes that the mystery that had consumed her waking and sleeping hours these last few weeks would finally be solved.

From time to time, she stopped to admire something in the shop windows: an antique necklace, furniture, rare books, finely tooled boots, and leather goods. There wasn't much to tempt her here. A teacher's income did not stretch to such luxuries. Besides, she was lingering for a purpose. In the last week or so, whenever she left the school, she'd felt vaguely uneasy, as though someone was watching her. It could be the result of a mild attack of conscience. Teachers weren't supposed to slip away during luncheon to attend to personal business. Questions might be asked, such as why she was using Pritchard's Bookshop as a mailing address when it was customary for teachers to have all their correspondence sent to the school.

The reflections in the shop windows showed nothing to alarm her. There were plenty of people about, for the shops in the walk were quite well-known, though not as prestigious as the shops in Mayfair—not that she ever ventured into that part of town. Bloomsbury was far enough away from Mayfair to make it unlikely that she would come face-to-face with any of her former acquaintances. And even if she did, no one would recognize her in the drab uniform that schoolteachers and governesses commonly wore. Ladies of fashion were clothed in expensive fabrics with bustles, flounces, and a profusion of decoration. Schoolteachers wore plain, serviceable gowns and modest bonnets to match their modest occupation.

Anyway, this was July. In the heat of the summer, the society ladies she once mingled with would have retired to their country estates or they would be visiting some fashionable watering hole.

A little bell above the door rang when she entered the shop. Mr. Pritchard was at the counter in conversation with a customer, but he greeted her with his usual friendly smile and salute. She turned to one of the book stacks and began to scan the various titles as she waited her turn. This part of the transaction always made her nervous, though she wasn't doing anything reprehensible. All she wanted was to protect her privacy. She didn't want strangers to know where she lived any more than she wanted her fellow teachers to know what she was up to. Too many letters arriving at the school for one teacher, a teacher who rarely received any letters, might lead to awkward questions she didn't want to answer.

When the bell over the door rang again, and another customer entered the shop, she opened a book at random and idly flicked through it. All was quiet in the shop, so she looked toward the counter to see if Mr. Pritchard was free. A man blocked her view, and her gaze shifted to him.

The light was behind him, so she narrowed her eyes as she studied him: dark hair, broad shoulders, lean frame. She could not see his face clearly. He might have been anyone, except that he exuded an aura of energy and confidence that touched a nerve deep inside her.

He took a step toward her, then another, and finally she could see his face. He was leaner than she remembered, his black brows knitted in concentration, his features hard and uncompromising, but there was the same keen intelligence in his tawny eyes, the same predatory gleam.

"Faith," he said. "I thought it was you."

James Burnett.

She was having trouble breathing. Her knees were buckling, and the book she had been leafing through slipped from her fingers to fall with a clatter to the floor.

When he held out his hand, she shied away.

"Faith," he said. "Are you all right?"

She had rehearsed in her mind what she would say to him if she ever had the misfortune to meet him again. No recriminations. No tears. No regrets. She would simply turn her back on him and walk away. She had not realized that her control was so fragile, especially now that he was here in person. All the pain and humiliation she'd thought she'd suppressed tasted as bitter and as fresh as though it had happened yesterday.

"Don't touch me!"

His hand dropped away. In contrast to her stinging tone, his was mild. "You looked as though you were about to faint. I only wanted to help."

Damn! Damn! Damn! She was cowering like a rabbit. This wasn't how she wanted to appear to this man. Her self-respect demanded that she act with some dignity.

Her chin lifted a fraction. "You startled me. I thought you were a stranger." She gave a choked laugh. "What am I saying? You are a stranger. I thought I knew you once, a long time ago, but I was mistaken. Please stand aside and let me pass."

He disregarded her dignified speech. "You're as white as a sheet. You'd better sit down before you fall down."

She steadied herself by resting one hand on a shelf. Half-formed suspicions began to crowd into her mind. The coincidence of his presence in Bloomsbury at the precise moment she stepped into Mr. Pritchard's shop was either the sheerest bad luck, or it was no coincidence at all. Was he the one who was stalking her?

"What are you doing in Bloomsbury?" she asked abruptly.

"I could ask you the same question. Look, can't we have a civil conversation?"

Her voice reeked of sarcasm. "You're eight years too late. We have nothing to say to one another."

With alarming deliberation, he took another step toward her and bent his head to hers. Her stomach lurched, but she kept her chin up. She'd been right to call him a stranger, she thought. He'd always seemed self-assured and capable of achieving whatever he wanted, but the hardness in him had been tempered by an odd charm. This man was as charming as a slab of marble.

"Speak for yourself," James said, his voice as hard-edged as his expression. "There's plenty I want to say to you."

She couldn't bear to go over ancient history. The thought of having her feelings stripped bare made her feel sick inside.

His eyes narrowed on her face. "Take my hand, Faith."

She pressed her fingers to her brow. "I'd as soon give my hand to a—"

She squealed when he stooped down and scooped her

into his arms. Her first instinct was to beat him on the head with her reticule, but the strings had become hopelessly knotted on her wrist, and she could not get to it. The urge to hit him passed when her head began to swim. Her arms and legs felt as if they'd turned to water.

"Mr. Pritchard," James roared. "Miss McBride is unwell. She needs to sit down."

Mr. Pritchard came hastening down the aisle, his chubby face furrowed with anxiety. "Through there," he said, pointing to a door at the end of the aisle. "My little parlor."

He pushed by them and opened the door. "Shall I send for the doctor?"

"A glass of water," said Faith, trying to sound decisive but managing only a pathetic wheeze. "I don't need a doctor."

As Mr. Pritchard hurried away to do her bidding, James settled her on a leather sofa. He then proceeded to remove her bonnet and began on the buttons of her coat.

That brought her to her senses. Slapping his hands away, she sat up. "Stop fussing!" Her voice was testy. "There is nothing the matter with me except that I have not eaten today."

She frowned when she saw the ironic smile drifting across his face. "What?" she demanded.

"It's common practice, when a lady has swooned, to loosen her clothes. Trust me, Faith, I have no designs on your virtue. I was simply trying to be helpful."

His words brought to mind other times he'd unbuttoned her coat, and not only her coat, but her dress, her stays, her...Hot color rushed into her cheeks, and she quickly looked up at him.

The mockery in his eyes faded, and he let his breath out slowly. "The electricity is still there, isn't it, Faith? We may not want it, but it's still there." He lowered his head to hers.

Against her lips, he whispered, "You feel it, too, don't you, Faith?"

She felt the swift rise and fall of her breasts. The muscles in her throat tightened. A heartbeat of silence went by, then another. She made a small sound of protest, then froze as his mouth touched hers.

He didn't increase the pressure. He was waiting for her to give him permission. It was all so familiar, just like the first time he'd kissed her. She hadn't known what to expect then and had been overwhelmed by the sudden rush of sensation that sensitized her skin and quickened her breathing. Without reserve, she had melted against him and fused her lips to his.

It wasn't going to happen this time. James Burnett had torn her heart and pride to shreds. She would be a lunatic if she let him do it again.

The thought was timely. With every ounce of strength, she strained against his shoulders and pushed him away. No words were spoken. Only the harsh sound of their breathing broke the silence.

Mr. Pritchard returned at that moment with the glass of water. Dragging her eyes from James's probing stare, Faith reached for it and drank greedily.

Mr. Pritchard hovered anxiously in the background. "Is there anything else I can get you?" he asked.

She managed a feeble smile. "No. Thank you. I'll be fine. Your customers will be wondering where you are."

Pritchard glanced from one to the other, as if he sensed the charged atmosphere and was reluctant to leave Faith alone with James. "If you're sure," he said slowly, looking at Faith.

Faith had no wish to be left alone with James, but she had even less desire to become involved in a public scene, so she nodded and smiled and asserted that she was feeling much better. On that assurance, Mr. Pritchard shuffled out of the room.

James's voice was laced with irony. "I beg your pardon. Shall we say that auld lang syne got the better of me? Old times' sake, Faith. That's all it was. It won't happen again."

She wanted to say something cutting, but she wasn't up to it. "Auld lang syne," she murmured. "Yes. That's all it was."

To give herself time to think, she began to sip slowly from her glass. She just wanted James to go away, but James Burnett had the tenacity of a bulldog. No one could make him do what he did not want to do. That was what had crushed her all those years ago. No one could make James Burnett do what he did not want to do. So he'd asked her to wait, had gone home to Scotland, and promptly become engaged to his childhood sweetheart.

She felt the sting in her eyes, and suddenly it was all too much for her. She put down her glass. Without looking at him, she said, "Do you think you could find something for me to eat? As I said, I haven't eaten a thing today, and I know Mr. Pritchard keeps a bag of biscuits under the counter."

Closing her eyes, she sank against the back of the sofa and sighed. James said something harsh under his breath, but it was not until she heard his steps cross to the door and proceed down the aisle that she came to life. She knew where the back door was, and it took her only a moment to gather her things and exit the premises into the lane. She didn't walk; she ran. One lane led to another, then another. When she was sure that he was not following her, she stopped in a doorway to catch her breath.

He had tracked her to Pritchard's. It would not be long before he tracked her to the school. At least when that happened she would be over the shock of seeing him again.

What did he want with her? That was the question that nagged at her mind. There was nothing he could say to make amends for his unscrupulous conduct. She'd thought she'd put the past behind her. It seemed inconceivable that he would want to rake over old coals.

Or perhaps she was making too much of it. Perhaps it really was a chance encounter. Perhaps he was as shocked as she, only he was better at concealing his true feelings.

She gave up trying to sort it out.

At least, if they should meet again, she'd have herself well in hand. No recriminations. No tears and no regrets. And no memories to shatter her control. James Burnett was dead to her.

She stopped in her tracks. Damn the man! Damn! Damn! Damn! He'd made her forget to collect her letters from Mr. Pritchard. She looked over her shoulder and suppressed a shiver. She couldn't go back, not after running away. What could she say to explain her behavior? She was over him. He was nothing to her now, and her exaggerated response was nothing more than...than...than...It was just as he said: auld lang syne.

Satisfied with her explanation, she struck out toward the school.

James was aware of her sudden departure when he'd done no more than take a few steps into the aisle. He didn't have to turn around and go back to the parlor to verify what he knew. His mind was so focused on Faith that he could feel the vacuum she'd left behind.

He wasn't sorry that she'd run away. He'd thought he was up to seeing her again, but he'd lied to himself. Faith McBride in person was far more lethal than his faded memories of her. Despite the passage of time, she was still as beautiful as he remembered; she still had that glow from within that softened her features. If only she'd been fat and frumpy, his brain might still be functioning, and he wouldn't be as hard as a rock.

His hands fisted at his sides. He had to get a grip on himself if he was to keep his promise to his granny. Next time he met the faithless McBride, he'd make damn sure that he kept his hands to himself.

On that virtuous resolve, he joined Mr. Pritchard at the counter and waited patiently as he served a customer.

This was not the first time he'd visited Pritchard's shop. He'd taken Alex's advice and started to read the morning newspapers from cover to cover. The clue to Faith's where-abouts had come in one of the advertisements.

"Wanted, information about Madeline Maynard, for-merly of Oxford. Apply to Miss F. McBride, Pritchard's Bookshop, Woburn Walk, Bloomsbury."

He hadn't known what to expect on his first visit—that she owned the bookshop or lived on the floor above it? He'd soon come to see that Pritchard's was not only a book-shop but also a letter box for people who either worked in the area or did not wish their mail to be sent to their own homes. It made him wonder what Faith had to hide.

Mr. Pritchard was a canny man and could not be made to divulge one scrap of information on Faith. Hence James's encounter with her today. Now that Pritchard knew that Faith and he were acquainted, however, the old man might be more forthcoming. Leastways, that was what James hoped. He had no wish to spend another morning patrol-ling back and forth along Woburn Walk on the odd chance that he might catch a glimpse of Faith. Besides, he doubted she would show her face in Pritchard's for a long time to come. In all likelihood, she would send a friend to collect her letters, and he would be none the wiser.

Pritchard counted out a customer's change, waited a moment until he was at the door and out of earshot, then turned to James with an anxious frown. "How is Miss McBride?"

"Much better," James returned. "I took her outside for a breath of fresh air, and she decided to return home at once."

Pritchard's bushy eyebrows snapped together. Bristling, he said, "And you did not go with her to see her safe to her own door?"

"She wouldn't allow it."

The old man's frown gradually relaxed. "School rules," he said and shook his head. "She'd find herself mired in trouble if she returned to the school in the company of a gentleman."

"She's a teacher, then?"

Pritchard's look was frankly suspicious. "I thought you and Miss McBride were friends."

James saw his mistake and quickly corrected it. "And so we were, a long time ago, when she was a..." He searched for the right word. "A debutante. I was surprised to see her today, surprised and dismayed. She seems to have..." He let his words hang, inviting a response.

Pritchard sighed and finished the sentence for him. "Fallen on hard times? That was my impression, too. A debutante, you say? I can well believe it. She's a lady, all right. Always a pleasant word from her, never forgets to ask after my grandchildren. Breeding, it always tells, you know." He sighed again.

The silence stretched. Finally, James said, "I'd like to help her. Oh, not personally, but I'm sure my aunt, who is the soul of tact, would be more than happy to make Miss McBride's acquaintance."

Pritchard scratched his chin and studied James thoughtfully, taking in the cut of his tailoring, his pristine neck-cloth, the quality of his leather gloves. Finally, he nodded. "The school is round the corner from Tavistock Square. You can't miss it. There's a sign out front, St. Winnifred's School for Girls. It's a big building on extensive grounds."

He broke off when two customers appeared at the counter. James thanked Pritchard for his assistance and promptly left. At the end of the street, he hailed a hansom to take him to his club in St. James's, and he settled back on the banquette to review what he'd learned from Pritchard.

He had, of course, lied to Mr. Pritchard. Faith had not been a debutante when he'd first met her, though in his eyes, no debutante could have held a candle to her. She was Lady Beale's paid companion, serenely beautiful, well-bred, and though her gowns were modest and Faith never pushed herself forward, she was the girl all the debutantes loved to hate. Envy was at the root of their dislike, of course, because Faith was the girl all the young bucks loved to moon over.

At nineteen, she'd been tall and slender, with glossy copper hair pinned in a simple chignon, a flawless complexion, and a cool-eyed stare that could depress any ardent young man who overstepped the line of gentlemanly conduct.

He'd watched the performance from the wings with a cynical eye. Those young bucks could moon as much as they wanted, but he doubted they had marriage on their minds. Marriage was a serious business, even in these enlightened times, involving dowries, contracts, and family connections. As a penniless orphan, Faith wasn't in the running, and she knew it.

She didn't fit in with the upper crust of polite society, mostly because she had to earn her own living. As he remembered, her father had been an Oxford don, but when he died, Faith had supported herself by taking the first job that offered: paid companion to Lady Beale.

Faith reminded him of himself when he'd been sent, against his will, to school in England. He hadn't fitted in, either. Looking back, he had to admit that it was largely his own fault. He'd got into one fistfight after another, proving to those superior English boys that he was as good as they were. It hadn't helped him to make friends. Those school years were the loneliest of his life.

Faith wasn't in a position to fight back, and Lady Beale seemed unaware of the snubs and slights her companion suffered, so he'd taken Faith under his wing. That was something that had always puzzled him—why he had decided to take a hand in things. He wasn't exactly a party animal. In fact, he only attended these functions because he'd been invited by men of influence who were crucial to financing his business ventures. Though he was very young, he'd already amassed his first fortune. Railroads were his passion, and though the railway mania was long over, there was plenty of money to be made in reconstruction, both in Scotland and in England.

So, he'd attended some reception or other, and that was where he had met Faith.

He was twenty-four to her nineteen. He should have known better than to think their friendship could remain platonic. He discovered his mistake at a Christmas ball when he'd kissed her carelessly under the mistletoe.

That careless kiss had rocked him back on his heels. After that, he couldn't keep his hands off her. One liberty led to another. He'd known damn well that the only solution for them was marriage. So they'd planned their lives together, but before they could publish the news of their engagement, his company in Scotland was threatened with bankruptcy, and he had to return to Edinburgh to set things right.

It had taken longer than he thought it would. Bankruptcy was the least of his worries. It seemed that his second-in-command had been bleeding the company dry for his own gain and had left James to face the lawsuits shareholders were threatening to bring against him. It hadn't been easy to raise the money to pay them off. And that was all he could think about: paying off his shareholders. It had never occurred to him that he had to worry about Faith, too.

He'd had to persuade some canny bigwig financiers that he could turn things around and make his company pay. In hindsight, he didn't know how he'd pulled it off. He was ambitious but, all the same, he was only a fledgling compared to them. Yet they'd taken a chance on him and made themselves a tidy profit in the bargain.

A memory slipped into his mind: Faith, her gray eyes wide and trusting when she'd promised to wait for him.

He'd known something was wrong when her letters stopped, so he'd traveled back to London to find out what was going on. No one knew where she was, not even Lady Beale. All she could tell him was that Faith had handed in her notice and gone off with some young buck called Alastair Dobbin, who was escorting her to friends in Dorset, or was it Derbyshire?

What it came down to was that Faith and Mr. Dobbin had disappeared into thin air.

The coach hit a pothole and lurched to the side. The sudden jolt cleared his head, and his mouth twisted in a humorless smile. So much anguish over so little! He wasn't the man he was then. As he kept reminding himself, there was no point in going over the past. It was the future he should be focused on. Faith was heading into danger. Why? How?

He dwelled on the advertisement he'd read in the paper. She wanted information on Madeline Maynard. Who was Madeline Maynard? How could he find out?

If he was to protect Faith, he had to get close to her, as close as her own shadow. There was the rub. She had made it perfectly obvious that he was the last person she would turn to.

He couldn't allow her feelings or his to stand in the way. This was a matter of life and death. One way or another, he would get close to Faith; then, when he was satisfied that she was no longer in danger, he would walk away and never look back.

Chapter 4

It was after supper before Faith had a chance to compare notes with her friend, Lillian Summers. At that time of day, the school was practically deserted, for nearly all the girls were day pupils. The boarders were mostly the daughters of diplomats who served in foreign embassies or girls whose parents lived far from London but wanted their daughters to have the cachet of having graduated from St. Winnifred's. That was the one thing that all the parents had in common: they wanted the progressive kind of education that was coming into vogue, the kind of education that would equip a young woman to go on to a university, or enter the professions, or fulfill whatever destiny she chose.

On entering the room, Faith went straight to the gas ring and put a kettle of water on to boil. Lily set out two mugs and measured two heaped spoons of cocoa powder into each one. She was a willowy young woman with flaming red hair that was tamed by a severe black ribbon. Her eyes, surprisingly, were as dark as the powder she was measuring into the mugs.

"Burnett!" she exclaimed, hostility making her voice vibrate. "At Pritchard's? Burnett the brute? The bounder? The scoundrel? *That* Burnett?"

Lily's outrage came as no surprise to Faith. She was a loyal friend. They'd known each other since they'd met when Faith was Lady Beale's companion and Lily was companion to Mrs. Rowatt, Lady Beale's sister, so they'd seen a good deal of each other. Their employers had not been demanding, but the girls had found that life on the periphery of society, where they were little better than servants, both wearing and depressing. They had become confidantes, sharing all the trials and tribulations—and the humor—of the daily round of a paid companion.

In spite of their different temperaments, they seemed to complement one another. Faith, however, had learned the value of diplomacy in her dealings with the upper classes. Her livelihood depended on it. Lily was fiery and outspoken. It was that tendency to speak her mind that had cost Lily her job with Mrs. Rowatt. According to Lily, it was the best thing that ever happened to her. She'd accepted a post as a teacher in a girls' school in Cheltenham where, she said, she'd found her calling. Lily was born to be a teacher.

Faith would have gone with her, but by that time, she had met James, and she couldn't bring herself to make the change. A year later, crushed and disillusioned, she was glad to make the change and even more glad that her closest friend was there to jostle her out of her misery. Lily had no patience with an easy sympathy. *Keep busy* was her remedy for a broken heart, and Faith tried to live up to it. In time, the pain became manageable and, as one year slipped into the next, the image of James Burnett faded to the darkest corner of her mind.

Until she had come face-to-face with him today. God in heaven, what had come over her? She'd felt as though a shard of glass had entered her heart, and she'd wanted him to know how much she despised him. After so many years, she should have felt nothing. What she should have done was turn on her heel and stalk out.

"Faith, did you hear me?"

Pulled from her thoughts, she looked at her friend. "Yes," she said, "*that* Burnett," and she pulled a chair up to the empty grate.

"What did he say?"

Faith winced. "I didn't give him a chance to say anything." She shook her head in disbelief. "Oh, Lily, you wouldn't have recognized me. I kept telling myself to be dignified, but when I opened my mouth, I let fly at him like a fishwife."

"Hah!" declared Lily. "When I remember what that bounder did to you, I'm surprised you didn't let fly at him with an ax."

Lily had a lot more to say about James's character, or lack of it, but Faith wasn't listening. She couldn't believe that one chance meeting, if it was chance, could have had such an effect on her. She felt like that young girl again, when she'd discovered that he'd become engaged to Lady Fiona Shand. She'd been numbed by grief and shock. The pain was so crippling, she hadn't been able to eat or sleep for weeks. She'd thought there was something special between them only to discover what a fool she had been.

He'd spent three months in Scotland, dealing with a crisis in one of the railway lines he was heavily invested in, with only the odd terse message to her, and the first real news she'd had of him was in the morning *Gazette*. It seemed that James's constant companion at every function and party that Edinburgh had to offer was Lady Fiona

Shand, and it was expected that their engagement would be announced within the week. Lady Fiona was the daughter of Lord Shand, one of Edinburgh's leading entrepreneurs.

Lady Beale wasn't surprised. She'd heard that James had lost a great deal of money in his railway venture and was only doing what many a man had done before him: taking a rich wife to pay off his debts. It had obviously never occurred to her ladyship that there could be anything between her paid companion and a man of his standing.

Faith didn't believe a word of it, but when his letters dwindled to few and far between, she'd decided to act. She'd handed in her notice, and she'd set off for Edinburgh to see James in person. She hadn't seen James, but she'd seen enough and heard enough to convince her that the gossip was true. James was going to marry Lady Fiona.

He was a widower now. Fiona had suddenly been struck down by typhus, that most lethal and dreaded disease of the age. Faith hadn't written him a letter of condolence. Somehow, it would have seemed inappropriate coming from her.

Lily's harangue eventually died away, and when they were drinking their chocolate, she said, "What have you told Robert about the bounder?"

Faith blinked and turned her head slowly to look at her friend. "Nothing. Why should I tell Robert anything?"

Lily made a clucking sound with her tongue. "I think he means to ask you to marry him."

"I hope you're wrong." With a weary sigh, Faith shrank into her chair. "In fact, I'm sure you're wrong. Robert and I are friends, nothing more." Lily's look of skepticism made her elaborate. "He doesn't think of me in that way, and I certainly don't think of him in that way, either. His father is on the school's board of governors. He's interested in the kind of education we provide and, of course, we have a common interest in all things Greek and Roman. That's all it is."

When Lily continued to stare at her with raised brows, she felt compelled to add, "I've never given him the slightest encouragement."

"You don't have to give him encouragement! All you have to do is be yourself. You listen to whatever he is blathering about and ask intelligent questions. With me, it's in one ear and out the other. Robert Danvers may be the biggest catch in Bloomsbury, but he's a bore, leastways, when he is with his father. When the cat is away, it's a different story. Robert comes out to play. Who can trust such a man—a model of virtue when his father is looking over his shoulder, and the gay cavalier when he gets out on his own? Rumor has it that his only interests, apart from pretty girls, are horses and gaming."

"Rumor!" Faith scoffed. "Don't believe everything you hear. And if he is interested in pretty girls, he is hardly likely to offer for me."

"All I'm saying is watch your step."

Lily's words had given Faith something to think about. It was only recently that Robert had taken to visiting St. Winnifred's regularly. Before that, he'd put in an appearance on special days, but that was only to please his father. When he'd heard, however, that her father had taught classics at Oxford, he'd taken an interest in her, or rather, he'd become interested in the books she could lend him to enlarge his knowledge of classical culture and history.

Leastways, she hoped that was all it was. He was a blond-haired Adonis whom all the senior girls were mad about, yes, and a few of the teachers, too. But not she. Her limited experience of men had taught her that a girl's best friend was between the covers of a book. And, if you didn't like what it said, you could throw it against a wall and stomp all over it.

She'd inherited her love of books from her father. Her

happiest memories as a child were tramping around England on the holidays, exploring the ruins of the ancient Romans. One day, her father had promised her, they would go to Greece and Italy and visit the places she'd only read about in books.

They never had, of course. Her father was a father first and a don second. He wouldn't go without her, and he'd never had the kind of money to take her with him.

Lily drank the dregs of her cocoa then said, "What did you mean, he doesn't like you in that way and you don't like him in that way either?"

Faith snapped out of her thoughts. "What?"

"You heard me!"

Faint color ran across Faith's cheeks. She'd been thinking of James. Even when she was an inexperienced young woman, a look, a word from him could turn her insides to custard, and that was before she'd come to know him. And today, when she'd least expected it, it had happened again.

She must need her head examined.

Hands on hips, Lily came to stand in front of Faith. Her dark eyes were rampant with speculation. "What is it you're not telling me, Faith McBride? Why don't you answer my question?"

That was the trouble with confidantes. They expected to be told every little secret. Well, this was one secret Faith was keeping to herself.

She shrugged. "Haven't you read *Jane Eyre*?"

Lily's nose wrinkled. "*Jane Eyre*? God and all his angels preserve us! If that is what love is like, I want none of it." A moment went by. "Is that what you had with James? Did you lose your head over him?"

"No!" came the snappish retort. "I was momentarily blinded. When I spoke of Robert, I meant that his presence or absence makes no difference to me."

Lily mumbled something Faith did not hear.

"What was that?"

"I said," Lily enunciated slowly and clearly, "I'm beginning to feel sorry for Robert. If you don't want him, some other young woman will snap him up. He's a fine-looking man and will come into money one day."

"I thought you said he was a bore."

Lily began to tidy up. "That's because he doesn't talk about what most interests me."

"And that is?"

Lily cocked a brow. "Me, of course."

For some odd reason, they both thought this was a huge joke, and they burst into gales of laughter.

As they washed their mugs in a basin of hot water that Faith had poured from the kettle, Lily said, "You haven't mentioned if there were any letters waiting for you at Pritchard's."

"I don't know. I forgot to ask."

Lily's eloquent eyebrows rose. "You forgot to ask?"

Faith's brows, on the other hand, took a downward turn. "I was distracted. I couldn't wait to get out of there, all right?"

A moment of silence went by. Shrugging, Lily said, "If there are any, they'll still be there tomorrow, and I don't suppose Burnett will hang around, not when he knows he might run into you again."

Not sure how she should respond, Faith merely nodded, but she was remembering James's words, that though she might not have anything to say to him, he had plenty to say to her.

Lily slanted her friend a sideways glance. "Or," she said slowly, "we could go to Pritchard's right now, before the staff meeting, you know, to take the air?"

"I'd forgotten about the staff meeting."

"We can't miss it. We're to finalize plans for Speech Day."

Faith nodded without much enthusiasm. Speech Day was when all the girls and their teachers were on display so that prospective students and their parents could wander the school at will, enter any classroom, and judge for themselves whether St. Winnifred's was for them. Most parents were amiable and asked their questions politely, but there were always a few who found fault with everything. The following Friday was Prize Day, when the school turned out in force to applaud the brightest and best for work well done. Then the summer break would be upon them. Faith could hardly wait.

"Well?" Lily prompted.

"I think the shop will be closed by now."

"Mr. Pritchard lives above the shop, doesn't he? I'm sure he'd be willing to open it for you. For some reason I cannot fathom, you're the apple of his eye."

Faith grinned. "That's because I talk about what most interests him."

"Himself?"

"No. His grandchildren."

Laughing together, they finished tidying up and got ready for their walk.

The headmistress's name was Miss Elliot, and she ran her school with the discipline of a benevolent tyrant. No teacher dared daydream when Miss Elliot held the floor. She might be pounced on and asked for her opinion, and woe to that teacher if she fumbled her words.

So Faith fixed her gaze on the headmistress, but her mind kept straying to the letter that had been waiting for her at Mr. Pritchard's. She'd recognized the feminine script on the envelope, and her heart had done a flip-flop inside her chest. She'd had several replies to her advertisement, but most of those were demands for money from unscrupulous swindlers who could not put two grammatical sentences together. Only one letter had seemed sincere, the letter that was signed simply "C." The writer was cautious and would not meet with Faith until Faith had explained her connection to Madeline and her reason for trying to find her. Faith replied, then waited with growing impatience for a response. The letter she had received today made the waiting worthwhile. Lady Cowdray, she'd read, would be happy to see her when it was convenient for Miss McBride.

There was a small problem. Her ladyship did not live in London, but a mile from the village of Chalbourne. To get to the village necessitated a two-hour journey by train, and Faith did not know how she could find the time. Saturday was usually free, but this Saturday was Speech Day, and every teacher had to be at her post. That meant she'd have to contain her impatience till the Saturday after that, and patience had never been her strong suit.

"Be patient," he'd said. "Wait for me. We'll wed as soon as I return."

So she'd waited patiently for three months, until she'd traveled up to Scotland and discovered the truth for herself.

She crushed the thought, furious with herself for allowing James Burnett to creep into her mind yet again. Did every stray thought have to lead back to him? Banishing him to oblivion, she concentrated on Miss Elliot's closing remarks.

The headmistress invariably sent her teachers on their way by firing up their enthusiasm for the grand work they had undertaken. Today was no different. Theirs was a vocation, not a job, she told them, and long after they were gone, their influence would live on in the hearts and minds of the girls. Their efforts would make the world a better place.

The staff meeting ended on that high note, and the

teachers, eyes glowing with the fervor of their mission, began to file out in ones and twos. Faith could never quite match their zeal. Though she enjoyed teaching, she did not think of it as her vocation. Her father's influence was at work in her, and her ambition was to dig among the ruins of Greece and Italy.

It wasn't an ambition. It was a fantasy. Single women who had to earn their living did not go gallivanting all over Europe. It would be different if she were rich. The new breed of women flouted convention and chose to go off exploring just like men. Someone with her limited means would be much better off digging in Bath, where excavations were already under way beneath the Pump Room. If only her father had lived to see it!

A stray thought flashed into her mind, startling her. If she married Robert, he would be happy to take her to Bath to dig among the ruins. He might even be persuaded to take her to Italy.

Mercenary! she chided herself. She couldn't use Robert that way. Then she would be no better than James.

She looked around for Lily, but she was deep in conversation with Miss Elliot, so she went up to her room alone.

The letter from Lady Cowdray was in a hidden compartment in her sewing box, as were all the other responses to her advertisement. She wasn't suspicious so much as careful. Girls barged in and out of teachers' rooms at all times of the day. Anything left lying around was fair game for their curiosity.

She retrieved the letter, sat at her desk, smoothed it out, and read, for the twentieth time, the few sentences on the single sheet of notepaper, sentences that dealt mainly with directions on how to get to her ladyship's house from the station.

Patience, she reminded herself. Meantime, she had to

prepare a lesson for Speech Day, nothing too difficult but something that would make prospective students and their parents sit up and take notice.

Her father had given her a thorough grounding in classical languages, and it was a selection of his library books that stocked her bookshelf. She went to it now and ran her fingers along the spines of the leather-bound volumes. She passed over the Greek and Roman philosophers, knowing that the girls would find those too difficult to translate. Aeschylus almost burned her fingers. Euripides tempted her, but she shook her head and found what she wanted, her father's commentary on the works of Herodotus. The girls would find Herodotus well within their capabilities.

Her father's commentary was well worn and showing its age, but Faith regarded this book as her most precious possession. She reverently traced the name of the author on the front cover: Malcolm McBride.

As the teacher, she had to be aware of any and every irregularity of grammar and syntax, so she made herself comfortable on the chair by the fire and began to read her father's book. Before long, memories flooded her mind, and her eyes teared. She could almost hear her father's voice, teasing her for her fanciful translations. "Stick to the text," he would say, "and don't elaborate." So she'd stuck to the text with a vengeance and had the pleasure of having him hoot with laughter.

Her mother had died in a boating accident when Faith was only six, so her memories of her were very sketchy, but her father had tried to fill in the gaps. Mama, he said, always went with him on his excursions to the various Roman ruins in England, but that was before Faith was born. After that, Mama stayed home to look after her baby.

Was it all a lie? Why would her father lie to her?

She riffled idly through the pages of the commentary as another memory came back to her.

"I remember when Mama..." he'd said, then his face had gone all sad and he'd stared into space.

"What about Mama? I want to know about her. Tell me!"

His expression cleared, and he smiled at her. "She was enchanted with Herodotus's histories and took up Greek just so that she could read them the way Herodotus had set them down. She would read them aloud to you whenever you cried or were fractious. The sound of the words always distracted you, and you'd stop crying and listen to the sound of Mama's voice. She had a beautiful voice."

Was that a lie, too?

Restless now, she set the book aside and wandered over to the window. There was little to see. A sudden fog had swept in from the coast, and the grounds were veiled in a diaphanous haze. The school was practically deserted at this late hour, so no sounds reached Faith through the open window. She might as well have been alone in the world.

The thought made her shiver.

She was just about to shut the window when a movement caught her eye. Someone was down there, in the bushes close to the school. At this time of night, all the girls should have been in their rooms, and it hardly seemed likely that a teacher would conceal herself in the bushes as though waiting for someone from the outside.

Her lips flattened. Every school had its renegade, and St. Winnifred's was no exception. A name came instantly to mind: Dora Winslet. Everything came effortlessly to Dora: languages, mathematics, the sciences, boys. Especially boys. She was a tearaway and would have been expelled long since had she not possessed one of the finest brains

Miss Elliot had ever encountered in her long teaching career. The headmistress expected great things from Dora.

Cursing softly under her breath, Faith opened the door and quit her room. She let herself out of the school quietly and, after a few steps, paused, straining her ears for the sound of Dora's voice. There was nothing. The fog swallowed up every sound and landmark.

"Who's there?" Her voice was barely above a whisper. "Dora, is it you?"

The silence was unnerving. Then it came to her, the sound of someone breathing. A twig snapped, then another. Whoever it was was edging his way toward her.

Was this the person she'd sensed had been stalking her? She swallowed the knot in her throat, then swallowed again.

Another name came to her: James Burnett! That settled her nerves as nothing else could. Turning on her heel, she walked smartly back to the school and shut the door with a satisfying bang, then locked it and made for the stairs.

Once in her own room, she marched to the window. If Dora was out there, she would find herself locked out. The only way in was through the front door, and the porter on duty would report the girl for breaking school rules. And if it was James Burnett come to harass her, the porter would turn him away with a blistering scolding.

Her anger cooled when she turned from the window, and her gaze came to rest on her desk. The letter she had received from Lady Cowdray was exactly where she had left it. What was out of place was her father's commentary. It was on her desk, too, and she distinctly remembered setting it on the little table beside her chair.

A picture flashed into her mind. Someone had entered her room when she was outside chasing down Dora and had picked up the book she was reading. Finding nothing of interest there, he or she had wandered over to her desk still carrying the book. The book was discarded in favor of the letter.

Thoughtful now, she walked to the desk and picked up the letter. She'd left it folded. Someone had smoothed it out. Someone now knew about Lady Cowdray and Madeline Maynard. They'd easily deduce that she would be going out to Chalbourne. But why would anyone care?

She sat on the edge of the bed feeling all at sea. A few moments' reflection cleared her brain. This was a girls' school. One of her pupils had probably come to see her about something, and finding the door unlocked, had allowed her curiosity to get the better of her.

What else could it be?

Chapter 5

❦

It was late in the afternoon when a hansom cab pulled up at the gates of St. Winnifred's School for Girls. James stepped down and helped his aunt, Mrs. Mariah Leyland, to alight. She was in her mid-sixties, pleasantly rounded, with a spark of humor lurking in her bright sparrow's eyes. She was not dressed in the height of fashion, but the quality of her garments indicated that there was no shortage of money.

"So this is St. Winnifred's," she said. "I wish there had been schools like this in my day."

James gave a dry smile. He'd made it his business to find out as much as he could about St. Winnifred's this past week, and he doubted that his aunt could have learned anything here that she had not learned in her full, if rather unconventional, life. She wasn't so much the black sheep of the family as the rebel, and when her temper was up, she could be a firebrand. He liked her immensely, but that had not prevented him from pitying her late husband, the colonel.

What puzzled him was how Faith had ended up here. The girls in this school were being educated to turn the world on its ear—his comfortable, masculine world, he supposed. That's not how he remembered Faith. The Faith he remembered was softer, generous, vulnerable...And as it turned out, he hadn't known her at all.

A gust of wind caught at his hat, and he held on to it with one hand. Minding his manners, he offered his aunt his arm. She took it automatically, but her eyes were taking in the splendid parklike setting and the handsome three-story Georgian building at the end of the drive.

"How did a girls' school come to be situated in this lovely house?" she asked. "Was it bequeathed to St. Winnifred's by a former pupil?"

"Yes," he acknowledged, "an eccentric lady much like you, Aunt Mariah."

She laughed, taking his words as a compliment. "And how do you come to know so much?"

"It's amazing what one can learn in one's clubs."

And from his cousins. No psychic visions were involved. All that was required was a little sleuthing, a quiet word to his aunt, and he had the perfect entrée to St. Winnifred's annual Speech Day. Aunt Mariah had published a number of biographies on the remarkable women of her own generation and was frequently asked to address a few words to women's groups. This time, she had offered to speak to the girls of St. Winnifred's, and her invitation had been accepted with alacrity.

"And such a lovely park, too," his aunt enthused.

James's steps slowed, and he halted. He, too, looked around the park, but it wasn't to admire it. He could feel the fine hairs on the back of his neck begin to rise, a manifestation of his growing powers, and he narrowed his eyes to take in the scene. There was too much shrubbery for his liking, too many weeping willows and other places for trespassers to hide. He was wishing he'd invited Gavin and his dog along. Macduff would soon nose out any undesirable characters.

There were plenty of people about, most of them making for the front doors, but others were in clusters, enjoying the picturesque grounds. The sun was shining, flowers were blooming, but the wind was fresh and smelled faintly of the sea. Some ladies wore stoles, others were in pelisses. The gentlemen were dressed much like James: dark coat, buff-colored trousers with matching waistcoat, and of course, the ubiquitous top hat.

Mrs. Leyland edged him forward. "Miss Elliot," she said, "wants to have a few words with me before I address the girls. Frankly, James, I'm beginning to be sorry that I allowed you to talk me into this, and on such short notice, too. I've hardly had time to set my thoughts in order. I'm not used to talking to young girls, and I may talk above them, or my mind may go blank."

He gave her a level look. "Tell them about Florence Nightingale and how you helped her found the institution for training nurses. Tell them about Mrs. Beeton and how she turned her husband's fortunes around by writing her treatise on household management. Trust me, Aunt Mariah, your mind won't go blank. It's getting you to stop talking that will be the problem."

Her irreverent snort turned into a chuckle. "Very true," she remarked with a sideways glance at her nephew, "but at the end of the day, you must tell me the real reason for this visit to St. Winnifred's. No. Don't try to put me off with evasions and half-truths. I think I've earned your trust, don't you?"

The truth, James reflected, would sound absurd. What could he say? That a teacher at the school was in danger and that he was the only one who could save her? That he did not know who or what threatened her and hoped to find some clue at the school to point him in the right direction? His aunt was a Burnett, like his father, and to them the McEcherans were prone to flights of imagination. No. The truth would not do.

Conscious of the gleam of speculation in his aunt's eyes, he replied easily, "Alex is on a case, and he asked me to keep an eye on one of the teachers. I'm sorry, Aunt, I can't say more than that."

She looked as though she would argue the point but merely sighed and shook her head. "You and Alex," she said. "You always blamed each other when things got sticky. And what do you mean, 'he's on a case'? Is it true what they say? Does he work for Scotland Yard?"

James shrugged. "It could be the Special Branch or the War Office. Your guess is as good as mine."

She opened her mouth, but before she could blister him, a lady with iron-gray hair and penetrating blue eyes called from the top of the stairs. "Mrs. Leyland! It is you, is it not? How do you do? I am Miss Elliot, and I do thank you for coming to speak to our girls."

The headmistress swooped down and swept Mrs. Leyland up the last few steps and into the school. James followed in their wake.

It was a shameful way to repay Alex for his invaluable advice, James thought with a faint smile, but Alex would have done the same if their positions were reversed. It was Alex who had suggested that Aunt Mariah would be welcomed with open arms at St. Winnifred's since her name was a household word among women with radical opinions. James was the one who would stick out like a sore thumb.

He must remember to keep his mouth shut.

* * *

James was right about his aunt's aptitude with words. It wasn't, however, that she didn't know when to stop so much as her audience would not let her. She was the last speaker and was laying forth on all the exceptional women of the nineteenth century that they should take as their examples, and her audience applauded wildly each time she paused, encouraging her to go on.

This didn't have the feel of a Speech Day to James, least-ways none of the Speech Days he'd attended when he was a schoolboy. He'd once, inadvertently, attended a Method-ist revival. The same religious fervor he'd sensed then was present in this hall. The words were different, but the mes-sage was the same: "Go forth and make converts."

All the teachers and girls were sitting in rows facing the lectern, but James's eyes were trained on Faith. He wasn't a member of the audience but had positioned himself at the side of the hall so that he could watch her unobserved.

He could tell from her pinched profile that she was aware of his presence. From time to time, she turned her head to speak to her neighbor, but her eyes never lifted to meet his. He recognized her friend but couldn't put a name to her: Iris? Daisy? Fleur? Something like that. As he remembered, she'd been Faith's friend when they'd met during the season all those years ago. Her back was to him, but he could read that rigid spine without reference to his psychic powers. Her hostility to him was equal to Faith's.

It was the person on the other side of Faith that he found irritating: a flaxen-haired gentleman, perhaps a year or two younger than himself, with a mobile mouth that smiled too much. And those smiles were all directed at Faith.

He gave a start when someone touched his arm. Looking

down, he saw one of the senior girls, about seventeen years old, eyes vividly blue and full of curiosity, with a Mona Lisa smile dimpling her cheeks. Though she was dressed in the school uniform—a plain gray round gown without embellishment except for its white lace collar—she had an air about her that didn't seem quite appropriate for a St. Winnifred's girl. In short, she didn't look like one of the converted.

"How do you do?" she said. "I'm Dora Winslet, and I believe you are Mrs. Leyland's nephew."

James looked at her outstretched hand and bit back a smile. He didn't expect a curtsy, but this masculine mode of greeting was highly amusing. They shook hands.

"How do you do?" he said. "I'm James Burnett of Drumore. Yes, Mrs. Leyland is my aunt." He gestured at the chairs facing the podium. "Shouldn't you be with the other girls, listening to the speeches?"

"Oh, the headmistress warned me off. I ask too many awkward questions, you see. My job is to wander around and take care of visitors, you know, make myself useful. If there is anything you want to know, you need only ask."

She was a taking little thing, but a tad precocious. He wasn't surprised that the headmistress had warned her off. He was searching his mind for a suitably intelligent question that would not make him sound condescending or pompous, when Miss Winslet spoke first.

"Are you acquainted with Miss McBride?"

He was taken aback. "Why do you ask?"

Her dimples flashed. "You look at her a lot. Or is it Mr. Danvers you know?"

He drew in a long, calming breath. "I am not acquainted with Mr. Danvers." Then cautiously, "Who is he?"

"He is the gentleman on the right and is the son and heir of the chairman of St. Winnifred's board of governors. You may have heard of them, Danvers and Danvers of Fleet Street? They're bankers."

He nodded. The name was familiar, and it had just occurred to him that Danvers Junior looked familiar, too. Had he met him at one of his clubs or seen him at the bank? "Is he on the board of governors, too? Is that why he is here?"

"No. We girls think that he is sweet on Miss McBride."

His voice rose. "Faith?"

"So you do know Miss McBride!"

He shrugged. "I knew her once, a long time ago. I doubt that she remembers me." He hoped Miss Winslet would take the hint and drop the subject.

She turned to look in Faith's direction. "Do you think so?" When she looked up at him, she was wearing her Mona Lisa smile. "Do say you'll come to our class after the luncheon. We're translating Herodotus, demonstrating our facility with the language, so to speak, but few parents are interested, so we rarely have visitors. It's not fair to Miss McBride. She goes to a great deal of trouble to prepare us. You should come out if only to support her, and us girls, too, of course."

James's mind was reeling. Faith taught the classics? He'd known, of course, that Faith's father was a university don, but he hadn't known that she'd had any interest in his work. He remembered his own university days, when Greek and Latin had bored him to tears. That's what he'd always told himself. The truth was, he was too lazy to apply himself.

He looked down at Miss Winslet. "How many girls are in Miss McBride's class?"

"There are only six of us senior girls left, though we started with twice that number. Some people have no stamina."

"I'm surprised that there are still six of you left."

She gurgled with laughter. "You wouldn't say that if I were a boy. We can't help being horribly clever. That's why we're encouraged to take Latin and Greek. Besides, we'll need them when we go on to university."

"University? You mean Oxford and Cambridge?"

"Yes. To the women's colleges. Not that—"

Her words were drowned out by thunderous applause. The speeches were over. "Do say you'll visit our class," she begged. "It's very informal, and it will give you a chance to renew your acquaintance with Miss McBride."

Not only was the chit horribly clever, she was also horribly tenacious. Nothing seemed to depress her. He did the only thing that was left to him. He gave her a tight smile and conceded the point. "I'll be there. You may depend on it."

"Thank you, Mr. Burnett."

He heaved a sigh when she moved away. In point of fact, he'd had every intention of visiting Faith's class before Miss Winslet had cornered him. He wasn't going to stay more than a few minutes, only long enough to make sure that Faith was out of the way when he broke into her room to look for the replies she'd had to her advertisement. It was possible that she had destroyed them, but it was worth a try. He had to know what kind of trouble she was in.

Now that the speeches were over, people were milling about in the hall, conversing in small groups and, of course, waiting their turn to speak to his aunt. Maids with laden trays were hurrying into the hall and setting things out on long tables to tempt the appetites of honored guests.

He was swallowing his third bite-sized cucumber sandwich when there was a sudden hush, and the headmistress announced that the rector would say grace before luncheon was served. He looked over at Faith and caught her staring right at him. Her brows were down. Feeling like a thief who had been caught red-handed, he put his fourth sandwich back on the plate and bowed his head. When the rector had given the blessing, James straightened. As he anticipated, Faith was one of the first to break from the herd and come straight for him. He looked over her head to see where Danvers was and noted that the abominable Miss Winslet was carrying on a one-sided conversation with the gentleman and thus preventing him from following Faith. Danvers looked impatient, but that did not stop Miss Winslet.

What was the chit up to?

Faith's voice was clipped and intense. "I should like a word with you in private, Mr. Burnett."

"I thought you might." The sizzle in her eyes pleased him enormously, but he was careful not to show it. "Shall we take a turn around the hall?"

"No. I said 'in private.' There are too many people here. Let's take a stroll in the grounds."

He looked over at his aunt. She was surrounded by a press of people and seemed to be having the time of her life.

"Lead the way, Miss McBride," he said.

He didn't know which pleased him more, the view of the park with its stately oaks and stands of beeches and cedars that seemed to stretch toward the distant houses, or the view of the young woman who strode ahead of him, her trim figure clothed in a gown of some indeterminate color that brought out the copper glints in her hair.

And the fiery glint in her eyes, he inwardly amended when she stopped suddenly and turned to face him.

He was fascinated by the way her breasts rose as she inhaled a long breath. "I do not appreciate your hounding me like this! First at Mr. Pritchard's and now at the school. Say what you have to say, and be done with it."

And he was irritated at the way she snapped at him. He wasn't here by choice, but, of course, she could not know that. As pleasantly as he could manage, he said, "Hounding is too strong a word. Say, rather, that I've followed the trail you left. Shall we walk as we speak?"

She ignored the arm he offered, but she fell into step beside him. "So you weren't in Mr. Pritchard's shop by chance?"

"Ah, no, I saw your advertisement and decided to follow up on it. Old Pritchard told me that you usually collected your letters over the noon hour, and the rest you can guess."

"I think there is more to it than that. You're been having me followed. Don't think I'm not aware of it. What I can't understand is what you hope to gain."

He had stopped in his tracks, his jaw slack. "Someone is following you?"

She retraced the few steps that brought them face-to-face. "You mean it wasn't you in the grounds the other night, stalking me when I came out for a breath of fresh air? And you didn't go to my room and go through my correspondence?"

"No," he said violently. "I did neither of those things." Not yet, he hadn't.

He'd trusted his psychic powers to forewarn him of any threat to Faith. The trouble was, he was a novice. He wasn't easy with the gift Granny McEcheran had passed on and, as far as possible, he tried to ignore it. What a complacent fool he had been.

His eyes searched hers. "Did he threaten you? Would you recognize him again?"

Her gaze was level, measuring him. Finally, she gave a shaky laugh. "No. In fact, I'm not sure of anything. Perhaps my imagination was playing tricks on me, or perhaps one of the girls came out for a breath of fresh air, too. She'd be breaking the rules and wouldn't want to be caught."

"Any other episodes?"

She made a face. "I get the odd feeling occasionally that someone is watching me, and the fine hairs on my neck begin to rise."

James nodded. "I know the feeling. You should trust it."

"But when I turn around, either no one is there or no one is looking at me. I've become nervous, I suppose, since I put that advertisement in the London papers."

Her voice suddenly died, and she frowned as though she were annoyed with herself for telling him so much.

They walked on in silence.

"Maybe," James finally said, "someone *is* following you. Maybe it *is* related to the advertisement you put in the papers. Who is Madeline Maynard, and why are you trying to find her?"

He'd hoped that Alex could help him discover the woman's identity, but Alex had left for destinations unknown, and James hardly knew where to begin to look. Apart from that, he wanted to be discreet. He didn't want anyone to know what Faith was up to in case he stirred up a hornet's nest. On the other hand, she'd said that someone was stalking her. Maybe the time for discretion was past.

Her lips tightened. "That's personal business and can be of no interest to you. So, what brings you here? What is it you want to say to me?"

A quick look at her profile convinced him that he wasn't going to get any answers out of her, at least for the moment. He suppressed his impatience and took a moment to frame his thoughts. "I thought...that is...I hoped..."

When he faltered, she looked at him curiously. He couldn't tell her the truth, but the explanation he'd hit upon seemed feeble now that he had to say the words aloud.

"I hoped," he said, "that we could lay the past to rest. Life is too short to carry grudges, and we were very young"—he smiled a little—"and hot and impetuous. I always wondered what had happened to you. You did not leave a forwarding address." The old feelings of betrayal were beginning to stir, and he finished hurriedly, "When I saw your advertisement, I knew I had to trace you if only to assure myself that things were going well with you."

She said incredulously, "You went to all this trouble just to tell me that? I buried the past a long time ago. Believe me, I'm not carrying a grudge. Anyway, you could have written to me care of Mr. Pritchard, couldn't you?" She gave a choked laugh. "I forgot. Writing isn't your forte, is it? I think I can count on one hand the number of notes you wrote to me from Scotland." She shook her head. "Let's not go down that road, or we'll be here till doomsday, and I haven't got the time. I have to look over my notes for the lesson I'm giving, and, oh, mix with parents of my students. If it's forgiveness you're looking for, you have it."

"I am not looking for forgiveness!"

"In fact, I can say now that your engagement to another woman was the best thing that ever happened to me. It made me realize that I was stronger than I knew."

He took exception to her easy dismissal of something that had devastated him, but tried not to show it. He didn't want to quarrel with her. He wanted to protect her, only this hard-eyed reincarnation of the girl he'd once loved was beginning to annoy him.

Suddenly, her expression changed, and she said softly, "I'm sorry I spoke so harshly. I read somewhere that you were widowed not long after you were married. What happened between us must pale to a triviality compared to that. I'm truly sorry."

This was the Faith he remembered: soft, giving,

misty-eyed and...and, he must never forget, treacherous. The old magnetism was still there, but he was older and wiser now. He wasn't going to give in to it.

In the same soft inflection, she went on, "You went to South America, didn't you, after your wife died? And built railways there? I heard you did very well for yourself."

He'd gone to where he could make the most money to pay off his creditors, and that was before Fiona died. He'd been glad to get away from his wife, but he owed Faith no explanation, so he did not bother to correct her.

His voice was clipped. "You seem to be well-informed about me. I, on the other hand, know very little about you, except that you hared off with that Donkey fellow without giving me a chance to explain."

Her voice was as icy as her eyes. "His name was Dobbin, not Donkey. As for how I come to know so much about you, I read the papers. You're a celebrity, James, you know, the railway magnate who made his fortune building railways in South America."

She made it sound as though he'd robbed widows and orphans. A look of hauteur settled on his face. "Dobbin? I was sure he was one of the Donkeys of Derby, but I'm not very good with names."

"No, and you're not very good at laying the past to rest, either. That's what you said you wanted, isn't it, to lay the past to rest? Well, consider it done."

With that, she turned on her heel and started to walk back to the house.

He tried to be angry. He thought that he *should* be angry, that he had a *right* to be angry, but all he could feel was a strange sense of exhilaration. The carnal delights of the Golden Fleece could not compare to the slings and arrows of one disastrously righteous woman.

What delights? What Golden Fleece? Since the night of

his granny's apparition, he'd sworn off women, sworn off gambling and, sadly, sworn off whiskey and concentrated all his thoughts on one provoking problem: Faith. And he felt more alive, more in tune with the world than he'd felt in an age.

The half smile on his lips died the moment he recognized the gentleman who was coming from the house toward Faith: Mr. Danvers, the man who smiled too much. He greeted Faith like a long-lost friend, laughing, talking across her words. Cozy. Exclusive. Then Mr. Danvers glanced over Faith's shoulder and shot James a look that was easy to read: *Keep your distance* was the unspoken message. *She's mine.*

Never tardy in taking up a challenge, James strolled toward them. He checked himself when he became aware that the precocious Miss Winslet was avidly observing everything from the shade of a weeping willow. He remembered Alex's advice, to do nothing to draw attention to himself and to keep his mouth shut.

He had come here for a purpose. Time to get on with it.

Mr. Danvers said, *"Who is that gentleman you were talking to?"*

It came to Faith, then, that she really didn't like Robert Danvers. He took too much upon himself. He was easier to bear when he was the gay cavalier, but when he transformed into a model of virtue, she could hardly keep her distaste from showing.

She answered him shortly, "He is an acquaintance of my former employer, Lady Beale. I haven't seen him for years. The other day, I met him quite by chance in Pritchard's Bookshop."

"And his name?"

When she looked at him sharply, he gave her an engaging smile. "He looks familiar, but I can't quite place him."

"James Burnett," she replied without elaborating.

He repeated the name softly. "Burnett. James Burnett. The railroad magnate?"

"He builds railroads, if that's what you mean."

He spoiled his handsome face by beetling his brows. "But what on earth would bring a man like that to St. Winnifred's?"

"His aunt, I presume. She gave one of the speeches."

With that, she hastened her steps to avoid any more questions on a subject that brought her nothing but embarrassment and pain.

Chapter 6

James made his plans with military precision. The object was to break into Faith's room and search for all the replies she had received to her advertisement. Had she confided in him, it would not have been necessary for him to go to such extremes. Since she hadn't confided in him, he felt he had no other choice.

It was remarkably easy, as easy as reading a railway timetable. First came the speeches, then came a luncheon, and after a short break in the program, the teachers and their students were to go to their classes, where parents and guests were welcome to observe. It was the perfect time to slip away without being seen.

He'd based his plan on the school's prospectus, which he'd obtained a few days before. It described the principles on which the school was founded, the kind of girls St. Winnifred's wanted to attract, and a list of former alumnae who had made a name for themselves in their chosen professions. It was a formidable list. It seemed to him that the era of compliant, indolent ladies who had nothing better to do than make some man happy, namely their husbands, was on its way out, or it would be if the graduates of St. Winnifred's had their way.

The last item in the prospectus was, for his purposes, the most important. It gave him a list of teachers' names and their room numbers. This was for the benefit of students who wanted to discuss a problem when school was over, or needed tutoring in some subject, or merely wanted to visit because they had nothing better to do.

It seemed to him that the teachers at St. Winnifred's had hardly a moment to call their own, and he wondered whose job it was to minister to *them*.

He stopped at the door of the classroom where Faith's lesson was in progress, just to make sure that she was where she said she would be, then he boldly mounted the stairs to the top floor of the house where the teachers' rooms were located. He held a book in one hand so that if he was challenged, he would say that he was returning it to Miss Elliot's room at her request. He doubted that anyone would chase down the headmistress to verify his story.

The door to Faith's room was locked, but he had come prepared. A length of wire inserted in the lock, a twist of the wrist, and the latch clicked open. He looked left and right, saw no one, and entered the room.

It was small, much smaller than he had imagined, though he should have expected it, knowing that before it was a school, the building had been the home of some wealthy family, and these were the servants' quarters. The room faced south and was comfortably furnished: upholstered chairs by the empty grate, a small mahogany table with two upright chairs, the washstand by the window, a lady's desk under a gas lamp, and beside it, a bookcase crammed with books. What the room lacked in elegance, it made up for in simplicity and charm. The occupant of this room did not follow the prevailing fashion of covering every nook and cranny with tasteless curios or suffocating the light with heavy drapes.

There was another door that he supposed concealed the clothespress. He opened it first. There was little enough to see. Teachers had no need for an extensive or elegant wardrobe. Even as a paid companion, Faith had had more garments than these, and of far better quality.

He went through the room methodically, and the more he searched, the more he began to feel like a Peeping Tom. The paucity of Faith's belongings told him far more than she would have wanted him to know. He had to keep reminding himself that he was doing this for her, that his motives were noble. He didn't feel noble. He felt angry and restless. Where were the cursed letters? Had she destroyed them?

On the stand by the bed was a leather-bound volume. He picked it up and read the gold lettering on the front cover: *A Companion to Herodotus* by Malcolm McBride.

A small smile touched his lips. She'd told him, a long time ago, that this book by her father was her most precious possession. One day, she would have it bound again and would pass it on to her own children.

Where are your children now, Faith? His smile gradually faded.

That was what she had wanted: a home and a family. She was an orphan, and those things were important to her. All he had wanted was Faith.

A shaft of light suddenly blazed through the gauze drapes, momentarily blinding him. It was enough to empty his mind of extraneous feelings and focus him on his impressions. Some small detail had registered, nothing sinister, but something interesting. What was it? He turned his head and gazed at the sewing box at the side of one of the upholstered chairs. He'd already been through it and had found nothing untoward. He crossed to it now, lifted it up, and carried it to the table.

It was a handsome piece, rosewood and inlaid ivory, too handsome to belong to the school. He'd decided that it must be Faith's personal property, something she had brought with her when she'd taken up residence at St. Winnifred's.

As carefully as before, he removed the contents, article by article: spools of thread, pincushion, scissors, needles, and all the paraphernalia peculiar to this womanly art. There was something different this time, not in the various articles, but in him. His fingers seemed to have developed a will of their own. His brain told him that the box was empty, but his fingers were not ready to give up. They smoothed the black velvet lining at the bottom of the box, and then he found it, a tiny flap that was almost invisible.

The bottom of the box came away easily, and he grinned. The secret compartment was stuffed with letters. He went through them quickly. There were eight responses altogether but only one that wasn't asking for money. It was from Lady Cowdray, giving Faith instructions on how to get to the house when she arrived at Chalbourne station on Saturday next. Then she would tell Faith all she wanted to know about Madeline Maynard. It ended with: "I have something of Madeline's that may interest you."

Lady Cowdray. The name meant nothing to him, as little as Madeline Maynard's name. How were they connected? Faith had always been selective in whom she confided, and he was the last person she would confide in now. He wasn't going to let that stop him. She was heading into danger, and the only clue he had to go on was her interest in finding Madeline Maynard.

Who are you, Madeline Maynard?

Girlish giggles on the other side of the door jerked him from his thoughts. It was time to go. He put everything back as he had found it and quit the room.

In the classroom one floor below, Faith's nerves were just beginning to settle. There were only half a dozen visitors present, but her girls performed as though Her Majesty herself was one of them. Their Greek recitation of Herodotus was flawless; their translation into English was fluent and accurate. To a certain degree, she was proud not only of them but of herself as well. On the other hand, these were the cleverest girls in the school, far cleverer than she was. It was easy to teach clever girls, so she couldn't take the credit.

Her eyes kept straying to the door. There was no sign of James, though Dora had told all the girls that he'd promised to visit. She hoped that this was one promise he would break. She couldn't order him out of her class just because he confused her. The headmistress would expect her to treat him with all the deference due a wealthy gentleman who might be induced to make a donation to the school's foundation fund.

Her mind was jerked from her anxieties when the visitors broke into a round of spontaneous applause. Cries of "Well done!" and "You should be proud of yourselves!" as well as one "Bravo!" had the girls preening like peacocks. All the tightness across Faith's shoulders relaxed, and she smiled. The hard part was over. The last few minutes would be taken up with questions from their visitors, and these visitors were obviously well-wishers and committed to what St. Winnifred's had to offer, except perhaps for one elderly lady, Mrs. Elphinstone. She was of the old school and didn't mind letting everyone know it, but she knew her duty and came every year to support her granddaughter. Thankfully, her son, the barrister, was there, too, and he knew how to handle his mother.

The first question was of a general nature. What did the girls want to do when they graduated from the school? Each girl answered in turn, and it was obvious that they had set the bar high. One wanted to be a doctor and had already enrolled at the Royal Free Hospital, one of the few hospitals that allowed women students into the operating room. Another wanted to go on to Somerville Hall at Oxford, the new women's college, to read history, and Dora was looking forward to, as she put it, "Playing around with numbers," if she was accepted at Cambridge.

"What Dora means," said Faith in answer to all the blank looks Dora's words had evoked, "is that she will be studying mathematics and physics." She nodded at their looks of astonishment. "We fully expect that Cambridge will welcome her with open arms."

This provoked a derisory snort from Mrs. Elphinstone.

"Now, Mama," said the barrister, "we live in a different age. Girls want more than they used to. Let them have their chance. That's what I say." To Faith, he said, "You're doing a splendid job, Miss McBride. Keep up the good work."

He got to his feet and helped his mother to rise, but Mrs. Elphinstone had more to say and stood her ground. "What good will all this education do them? No one wants to listen to clever women. Whatever happened to small talk? That's what a woman needs to know. If you want my opinion, an education is wasted on women."

There was more in this vein, but the barrister possessed the same determined streak as his mother, though he was more tactful with it, and before the old lady could completely mortify her granddaughter, whose face was already flushed with embarrassment, he steered Mrs. Elphinstone through the door.

Faith was racking her brains for something to fill the silence before it became awkward, when a soft, Scottish brogue had all heads turning to the door. "The lady has a point," said James Burnett.

He was lounging with one elbow propped against the doorjamb. A collective sigh from the girls went up. It never ceased to amaze Faith that even clever girls could lose their heads over a handsome face and a pair of broad shoulders. A Scottish brogue! That was all for effect. James Burnett's accent was as English as hers. But his charm was working. Even the mothers who were present were breathing a little faster.

"Mr. Burnett," she said, "to what do we owe the honor?"

He strolled into the room and took an empty chair in the front row. "Curiosity," he replied with an easy smile, and he stretched one arm along the back of the next chair. "I met Mr. Danvers Senior on the stairs, and he suggested I consider a contribution to the school's foundation fund. I never buy a pig in a poke, so here I am."

The girls giggled. The visitors chuckled. Faith managed a tight smile. She wasn't impressed, or intimidated, or won over. He wanted to take the measure of her girls? Let him! She had prepared them well.

"Perhaps," she said, "you'd like to hear the girls translate a passage from the histories of Herodotus? They have their books right in front of them."

"Ah, no." He rubbed his chin with his index finger. "I expect them to be word perfect with you as their teacher, Miss McBride. What I want to know about is their hopes and aspirations. You see, I couldn't help overhearing Mrs. Elphinstone's words as I approached the door, and that set me thinking. What do these young women see in their future? I know they are preparing themselves for the professions, but what about marriage? Children? A home of their own? And dare I say it—a husband?"

Faith's confidence began to waver. She wasn't worried about the girls but about the visitors. Some of the opinions that the girls would express, she was sure, would make their hair stand on end. She gazed briefly at these unsuspecting pillars of the community: the Bishop of Hemmel and his wife, Mrs. Powell; Mrs. Brown and her husband who was a member of Parliament; Lady Frances Hollister, an advocate of universal suffrage. How much did they know about what went on inside their daughters' heads?

She opened her mouth to tell James, pleasantly, of course, that he was out of order, but he spoke first.

"Shall we let the girls speak for themselves? Miss Winslet, I'm sure you have given the matter some thought. What say you?"

Dora stared at her open book as though lost in thought. When she looked up, her dimples were flashing. "Why is it," she said, "that no one ever asks a boy what place marriage has in his future, leastways not until he has reached his thirtieth birthday and his doting parents are becoming impatient to dandle their grandchildren on their knee?"

Faith gave a heartfelt sigh of relief. The girls murmured their approval.

Dora wasn't finished yet. Adopting a playful tone, she went on, "We might ask you the same question, Mr. Burnett. What about marriage? Children? And dare we say it—a wife?"

James blinked then slowly nodded. "That's a fair question. I was married once. Perhaps you didn't know that I'm a widower?"

Dora had the grace to look contrite. "No. I'm sorry. I didn't know."

Faith interjected tactfully, "Perhaps we should stop there? In another five minutes the bell will ring."

Dora ignored the hint. "Does that mean you will never marry again? Are you confusing marriage with love?"

"Dora!" protested Faith. "That is a personal question."

She looked at James and was taken aback by the intensity of his stare. His look spoke volumes, but she did not know what to make of it.

The ever precocious Dora was not cowed into silence. "Love," she said, "is not the same as marriage. Love is freely given and taken. It's what the poets write about. Marriage is about money and contracts. It's how solicitors make their living."

"Miss McBride?" Lucy Elphinstone held up her hand.

"Yes, Lucy," replied Faith, glad to have a reprieve from Dora.

"Love can come after marriage, can't it? If two people like each other?"

Faith was beginning to feel as though a creature of the wild had been unleashed in her class. She felt trapped. Smiling as pleasantly as she could manage, she said, "Since I have no experience of love or marriage, I am reserving judgment."

When the girls made hissing sounds to demonstrate their displeasure at this evasive answer, she held up a hand to silence them. "Just because you are St. Winnifred's girls does not mean that you have to have an opinion on everything. It's all right to say, 'I don't know.' No, no more arguments. I want you out of here when the bell rings, so let's not begin a discussion we won't have time to finish."

She ignored James and braced for the comments of the

esteemed visitors. The bishop beamed at her. "Solomon could not have said it better," he enthused when he came up to her. "Too many people spout their opinions on something they know nothing about."

His wife gave Faith a commiserating look. "Are they always like this? Poor Miss McBride. If I had charge of them, I'd be tempted to beat them all soundly and send them to bed."

The bell rang. The ordeal was over. As the room began to empty, Faith went around the room collecting Herodotus's histories and other texts that were on display for the benefit of the visitors. "Dora," she said, "will you stay behind and help me?"

James deposited a pile of books in her arms. Keeping her voice low so that Dora would not overhear her, she said crossly, "You certainly know how to put a cat among the pigeons. What was that talk about marriage and love in aid of?"

He answered mildly, "I was testing your girls. Seems that they're more conventional than you give them credit for."

"And you approve, I suppose?"

He chuckled. "Of course I approve. It gives me hope that the human race will not become extinct."

She made a harrumphing sound.

"I was surprised," he said, "when you said you'd never been in love. Didn't you love me, Faith, when you agreed to marry me?"

"Was it love? It was so long ago I don't remember."

Fearing that she would explode, she marched to the book cupboard with a stack of books in her arms and came to a sudden halt. She couldn't open the door without dropping the books.

"Dora?" she said in a pleading tone.

The door was opened, and she entered the cupboard that stored not only school texts but also as much as she'd been able to salvage from her father's library. The only light came from a small window high on the back wall. There was a small stepladder that she used to reach the topmost shelves.

She stepped on it, climbed to the next step, and began to totter. In her determination to ignore James, she'd forgotten to hike up her skirts, and now the hem was caught beneath her shoes. She wiggled, she jiggled, she twisted this way and that. The result was, the books flew out of her arms.

"Bloody hell!" said James Burnett from the bottom step. "That hurt!"

Quite forgetting her precarious position, Faith twisted to look down at him. That last twist was her undoing. She lost her balance. With a cry of fright, she toppled straight into James's arms, then he, too, went toppling to the floor.

The door clicked shut.

Chapter 7

✺

In the fall, James's elbow had inadvertently connected with Faith's chin. Spots danced in front of her eyes, and she collapsed against him.

"Bloody hell!" James tried to ease from beneath her, but one side of his head struck a shelf. "Bloody hell!" he repeated, but this time more viciously. Spots were dancing in front of his eyes, too. Faith's whimper brought him to his senses. "Talk to me, Faith," he said. "Are you all right?"

Faith moaned and came to herself slowly. Tears of pain welled in her eyes and spilled over. Her words were punctuated by the rasping gasps of air she tried to draw into her lungs. "A few scrapes and bruises, that's all." Then crossly, "You shouldn't have closed the door. It only opens from the outside. Now what are we going to do?"

He was still trying to ease from beneath her but stopped at her words. "I didn't close the door," he said, "but I can guess who did."

He was remembering Dora Winslet and all the impertinent questions she had asked. Was this the conniving chit's way of getting Faith and him back together? And how did she know about Faith and him? Were they so obvious?

Similar thoughts were going through Faith's mind, but she was more alive to the perils of their situation. "We can't be caught here like this," she cried. "What will the headmistress say? And the girls? We've got to get out of here before we're discovered."

James's thoughts had taken a different turn. He'd wanted to get close to Faith, and he couldn't get much closer than this.

She raised her head. "Are you smiling?"

His lips flattened. She was right. He had been smiling, and there was nothing in this situation to smile about. This is what had gotten them into trouble in the first place.

He tried to force himself not to think of the warm woman's flesh that was intimately wrapped around him. He tried to remove his hands from the undersides of her breasts, breasts that he had once kissed and petted so intimately. *Intimate.* The demon word kept popping into his brain.

"Don't be daft," he said. "I wasn't smiling. Anyway, There isn't enough light in this box to see your hand in front of your face."

She snorted and made to move off him then stopped.

"What is it?"

"I think I've twisted my ankle."

There was more to it than that. She felt light-headed, not because of the fall, but because things that she had forgotten were forcing their way into her head. He smelled of soap and freshly starched linen. He was hard and lean but with the gentlest hands of anyone she had ever known. And those hands . . .

They were clasping her waist, but his thumbs were feathering the underside of her breasts. Wide awake now, she swallowed a breath. Her skirts were hiked to her thighs, and her knees were spread on either side of James's flanks. He was half propped against the door, and she was clasping his shoulders for support.

She tried to push away from him, but the pressure on her ankle made the pain worse. She was in agony, and he was smiling again!

"You think this is funny? I could lose my job! I can't be found here like this with you."

He tried to straighten his lips, but they wouldn't obey the commands of his brain. He tried to remind himself of his resolve to keep his hands to himself, but his hands wouldn't cooperate, either.

What the hell, he thought, giving up the struggle. They were in a tiny cupboard with no room to move. How much trouble could they get into?

"If I'm smiling," he said, "it's because I'm remembering the day of that awful storm when we took shelter in the summer house."

"I don't remember."

"Of course you do. It was at the house party at Mrs. Rowatt's country place. We went out riding early in the morning, under a cloudless sky."

He could almost feel the warmth of the sun's rays on his face and the pleasure of being with Faith. She was so easy to talk to, so interested in the things that interested him. Whenever he'd mentioned the word *railroad* to other young women, they'd nodded and smiled, but he'd known that they were bored out of their minds. With Faith, it was different. She'd asked intelligent questions. She'd understood that he wasn't investing every penny he possessed just for the profits he hoped to make. He loved railroads the way his father loved Drumore. He loved their smell, their clean lines, their speed. And he'd wanted to be part of that world.

He could see in retrospect that he'd taken a great deal for granted when he'd left Faith in London, while he went north to salvage his company. She hadn't given him a chance to explain. They had planned their lives together in that summer house. How could things have gone so wrong?

"I wish we could turn the clock back to that summer house," he said, voicing the thought that came to him. "A ferocious storm came up, don't you remember? And we dismounted. We were walking our horses when lightning hit the ground. They bolted, and we were lucky to find shelter in that neglected summer house. We didn't realize that the main house was just beyond the wilderness of trees and brush."

The memory was burned into Faith's mind. They'd reached the summer house before the rain became a torrent, turning day into night. She'd groped her way past obstacles only to trip over her own feet and had landed with a thump on a sofa that smelled revoltingly of dogs. James tried to help her up, but another thunderbolt shook the ground, and she'd grabbed for him. He fell on top of her, and that's when the trouble started.

"I don't want to think of that day." Her tone was belligerent.

His was whimsical. "Don't you? It was magical, wasn't it, Faith? We were so young and impetuous. We were in love—don't deny it—how could we help ourselves?"

She had to swallow the lump that was stuck in her throat. Of course she remembered every little detail: how he'd laughed softly before he kissed her, how she'd clung to him, how one caress had led to another. And she remembered with breathtaking clarity the moment when the slow-burning fire that he'd ignited inside her had suddenly blazed to a white-hot inferno. Just thinking about it made her shiver with anticipation.

"You were trembling, then, just as you're trembling now," he said.

His voice was low and husky and had taken on that soft Scottish burr that she'd always found irresistible. Her erotic memories, the suggestive position they were in with her knees splayed over his flanks, his beguiling voice— everything was conspiring to make her excruciatingly aware of how her body was responding. Her breasts were beginning to swell, the crests were tingling, the slickness in the core of her femininity made her flush with embarrassment—or was it desire?

"What is it, Faith? Are you cold? Here, let me warm you." He opened his jacket and wrapped it around her, enveloping them both in a warm cocoon.

She had the strangest sensation that this wasn't real, that she was dreaming. A frown puckered her brow as she looked at him. His eyes seemed black in that dim light, dark and intent as they gazed back at her. He wasn't smiling now.

She wanted him to make love to her, just as she had on that long-ago morning in the summer house. She'd been the brazen one then. "Make love to me, James," she'd begged. He wouldn't hear of it. They could wait a little longer, he told her. When he returned from Scotland, they would marry. All she had to do was be patient.

She wished the empty years of loneliness and heartbreak had never been. If only she had never met him. If only she had never loved him. If only . . .

Sensing the change in her, he raised his head and took her lips in a searing kiss. His hands weren't idle, either. He grasped her posterior and dragged her against the bulge that strained against the cloth of his trousers.

Holding her fast, he ground himself into the core of her femininity.

Faith choked back a helpless whimper. This couldn't be happening. This shouldn't be happening. She had to gather her wits and make him stop. But her body was telling her a different story. It ached to give him whatever he wanted, what they both wanted.

His breathing was harsh, fierce, difficult. Through clenched teeth, he grated, "I've damned myself a million times for being so noble in that cursed summer house."

Noble? That's not how she remembered it. He'd kissed her and caressed her with such passion that she hadn't known how they could possibly become more intimate. But she'd wanted to know. Nothing had changed. He could still make her ache with need.

Her thoughts scattered when his hands brushed over her frilly drawers, but when his fingers probed gently between her thighs, she bit back a scream and flung back her head. They had never gone this far before.

"You're wet for me," he said.

She was wet and ready for him, and he was more than ready for her. A smile of supremely masculine satisfaction spread slowly over his face. Gradually, the smile faded.

It was at this point that he seriously began to question his sanity. There was no room to lie down in that small cupboard and barely enough room for the two of them to stand. It was still possible to make love to her, but only if they remained as they were.

And what about his resolve? He'd made a promise to himself not to become beguiled by the winsome ways of the treacherous Miss McBride. Sweat broke out on his brow. She was driving him crazy with the soft, trilling sounds of arousal she made. Fine. He would give her something to remember him by, something to drive *her* crazy whenever she remembered how close they'd come to making love in her classroom cupboard.

The slow slide of his fingers was making her frantic. She couldn't think; she didn't want to think or debate the rights and wrongs of what she was doing. Her whole world was centered on the incredible tormenting sensations between her thighs.

She opened her eyes wide when tiny, rippling shudders started deep inside her, then she clutched at his shoulders as she convulsed in wave after wave of mindless sensation. She would have screamed at the wonder of it, but she couldn't find her breath. When the tremors died away, she sank against his chest and buried her face in the crook of his shoulder.

The world came back to her slowly: the scent of their lovemaking, the heat in that closed space, the hard-muscled body that cradled her so carefully. She raised her head to get a better look at him—and that insufferably complacent smile on his face.

This wasn't the man she remembered. This man was too knowing, too skilled, and too damn carnal to be the knightly lover she had once known. In eight years, her experience amounted to zero. She'd bet her last farthing that he couldn't say the same. Then what was she doing, sprawled across him like a wanton out of a bawdy house?

Since she couldn't scream her frustration at him, she took refuge in the logistics of their situation. "We have to get out of here," she said, "before—"

The unmistakable sound of voices carried to them from the corridor. "Do something!" she cried. "It's Robert."

Whether it was the pain from her fingers biting into his shoulders or the stark horror in her voice that made James suddenly rear up was immaterial. The result was that Faith was thrown back, knocked her head on the edge of a shelf, and cried out in fright.

James got to his feet. "Get us out of here!" he bellowed at the top of his lungs.

They heard the tread of footsteps crossing to the cupboard. When the door was flung open, James was on his feet and filled the entrance, blocking Faith from view. Staring up at him with shocked expressions were Faith's friend and Robert Danvers.

"What took you so long?" demanded James, feigning annoyance. He hoped that Faith had the presence of mind to straighten her clothes. "Didn't you hear me shouting?"

Robert eyed James with patent suspicion. Lily was bobbing this way and that, trying to see past James. "Was that Faith's voice I heard? Is she in there with you?"

Robert said, "What's going on here?"

James turned his back on Robert. "I'll tell you what's going on." He took a moment to help Faith to rise. She looked disoriented and close to tears. "One of those abominable girls shut the door on us when I was helping Miss McBride stack the books."

Breathless and slightly disheveled, Faith stepped out of the closet and put a hand to the back of her head. "I banged my head," she said plaintively, "and Mr. Burnett tried to help me." When she took her hand away, there was blood on her fingers. She moaned but was careful not to overdo it. What she wanted was to convince her friends that nothing untoward had occurred when she was locked in the cupboard with James.

Her ploy worked. The stiffness in Robert's spine softened, and he adopted a commiserating look. "One way or another," he said, "I'll find out who played that filthy trick on you."

"Please don't bother," Faith replied. "Whoever it was, I'm sure she meant it as a joke."

Lily's expression was more knowing than sympathetic. She shot a look at James then studied her friend. "Well," she said, "no harm done. Let's get you to your room, and I'll take a look at that cut."

Flanked by Robert and Lily, Faith hobbled to the door. James crossed his arms over his chest and watched them with mounting irritation. He might as well have been invisible.

At the door, Faith turned to face him. "Thank you for your assistance, Mr. Burnett. I'm sorry to put you to so much trouble."

He gave her a smile that was little more than a baring of his teeth. "Don't mention it, Miss McBride. I was more than happy to be of service."

The others saw nothing amiss in these words, but faint color ran under Faith's skin. A moment later, James was alone.

All unsuspecting, Faith was walking into a trap. James knew that he was dreaming, but that did not lessen the sense of panic that squeezed his throat. He was inside the mind of a killer who would go to any lengths to get the book.

What book? What book? What book? The words throbbed inside James's head, and his hold on the killer's mind relaxed, allowing him to slip away.

Panic wasn't helping him. He had to think! Concentrate! Focus! Where was Faith?

A gray mist, like gauze drapes fluttering in the breeze, swirled around him, blinding him.

Come on, Granny McEcheran, help me.

Pictures flashed in front of his eyes. A house, a bridge, a waterfall. Faith was there, running for her life.

Where was the man who wanted to kill her?

Focus. Concentrate. Infiltrate.

As easily as an otter slips into water, he entered the killer's mind.

The killer didn't hate Faith. He wasn't enraged. Killing her was a matter of expediency. But first, she had to give him the book.

The mist thinned then slowly lifted, and he saw everything. He knew where he was and what he had to do. He was on the grounds of Lady Cowdray's house, and he had to get Faith and her book safely away.

The dream changed. The sun beating down on him was almost blinding. He raised a hand to shade his eyes. Off in the distance, he saw pyramids and sphinxes and desert as far as the eye could see. The sound of laughter brought his head around. He was in the courtyard of what he knew was a hotel, though not the sort of hotel he had ever stayed at. It reminded him of the Moorish buildings in southern Spain.

The people here were British. Someone was herding them together to take a photograph. Then he saw her, Faith, head bent, in the shade of a palm tree, scribbling in a notebook. She set the notebook aside, got up, and joined the others.

The sun beat down relentlessly. He could feel the pressure of it behind his eyes. It was blinding him. He couldn't see Faith. Where was she? Where—?

He wrenched himself up and opened his eyes. He was in his own bedchamber. The gas lamp on the wall was still lit, though it had been turned down. His lungs felt as though he'd been running for miles.

Heaving the tangled covers aside, he got out of bed and strode to his dresser where he'd left the glass of whiskey his butler had brought for him. It was untouched, but not for long. Two healthy gulps chased his panic away. He put the glass to his lips again then changed his mind. The last thing he needed was to blunt his powers of deduction. He had to relive the dream until he made sense of it.

He didn't need Granny McEcheran to tell him that this was no ordinary dream. The fine hairs all over his body were bristling. The episode with Faith was easy to grasp, but not the second episode. Pyramids, sphinxes, and deserts could only mean Egypt.

What did Egypt have to do with anything?

He put the glass down and began to pace. Egypt could wait. What was critical was keeping Faith safe. Faith would be on the train to Lady Cowdray's place, but if she caught sight of him, she might turn tail and run. Or she might start asking questions, such as how he knew that she would be on the train. He didn't relish the idea of telling her that he'd broken into her room and found Lady Cowdray's reply to her advertisement.

He went back to bed, but he was in no mood to sleep. Resting his neck on his linked fingers, he stared blindly up at the ceiling and forced himself to think of something else. The girls at St. Winnifred's made no bones about what they wanted out of life. They wanted it all: love, marriage, children, and a satisfying profession where they could exercise their formidable gifts. He wondered what Faith wanted out of life.

His thoughts turned to his erstwhile wife. Having lost Faith, he'd drifted into marriage because he did not care whom he married and, of course, their families were ecstatic. Who could have known that the sweet and biddable Lady Fiona was a harpy in waiting? The temper tantrums! The scenes! The constant quarreling over trifles! She seemed to think that after they were married, he would give up his interest in trains and railroads and dance attendance on her. And her heart was set on becoming the foremost hostess in Edinburgh.

His heart, on the other hand, was set on building railroads in South America. It gave him an excellent excuse to put some distance between himself and Fiona. It also helped to replenish the family's fortunes. What it did not do was bring him happiness. He was at a crossroads. He still loved trains as much as ever, but he'd set up his company with good men at the helm, and there was little for him to do.

What was next on the horizon?

He made a face. It was too bad that his ability to see into the future did not apply to himself. If it had, he would never have kissed Lady Beale's companion under the mistletoe, never have found shelter from the storm in Mrs. Rowatt's dilapidated summer house, never have married Fiona, and never, never have walked into the closet to help Faith stack her books. Now he could not get her out of his mind.

Gritting his teeth, he focused his thoughts on his dream. Someone wanted to kill Faith but only after he had the book. Faith was making notes in a book. Faith was in a photograph. Who took the photograph? Who else was there? Why did he see pyramids out in the desert?

The pieces of the puzzle kept floating around his head, but try as he might, he couldn't fit them together. A thought entered his brain like a shaft of light. Lady Cowdray had written that she had something of Madeline's that might interest Faith. Was this the book the killer was after?

He was still mulling over that thought when he finally fell asleep.

Chapter 8

It was a miserable, foggy morning when Faith boarded the train at King's Cross station. It seemed to her that three of the passengers in her carriage were men of business. They would probably be going on to Manchester or other big centers of commerce. They looked bored, as though they'd made this trip many times. She'd rarely traveled by train, and she was looking forward to the journey. There was, however, more to her anticipation this time. She would finally learn the truth about Madeline Maynard.

The journey was a bit of a letdown. She'd hoped to get a good view of the passing scenery from the train window, but the countryside was shrouded in a mist that was almost impenetrable.

Lily had offered to come with her, but Faith wouldn't hear of it. Lily's brother and his family lived in Brighton and were expecting them both to spend the first two weeks of their holidays with them, as was their habit.

"I don't need a chaperone," Faith had protested. "There

will be plenty of people about. You go on to Brighton, and I'll join you as soon as I can."

"You think Lady Cowdray will ask you to stay the night?"

"It's possible, but I couldn't accept. We're strangers. I don't want to impose. Besides, I'd feel awkward after writing that I only wanted an hour of her time."

Lily nodded. "And I'd just be in the way, I suppose." There was no rancor behind her words. Lady Cowdray had agreed to see Faith. An uninvited guest might not be welcome. They both understood that.

"Lily, I'm a big girl, now. Don't worry about me. I'll be back in time to catch the last train to Brighton."

"Well, at least I can look after your traveling case. You don't want to be lugging that around when you're running for trains."

And that's how it was left.

Since there was nothing much to see from the window, Faith turned her attention to the people in her compartment. The men of business looked very important as they read the morning paper. The fourth passenger was an elderly lady who was dozing with her chin on her ample bosom. No one spoke or tried to catch her eye. They were traveling second class, and that was the thing about second-class passengers: they were all locked up in their individual coaches like cattle going to market. There was no escape if a quarrel got going, so they kept themselves to themselves.

James, of course, could travel any class he wanted, and he didn't always choose first-class. He was as interested in the interior design of the coaches as he was in building the tracks to carry them. She wasn't surprised that he'd made people believe in him, or that he'd found backers to invest in his companies. His enthusiasm for railroads was infectious.

Maybe Miss Elliot should have invited *him* to be one of the speakers on Speech Day.

That was the last time she'd seen him, the day that would be forever branded into her mind, not as Speech Day but as the day of the locked closet. Gingerly, she touched a hand to her face. Her skin felt as though she was coming down with a fever. Good Lord, the man wasn't infectious, he was *lethally* infectious, no matter what he was selling.

Shoving all thoughts of James from her mind, she forced herself to focus on the approaching interview with Lady Cowdray. She felt at a disadvantage because she knew next to nothing about her ladyship, while she had been obliged to give an account of her life with her father and subsequent career as a lady's companion and teacher at St. Winnifred's.

And if that were not enough to convince her ladyship to see her, she'd included a photograph of Madeline, the mother who, she was led to believe, had died when Faith was six. She'd discovered the photograph by sheer chance among her father's papers. On the back was written in her father's script, "Madeline Maynard."

What troubled Faith was that the woman in the photograph was forty if she was a day, but she'd been told that her mother was twenty-six when she died. Faith had speculated endlessly on what it might mean. Now, at last, she hoped to learn the truth.

Chalbourne was the first stop the train made, and many of the passengers got out either to stretch their legs or to use the station's conveniences. When the guard blew his whistle ten minutes later, people hurried to reboard the train. The engine belched a cloud of steam and smoke then jolted into motion, leaving Faith alone on the platform.

She was supposed to be picked up by her ladyship's driver, who would convey her to Cowdray Hall. Feeling a tad conspicuous, she sat on a bench against the waiting room wall and looked this way and that. Her gaze became riveted on a figure, shrouded in mist, who was lounging under a tree at the far end of the platform. Was he Lady Cowdray's driver? She got up and took a step toward him then halted. The mist had swallowed him up.

She jumped when someone spoke at her back. "Miss McBride?"

Turning quickly, she saw a short, stocky man, hat in hand, revealing a shiny face and a bald pate. "You must be Lady Cowdray's driver," she said.

He nodded. "Farr's the name." Not a smile cracked his face. "Shall we go?" And turning on his heel, he walked away.

Faith picked up her skirts and hastened after him.

They had to pass through the main thoroughfare to get to the house, and as the buggy jogged along, Faith asked the odd question about her ladyship just to be friendly, but Mr. Farr's short replies did not encourage her to continue. On one stretch of road, they stopped to let a dray cart going in the opposite direction pass them, but other than that, it was an uneventful journey that lasted no more than twenty minutes.

Her first view of the house might have been taken from one of the gothic novels she enjoyed—a castle rising above the mist—but as they got nearer, she saw that the house was much smaller than she imagined. There was no turret or battlements, only graceful Ionic columns that flanked the stone steps leading up to the front door.

A butler, who was as stony-faced as Mr. Farr, ushered

her into the great hall and told her to wait. She took in the giant pilasters lining the walls, the wall niches with sculptures, but what riveted her attention was the enormous sculpture of a reclining woman with only a sculpted shawl covering the lower half of her naked body. Whatever the artist's intent, it certainly did not preserve the lady's modesty. Faith moved closer. Modesty or not, the model, she thought, was truly lovely, and this was a work of art.

She did not have long to wait. The butler returned to conduct her to her ladyship, but this time, he might have been a different man. The starch had gone out of him, and though he did not smile, his manner was not intimidating. Encouraged by this, Faith followed him through one of the three doors into the great hall and was almost immediately shown into a large room that seemed to be part library and part sitting room. Her first impression was of untidiness, but it was an appealing untidiness and reminded her of her father's study.

Her gaze shifted to a lady who was pouring what seemed to be sherry into two crystal glasses. Her gown was simple, a pale green silk that suited her silver hair. It was hard to tell her age, but Faith judged her to be close to sixty, though a youthful sixty.

"Milady," protested the butler, quickly crossing to her, "allow me."

Her ladyship waved him away. "Go and find something useful to do," she said. "Tell Cook to send us tea and sandwiches. Miss McBride and I have a lot to talk about."

As her ladyship closed the distance between them, Faith's jaw dropped. There could be no doubt about it. Though she was older and had a few lines on her face, Lady Cowdray was definitely the model who had posed for the sculpture in the great hall.

Her ladyship seemed amused. "You've seen the sculpture," she said. "Well, of course you have. Sir Arnold, my late husband, commissioned it when we were first married and very much in love. I hope it did not shock you."

"Not at all," Faith managed in a reasonably neutral tone. She suspected that Lady Cowdray liked nothing better than to shock people.

Lady Cowdray had a glass of sherry in each hand. She smiled into Faith's eyes as she offered her one. "I would have known you anywhere," she said. "You are the image of your mother. Sit down, sit down. I only wish Madeline could see you now."

Her thoughts in a whirl, Faith took the chair her ladyship indicated.

"I met your mother," said Lady Cowdray, *"at a lecture of the* Antiquarians' Society at Somerset House. The speaker was Aurora Blandford, one of the first women to travel to Egypt without male chaperonage. She didn't go alone, of course. Other women with a sense of adventure went with her, and whenever they required men to do the heavy work, they hired porters and servants on the spot."

A maid had brought a tea tray, and her ladyship passed a plate of tiny sandwiches to Faith. She ate them without thinking. Her mind could hardly take in what she had heard. The mother she thought had died when she was a child had led a separate existence that she had known nothing about.

Lady Cowdray smiled at Faith, and all the lines in her face became more pronounced. "Madeline and I took to each other at once. You may imagine that Aurora's address had us all fired up."

Faith nodded. She was thinking of Speech Day at St. Winnifred's.

"At any rate, one thing led to another. The following year, we set out for Egypt, and we took the route that Aurora had taken, you know, traveling down the Nile, making stops along the way to see the sights. It was glorious." Something in Faith's expression made her elaborate. "It wasn't as dangerous as it sounds. We traveled the Nile in a boat. Everything we wanted to explore was within easy distance: Cairo, the tombs, the pyramids. And there were plenty of other English people around with the same idea. We made many friends. Oh, before I forget."

She opened a book on the table by her elbow and withdrew a photograph, which she passed to Faith. "When I opened the package you sent me and saw Madeline's face staring up at me, I knew you were not some charlatan out to wheedle money out of me." She smiled and looked down at the photograph. A silence that seemed almost reverent settled on them.

"This was taken shortly before your mother died," her ladyship said softly. "It must have been the summer of seventy-five. The last time I saw this photograph was when I sent it to your mother's solicitor informing him of her death. That was our arrangement. If anything happened to Madeline, I was to let her solicitor, Mr. Anderson, know about it. I presume he gave your father the photograph of Madeline. I thought he should have something to remember her by."

Faith blinked back incipient tears. She had been seventeen when her mother died, old enough to know the truth. Why hadn't her father told her? She thought of something else. Thomas Anderson had been her father's friend as well as his solicitor. Now they were both gone.

Faith's eyes were intent on the older woman. "Why did my mother never write to me? Why did she never write to my father? I'm sure if she had, he would have kept her letters."

Her ladyship let out a tiny sigh. "I have no idea. Perhaps she thought that a clean break was best. I was a widow with no children to care for. There was nothing to stop me living the life I always wanted. I don't know about Madeline. We never discussed our past lives, not in any detail. She knew what she wanted and was single-minded in reaching for it. I admire that in people, male or female."

As the silence lengthened, her ladyship stirred her tea. Finally, looking up, she said, "I knew that Madeline had left her husband to follow her own path, but that was all I knew. I'm sorry to give you pain, but Madeline never told me more than that. Frankly, I was happy for her. I don't believe in putting birds in cages. I did not know she had a daughter."

Faith had heard words like these at St. Winnifred's more times than she cared to remember. She may have said some of them herself. But this was *her* mother they were talking about, and she resented the implication that her mother had regarded their home in Oxford as a cage. She resented it, but she could not argue against it.

"Tell me how my mother died," she said.

Lady Cowdray nodded. Obviously, she'd been expecting the question. "It was our third trip to Egypt, November seventy-five," she said, "and we were staying at the Grand Hotel in Cairo. On this occasion, we were a mixed party. By that I mean that Madeline and I had joined Sir Edward Talbot's expedition before we set out for Egypt, so he was in charge. That last night, Madeline was unnaturally restless. She said that she felt feverish and wanted to lie down and sleep off whatever was making her feel unwell. The rest of us were in the dining room having a party, I suppose you would call it. At any rate, your mother wasn't gone long. When she came downstairs, she said that she was feeling much better."

Her ladyship seemed reluctant to go on. Finally, she sighed and said softly, "She was found dead in her bed the next morning. There were no signs of violence. There was an English doctor there who said that Madeline had taken too much laudanum, that she'd probably been disoriented during the night when she'd wakened and had mistaken the dose she'd added to her glass of water. You can imagine how shocked we all were." She blinked rapidly and swallowed. "She is buried there, you know, in Cairo. Her grave is in the Coptic churchyard. There's a headstone. I didn't know what to put on it but her name and the dates of her birth and death."

Faith was trying to take everything in, but something the older woman said struck her as odd. "Why would you say that there were no signs of violence? Were you surprised that there weren't any?"

"No! It's just that..."

"What?"

Her ladyship spied her half-drunk glass of sherry beside the tea tray and reached for it. "It's just that odd things got me to thinking once I was home." She drained her glass before continuing. "That last day, Madeline told me that she thought she'd recognized someone, but she had her reasons for not mentioning it when they were introduced. I didn't think anything of it at the time, but once I was home and my maid had unpacked one of my traveling boxes, at the very bottom, she found Madeline's diary wrapped in one of her scarves. Then I began to wonder about it."

"How did it get into your traveling box?"

"It shouldn't have. Madeline was very careful to keep it with her at all times, because it contained all the notes she'd made of the places we had visited. Later, she would turn those notes into articles and sell them to a number of periodicals and newspapers. That is how she supported herself, and she did very well, too."

Faith was having a hard time taking it all in. Her mother was an explorer and had traveled extensively in Egypt. Now she was a writer and had made more than enough to support herself. Finally, she said, "She was a celebrated Egyptologist and she wrote for the newspapers? Wouldn't my father have recognized her name? Wouldn't I?"

Her ladyship's voice gentled. "She was celebrated in our own little circle of female explorers. Only men become famous. And she wrote under a pen name, Madeline Wolf. I don't think Madeline wanted to be recognized by any of her former friends."

Faith tried not to take umbrage at this easy tolerance of an event that had affected her own life so drastically. "My father did not live long after my mother. Did you know?"

"No, I'm sorry, but I doubt he died from a broken heart."

Faith's annoyance surged then quickly evaporated. No insult was intended. It would never have occurred to Lady Cowdray to express herself tactfully. It had nothing to do with rank, in Faith's opinion, and everything to do with how she had lived her life. Tact wouldn't have got her very far in what had always been regarded as a masculine preserve.

They had wandered from the point, and Faith turned the conversation to what most interested her. Gathering her thoughts, she said, "Could a maid have packed the diary in the wrong box, your box, when you were leaving Cairo?"

"I don't see how. Madeline and I didn't share a room. And it was at the bottom of my box, wrapped in her scarf. No. I am convinced that someone must have put it there deliberately."

Faith thought for a moment. "Who would do such a thing?"

"I have no idea. Madeline, perhaps? Anything is possible."

Faith was reflecting on Lady Cowdray's words, that though Madeline recognized someone, she'd had her reasons for keeping quiet about it when they were introduced. "Was there any clue in my mother's diary to the identity of the person she thought she had recognized?"

"I never read the diary. It was in some sort of code; Malcolm's code, she called it."

"Malcolm's code!"

Her ladyship's brows rose. "You know it?"

Faith nodded. "My father invented it. Codes were his hobby. A schoolgirl with a smattering of Greek could break it." She bit down on her lip. Now who was tactless?

Her ladyship didn't take offense. "That's what Madeline said. But I don't know any Greek." She got up. "I'll fetch it for you."

Faith was puzzled. "You never thought to have someone decode it? I mean, most educated men have some Greek."

"No."

"Why not?"

"Because I was afraid that Madeline's diary might stir up a hornets' nest. She knew things about people that she ought not to have known, did things that she would not want others to know about." She lifted her shoulders in a tiny shrug. "I was afraid of what I might find in the diary. I can't explain it better than that. But I know that the diary will be safe with her daughter."

Faith could only stare as Lady Cowdray left the room.

Chapter 9

Her ladyship was gone for only a moment or two, and when she returned, she handed Faith a small parcel that was wrapped in brown paper and tied up with string. If Faith had been alone, she would have torn the wrapping apart and made a beginning on decoding the diary, but this was not the time or place. It was evident that her ladyship wanted to talk. There were so many stories about her adventures with Madeline that she wanted to relate, and Faith was eager to hear them, so she set the parcel on her lap and gave Lady Cowdray her full attention.

One part of her couldn't help admiring these intrepid ladies who had traveled on the Nile. They'd had adventures that would make most women's hair stand on end. Another part of her felt let down. She could not get around the fact that Madeline had deserted her family without a backward glance, or so it seemed. Other questions were buzzing inside her head that only her father could have answered.

What had he done to turn her mother against him, and why had he lied to her all these years?

Those questions were too personal to share, and Lady Cowdray never thought to raise them, a small mercy for which Faith was thankful. She was a grown woman. She shouldn't, *wouldn't* become maudlin over something that had happened years ago. It wasn't as though she and her mother had been close. She had only vague recollections. Her memories came from what her father had told her.

Mindful of the time and that the train to London would soon be arriving at the station, she rose to go. Lady Cowdray got up as well.

"Can't I persuade you to stay the night? I haven't enjoyed myself this much in years."

Faith shook her head. "My friend is expecting me and will be worried to death if I don't turn up." Her eyes strayed to the clock on the mantel. "I don't want to miss my train."

Her ladyship nodded. "I'll have the footman arrange for Farr to drive you to the station."

This was soon done, but hardly had the footman left to do her bidding when her ladyship whirled around and quickly crossed to a low oak dresser. A moment later, she returned with a photograph and handed it to Faith.

"This," she said, "was taken on our last visit to Cairo. I'm sure you'll find your mother very easily. She looks just like you."

Faith's eyes began to tear. She remembered her father's words. "You're the image of Mama, Faith," and the sad look in his eyes when he said it.

Did she look like her mother? She couldn't tell. The solemn-faced woman who stared out at her was only one face among many in the photograph. There must have been a dozen or more people there, obviously posed for the occasion.

She looked at the older woman. "Lady Cowdray, you said earlier, before you went to get my mother's diary, that my mother knew too much about other people's affairs. I got the sense that you felt she might have incurred some-one's anger or put herself in danger."

Her ladyship's smile slipped, and she heaved a sigh. "I would not put it quite like that, but I will say this: don't broadcast the fact that you have Madeline's diary, not until you transcribe it and learn its secrets. If it's harmless, well and good. Just be careful, my dear."

In the next instant, she was reeling off names as she pointed out various people in the photograph, and Faith reluctantly let the subject drop.

Lady Cowdray shook her head. "I'm giving you too much information, am I not? You'll never remember all these names. Why don't you come out to the next meet-ing of the Friends of the Egyptology Society? You'll meet people there who knew Madeline, though a few of them, sad to say, are no longer with us."

"No longer . . . ?" prompted Faith.

"They died or moved away," elaborated Lady Cowdray. She was staring thoughtfully at the photograph she had given Faith. "I have a card somewhere—"

She went back to the dresser and returned in a moment with a card. "Here you are. The next meeting of our little group is on Saturday next at the home of Mr. Hughes. It's all there in the card. I'll be there and would be happy to introduce you to people who had so much in common with Madeline. Come with a friend, if you like. The more the merrier."

Faith glanced at the card then placed it, along with the

two photographs, inside her reticule. Her mother's diary was clutched securely under her arm.

Her ladyship went on, "The lecture is to be given by Professor Marsh."

The name meant nothing to Faith, but she was pleased to be invited, pleased and curious. She might get some insight into the world that had evidently meant more to her mother than her own husband and child.

"Thank you. I would like that," she said.

Next Saturday, she would be in Brighton, but she could always take the train to London in the morning and stay at St. Winnifred's for the night.

The butler saw her out. At the bottom of the stone steps, the buggy, with its hood raised to protect her from the elements, was waiting. When she climbed into the gloomy interior, she could just make out the driver and knew that it was not Mr. Farr. This man was less bulky and had longer arms and legs, but he was just as uncommunicative as all Lady Cowdray's servants appeared to be. His cap was pulled down over his brow, his collar was up, and he barely glanced at her. That suited her just fine. She wasn't in a talkative mood either.

There was something about Lady Cowdray that disturbed her. Faith did not believe that her ladyship had lied about the circumstances surrounding her mother's death. It was more a case of omission, not telling her the whole story. When she thought about it, she would have said that, in spite of her amiable and confident manner, Lady Cowdray was afraid. *Afraid* was too strong a word. *Anxious* was a better fit. But anxious about what?

They were moving at a sedate pace, too sedate for Faith's peace of mind. She didn't want to miss her train.

"I have a train to catch," she told the driver politely.

"Arr," was all he said in reply.

She hadn't been aware of her surroundings, but as they passed through the great iron gates of the estate, she saw that the mist was much thicker than when she'd arrived. As a Londoner, she was used to pea soup fogs, but those fogs covered paved roads that were well-lit and easy to navigate. In the country, it was different. There were no streetlamps to light their way or well-marked roads. If the driver wasn't careful, they could end up in a ditch.

"I'm going to miss my train, aren't I?" She knew she had stayed too long, but she'd been totally absorbed in the stories Lady Cowdray had told about her mother.

The driver's sudden response made her cower in the corner. He raised his whip, but it was only to crack it so that the horse harnessed to their buggy would pick up its hooves. He cracked it again, and the buggy took off, careening from side to side as it rattled over gravel. She had to clench her teeth to stop them from chattering. When she started bouncing, she'd had enough.

"I don't care if I miss my train!" she yelled. "I wasn't finding fault with you. Please, just stop—"

She screamed when the buggy hit a pothole and lurched to one side. Her parcel slid to the floor, and she quickly retrieved it. Panicked or not, she wasn't going to lose her mother's diary.

Bang!

Her eyes flared. "That sounded like a gun going off!"

Bang! Bang!

"Someone is shooting at us!" Her voice was shrill. "They must think we're poachers."

"Get down and hang on!" yelled a voice she recognized. "We're going over the bridge."

Her jaw dropped. James Burnett? *James Burnett* was driving the buggy? What was *he* doing here?

At the next bang she threw herself to the floor and curled

into a ball. A plethora of thoughts chased themselves inside her head. Someone had made a terrible mistake. They weren't poachers, or housebreakers, or thieves. They were law-abiding citizens. They should stop the buggy and give themselves up.

Where was Mr. Farr? What had the madman beside her done to him?

She braced for the shock of the buggy hitting the bridge, but it was the shock of a gun going off right by her ear that made her scream. She opened her eyes. James held the reins in one hand and a smoking revolver in the other. The acrid smell of powder made her stomach heave. It was his gun that had gone off.

The buggy slowed and finally stopped. "Bloody hell! I think our pony is lame." He jumped out of the buggy. "Well, don't just lie there like a sitting duck. Take my hand and jump. And don't forget your parcel!"

Clutching her parcel and reticule to her bosom with one hand, she heaved herself up, grabbed for his hand, and jumped. As her feet landed on the gravel, her teeth jarred, bringing tears to her eyes. Before she could find words to berate him, he was hauling her off the road and into the thick of the mist. She stumbled a time or two, but he had the instincts of a cat and seemed to know where he was going.

He mouthed the words in her ear. "There's a waterfall up ahead with a small cavern behind it. If you make yourself small you can crawl into it. Wait for me there."

"Where are you going?" she asked, alarmed.

"To even the odds." And with that, he was gone.

She could hear the rush of water straight ahead of her. As she emerged from the mist, her heart sank. *Small* wasn't the word for it. A pigmy would have trouble finding shelter under that fall of water. She wouldn't dignify it with the tile of *waterfall*.

She balked. She was a teacher at a girls' school, for heaven's sake, not a spy or a murderess. No one had reason to hurt her. This was all a colossal misunderstanding, and James Burnett had a lot of explaining to do. He acted as though the men who had shot at them were villains. They could just as easily be gamekeepers on the hunt for poachers.

Did gamekeepers shoot first and ask questions later? None that she had ever heard of. Her mind was suddenly made up for her by a volley of shots coming from the direction of the bridge. She didn't want to be mistaken for a poacher. After stuffing her reticule and parcel under the bodice of her coat, she edged her way under the waterfall and sank to her haunches.

The minutes ticked by with no more shots to frighten the life out of her. She might have been the only person in the world. As her fear ebbed, suspicion filled her mind. What was James doing here? What had he done with Mr. Farr? How did he know about this waterfall?

A sudden spray of water doused her cheeks, and she sucked in a startled breath. *Only a douse of cold water,* she told herself crossly as her heart gradually slowed. She grew impatient with herself. She'd just heard her mother's life story. There was nothing her mother would not dare. Then why was she, her mother's daughter, cowering in this foxhole like an escaped convict? She had done nothing wrong.

On that thought, she pushed herself up, flattened her back against the rock face, and edged her way out. Breathing deeply, she stepped away from the water's edge and promptly stumbled. Her shoes were wet, the hem of her coat soaked up water, and she was tempted to weep. As she got up, she allowed herself a small sniff then froze when she heard someone approaching.

"I've got one of them," a voice shouted, a cultured voice. Through the mist a shape emerged, a ghostly shadow, indistinct and horribly threatening.

The cultured voice continued, "No sign of the other one." Then to Faith, "Come over here and don't try anything."

Faith spoke clearly and reasonably with only a slight tremor in her voice. "This has all been a colossal misunderstanding. My friend seems to think that you are villains, and you seem to think that we are poachers. We're not. Lady Cowdray will vouch..." Her words died when she saw the revolver he was pointing straight at her. Her heart began to race, and she could scarcely hear the sound of the waterfall for the blood pounding in her ears.

Someone else emerged from the mist, someone whose voice had the broad accent of one of the locals. He was breathless from his exertions. "Three of our fellows are down. Do what you have to do, and let's get out of here before her friend comes after us."

Do what you have to do. She didn't like the sound of that. Where was James? Why had he left her to the mercy of these villains?

"Patience," said the cultured voice. "First she has to give us the book."

First she had to give him the book? What came second? As her mind made the connection, her fear took a gargantuan leap. He was going to kill her. She had only one chance, and she seized it. "James!" She yelled at the top of her lungs, as though she were yelling a battle cry, and she sprang at the man with the gun, the man she considered the leader.

He wasn't expecting her attack. Unbalanced, with a shocked yell, he teetered at the edge of the roiling stream then fell into it with an almighty splash. His companion was too slow for Faith. With a speed born of desperation, she dodged past him and darted into the mist.

Her feet had never moved faster. Her heart had never pumped so hard. Though she was running blind, only one thought gripped her mind: she had to get away.

A tall, shadowy figure suddenly loomed up in front of her. Faith put her head down and charged. He sidestepped the charge, grabbed her from behind, and clamped a hand over her mouth, cutting off her scream.

"Can't you do anything right?" he growled in her ear. "I told you to stay hidden. You were quite safe where you were. What were you thinking to show yourself and scream my name?"

At the first sound of James's voice, her body went lax. When he took his hand away from her mouth, she got out in gasps, "We've got to get back to the house. We'll be safe there."

"That's the first place they'll look. Have you got the book they were after?"

"Right here." She undid the top button of her coat and produced her parcel and reticule.

"What makes it so special? I mean, why kill for it?"

She shook her head. "I have no idea. It's only my mother's diary. Maybe when I have a chance to read it, it will tell me."

"Then let's get the hell out of here."

"Where are we going?"

"Back to the station to catch the train."

She would have protested that she could not make it that far, when the sound of someone whispering nearby made her heart jump. Swallowing her fear, she clutched James's coat and followed where he led.

When they reached the station, passengers were beginning to board the train. "If we run…" Faith stopped. She could hardly find the breath to go on. They'd covered the distance to the station in ten minutes, and her body was punishing her for putting it to such a test. Her legs felt leaden, her lungs were burning, and if it were not for James's arm holding her up, she wouldn't be moving at all.

"Hurry!" she managed to gasp out.

He was scanning the station just in case one of the thugs had arrived before them. Satisfied that his dream had not misled him, he gave his attention to Faith. "What did you say?"

"We'll miss the train."

"Oh, it won't go without me."

Now she was really annoyed. "Don't be stupid. Trains wait for no one."

"They do for me. Ah, there's the stationmaster. I want a word with him. This will only take a moment. Keep your head down and keep out of sight."

He moved so fast, she didn't have time to argue. With an arm around her shoulders, he rushed her to the front of the train, handed two tickets to the ticket master, then shoved her inside and stalked off to speak to the stationmaster.

She could see the stationmaster's face. He shook his head in response to something James said. A moment later, his eyes widened, and he nodded. At that point, Faith looked down the length of the platform. There was no sign of anyone who looked like a villain. Then again, what did she know about villains?

Her attention turned to the interior of the carriage that James had pushed her into. Naturally, it was first-class. It comprised two separate compartments, both empty, and a convenience at one end of a short corridor for, well, the convenience of first-class passengers.

The guard blew his whistle just as James climbed into

the carriage. "Let's take the last compartment in the carriage," he said. "I always find it more comfortable."

"I'm not interested in comfortable!" The impatience in her voice made his brows lift. "I'm interested in someone trying to kill me! I'm interested in what you said to the stationmaster! But most of all, I'm interested in what you are doing here in Chalbourne and how you knew I would be here."

There was the sudden grind of metal on metal, and a belch of steam billowed from the engine, engulfing the nearest carriages in its choking fumes.

James said, "Shall we take our seats before we are jolted off our feet?"

If there was one thing she detested, it was take-charge men. On the other hand, if he had not turned up when he did, she could be lying in a ditch right now.

Squaring her shoulders, she followed him into the compartment, sank into a well-upholstered banquette, and waited for him to join her. "Well, James Burnett, I'm waiting for an explanation."

When he began to laugh, she bristled. "Did I say something funny?"

He shook his head, but he didn't stop grinning. "Look at you," he said. "Look at me. We look like a couple of scarecrows."

She had to give him the point. They were both mired with mud, and leaves were sticking to their hair. She'd lost her bonnet, but at least her precious parcel was intact. She rested her hand on it in an unconscious protective gesture.

"Once the train gets going, you can tidy yourself in the facilities," he said.

Her interest was piqued. She'd always wanted to see all the amenities of first-class travel. "Later," she said. "First, I want to know what you were doing at Lady Cowdray's and how you knew those villains would be lying in wait for me."

He combed his fingers through his hair and threw her a strangely appealing look. Finally, he shrugged. "I have two explanations," he said. "The first is..."

"Yes?"

James linked his fingers and contemplated them in silence. He was remembering his dream, how everything had been laid out for him like a map: the house, the bridge, the waterfall, the lay of the land. He'd been inside the mind of the leader and knew where and how he had placed his men. It was like a game of chess. There was no way he could circumvent it. He couldn't stop Faith going to see Lady Cowdray nor did he want to. It was imperative that she get the book. All he could do was play to win.

He drew in a quick breath. "The first explanation is that I inherited the gift of second sight from the McEcheran side of my family, and I can see into the future—"

She cut him off with a disbelieving snort. "Do I look like a simpleton? This is not a joke. We are in serious trouble."

He regarded her steadily for a moment, then said, "According to my Scottish Granny McEcheran, I'm a Grampian seer."

"Yes, well, according to my Irish Granny McBride, our family can trace its roots back to Merlin, and that trumps any seer you care to name. Can we get on with it? You said you had two explanations. The second had better be more credible than the first."

He raised his shoulders in a gesture of defeat. "Have it your own way. It's just as I told you. I saw your advertisement in the paper and decided to follow up on it. When you told me that you suspected you were being watched, I decided to follow up on that, too."

She was breathing hard as she saw how it must have

happened. "You broke into my room and found my correspondence!"

"You wouldn't tell me anything. What else could I do?"

"You knew I was coming here today to meet Lady Cowdray?"

"And I'm not sorry I did." He sounded aggrieved. "Those cutthroats were lying in wait for you."

She pounced on this. "How could you possibly have known that? And don't give me that nonsense about second sight."

"I wasn't about to. I overheard them on the way up. They were waiting in ambush under the bridge." Leastways, he'd dreamed it, so it wasn't an outright lie. "They wanted the book. You were safe as long as you didn't give it to them."

Her brow knitted in a frown. "Where did you go when I was hiding under the waterfall? One of the villains said that three of their fellows were down. They're not . . . ?" She choked on the word.

"Of course they're not dead!" He shook his head in disbelief. "I knocked them about a bit, that was all. They'll survive."

She wasn't finished yet. "Did you follow me to Lady Cowdray's?"

"I was on the same train as you."

"But—"

He suddenly pounced on her. "Have done with these useless questions! You're alive! I'm alive! Things might have turned out quite differently. Don't be such a sobersides. Everything worked out for the best, didn't it?"

He was right. An intoxicating cocktail of emotions—delayed relief, joy, rapture—bubbled up, making her dizzy. "Yes, of course, it did."

"That's all I wanted to hear."

Then he kissed her.

It wasn't a gentle kiss. It was bruising, greedy, glorious, and just what she needed at that moment in time. She
was alive, desperately alive, and so was James. The need
to affirm that truth suffused every cell in her body. She
wrapped her arms around him and savored the strength of
the arms that wrapped around her. She thought she would
melt with the wonder of it.

When he touched his tongue to hers, the familiar quiver
began deep inside her. They couldn't get close enough. He
lifted her bodily to sit on his lap, and the hard bulge that
thrust against her made her ache with wanting. He kissed
her again and again, his mouth slanting across hers with
a passion that made her dizzy. His hands slid to her bottom, and he pulled her hard against his groin. When he
ground himself against her, she moaned with a need that
was building higher and higher.

She kissed his cheeks, his ears, his throat, and made
a small sound of pleasure when she felt the pulse in his
throat jump. Her actions were rash, but she wanted to be
rash. She was tired of being constrained by all the rules
that had been placed upon her, as her father's daughter, as
a paid companion, and as a teacher. She wanted to be more
like her mother. She wanted to squeeze as much out of
life as was humanly possible and damn the consequences.
There would be pain, there would be pleasure, but at least
the empty, hollow space where her heart should be would
know that she had truly lived.

Her ardor fired his like a flame to dry tinder. He undid
the buttons of her coat and dragged the bodice of her gown
to her waist. Her stays were easily dealt with, then he
feasted on her breasts, laving the hard buds of her nipples,
sucking until pain and pleasure became pure torment.

When he raised his head to look at her, they were both
breathing hard. His words punctuated his harsh gasps as

he drew air into his lungs. "I've never seen you like this before. What—"

She wasn't about to let him spoil it with words. She reached for the closure on his trousers and began to undo the buttons. "I'm not looking for love. I don't want a husband. I want to experience everything life has to offer before it's too late."

There was a moment of profound silence; then, as suddenly as he had grabbed her, he thrust her away and lifted her till she was sitting in her own place. She blinked rapidly as she came to herself.

"James," she breathed out, "what...?"

He was scowling, and she instinctively inched away.

"A new experience. Is that what I am?" His voice grated on her ears like sandpaper on a scab. "You don't know when to stop. This is what got us into trouble all those years ago: lust, sheer animal lust. Seems that neither of us has learned from our mistakes." He straightened and folded his arms across his chest. He spoke in a flat, neutral tone. "Shall we return to the subject at hand? I've answered your questions; now it's your turn to answer mine."

Faith stared at him wide-eyed as she pulled her clothes into place. She wanted to brain him. She wanted to throttle him. She wanted to spit on him and stomp all over him.

Lust. He must be right, because she could never, *never* love anyone as insensitive as James Burnett.

She turned her head and looked out the window. The mist was lifting, the sun was beginning to set, and she could see the lush English countryside in all its glory.

"Faith?"

She did not look at him. "What is it you want to know?"

Now his voice was soft and gentle. "Start from the beginning," he said. "Tell me what prompted you to put that advertisement in the paper."

Chapter 10

✹

She stared out the window so that he would not see how furi-
ous she was. She was a woman scorned not once but twice.
James Burnett, of all people! How could she have melted
for him like that? If she looked at him now, she'd reduce
him to a cinder.

She gazed steadfastly out the window as though she
were gathering her thoughts. "It began," she said, "in Ransome's bank about a month ago. Long before that, when I
left Lady Beale's employ, I deposited a trunk in their vault
with the idea of retrieving it when I was settled. With one
thing and another, I never got around to it."

She turned from the window to look at him. "I didn't
forget about it, but it contained nothing of interest as far as
I was aware. The trunk belonged to my father, and most of
the contents were his—deeds, business papers, mementos
from his university days, a package of old photographs,
that sort of thing. The only reason I wanted to look through
it was because I knew it contained my father's commentary

on Herodotus. Speech Day was coming up, and I thought it would help me prepare my girls with their translation."

James knew of the custom of depositing trunks in Ransome's vault. The clients who did this usually moved around a great deal: soldiers who were shipping out or debtors who were on the run from creditors. The thing about Ransome's was that they never threw anything away. A man could return years later, and his trunk would still be waiting for him.

She looked out the window again. "To cut a long story short, I spilled the package of photographs, and when I picked them up, I saw an inscription on the back of one. I didn't remember seeing this photograph before. It must have been stuck to the back of another one. At any rate, I'd missed it. 'Madeline Maynard,' it said. That was all."

When she paused, he said softly, "And Madeline Maynard was your mother's maiden name?"

"Clever you. With your psychic talents, I suppose you know why I was shocked?"

She was needling him, and he thought that perhaps he deserved it. The trouble was, Faith didn't know when to stop, though this time she'd certainly brought him to his senses with the icy splash of her words. He lusted after her. She lusted after life. Is that all he was? A new experience?

She was waiting for his response.

"Why were you shocked, Faith?"

"Because the woman in the photograph looked about forty. My mother died when she was twenty-six; leastways, that was what I was told. She died in a boating accident on Lake Windermere, my father told me, and her body was never recovered."

"You're sure the woman in the photograph was your mother?"

"Yes, I was sure. There were other photographs of my

mother, but they were of a much younger woman, and they were grainy and faded. This photograph was a portrait, only head and shoulders. There was no doubt in my mind that it was of Madeline."

"What happened to your father's trunk?"

"I cleaned it out. It was mainly packed with books I couldn't bear to part with and old deeds and papers."

"So you put your advertisement in the paper, hoping, I suppose, that your mother would reply to it?"

Her voice had a brittle edge. "I was curious, that's all. I wanted to find out where she was and what she was doing. I thought that maybe she had lost her memory or . . . I don't know what I thought." She shook her head. "That's not true. Don't ask me how, but I knew she was dead."

He said softly, "Where is the photograph now?"

She raised her reticule. "Right here. I had to send it to Lady Cowdray to establish my connection to Madeline Maynard. She returned it to me today when I went to see her."

After all she'd been through, he wasn't sure that this was the best time to question her. On the other hand, the optimum moment might never arrive. There was too much history between them to overcome.

Keeping his voice neutral, he said, "Tell me what happened at Lady Cowdray's, Faith. Help me understand why you are at the center of this storm that has suddenly exploded around you."

"I only wish I knew! As I said, it started when I put that advertisement in the paper." Slowly, haltingly, she related most of what she had learned at Lady Cowdray's, but there were many gaps. Finally, she said, "I don't think I'm at the center of the storm. I think my mother is." She patted the brown paper parcel that was on the seat beside her. "And when I've read her diary, I'll know why."

"We could read it now. I could light the lamp—"

"No! It's not that easy. It's in shorthand, a code, and I'll need time to decipher it."

"Tell me about your mother," he said. "What was she like?"

"My mother," she said, "was the kind of woman St. Winnifred's would be proud to claim as its own. She was an adventurer and an explorer, as was Lady Cowdray. They traveled by mule mostly, and visited areas that were accessible only to intrepid travelers like themselves." She turned her head on the banquette to look at him. "So you see, a husband and child would only get in my mother's way. That's why she left us and, as far as I can tell, she never looked back." She looked away. "She was buried out there, you know, in Egypt. There's a Coptic church. I don't suppose I shall ever visit her grave."

When she became lost in her own thoughts, he sighed inaudibly, but he did not prompt her to go on. *Patience,* he told himself.

At last she said, "Do you know, I've lived in England all my life except for one short jaunt to...to Wales? My mother was what is known as an Egyptologist. She wrote articles for newspapers on the places she had visited. That was how she supported herself. She had a pen name, Madeline Wolf. Obviously, she didn't want to be found."

He stretched out his legs and waited for her to go on.

"I have no idea why my father didn't tell me the truth."

"Maybe," said James, testing the thought gingerly, "he was afraid that he would lose you, too. You know, that when you were older, you might find her and join her."

"I doubt if she would have had me. I don't possess the kind of focus and direction that she had, or of the adventurous women who can be found at St. Winnifred's on Speech Day."

There was something challenging in the way she looked

at him, and he decided not to pursue the subject. He nodded in a noncommittal way before continuing. "Didn't Lady Cowdray give you some clue as to why these villains would be lying in wait for you and why they would want your mother's diary?"

"I'm not sure." Her brows knitted together as she focused her thoughts. "She seemed to think that my mother died in mysterious circumstances."

"What?" He was astonished. "And you've waited until now before telling me this?"

Her lips flattened, and she sat up straighter. "It's just a vague feeling that Lady Cowdray had."

"Well, I'm a great believer in feelings. So what did she tell you?"

She seemed to be holding her breath. Releasing it slowly, she went on to describe what had happened the night her mother died and how Lady Cowdray had found Madeline's diary in her box after she returned to England.

"And she doesn't know how it got into her box?" James asked.

"Apparently not."

"What happened to your mother's box?"

"Oh, I never thought to ask," she said in a dismayed voice.

He thought for a moment and said finally, "Lady Cowdray never thought to have someone transcribe your mother's diary?"

"So she said."

"Mmm." He sank back against the banquette, crossed one booted foot over the other, and steepled his fingers. "Sounds to me as though Lady Cowdray knows more than she is telling."

"That's what I thought, too, but I could hardly come out and say it."

They sat in silence as each became preoccupied with their own thoughts. Finally, Faith said, "What did you say to the stationmaster?"

He came to himself slowly. "The stationmaster?"

"Before we boarded the train."

"Oh." He straightened. "I told him that I'd heard gunshots coming from Lady Cowdray's estate and that you had appeared out of the mist screaming murder. I advised him to telephone her ladyship to warn her that there were ruffians on the prowl. Unfortunately, she doesn't have a telephone, nor does anyone in Chalbourne, but he said that he would get the police right onto it."

She shook her head in wonder.

"What?"

"Chalbourne is a small country town. I'm not surprised there are no telephones there. You can get where you want to go in five or ten minutes. Everyone is practically within hailing distance."

"Not if you live in London and want to speak to the police in Chalbourne."

Something else occurred to her. "And Mr. Farr? What is going to happen when he tells the authorities that you stole his buggy?"

He spoke to her as though she were a slow-witted child. "Mr. Farr isn't going to say anything about me. I have more sense than to let my face be seen when I commit a criminal act. No. As I see it, they'll suspect the same people who shot at us."

She gazed at him for several long moments with unseeing eyes. Nodding imperceptibly, she said, "Am I in a lot of trouble, James?"

He shrugged. "I don't think there is any doubt of that. You have the book the villains want. Whoever is directing them must be wondering whether you have read it or not and whether there is something in it that he doesn't want anyone to know."

"If he is willing to kill to get it, that means..."

"He must have something serious to hide, something that could discredit him completely or, perhaps, take him straight to the gallows."

She was silent for a long time, then whispered, "But how did he know about my mother's diary? I didn't know of its existence until Lady Cowdray gave it to me."

"Maybe she told someone about it?" His eyes narrowed as he sifted through various impressions. He turned his head to look at her. "I think someone read Lady Cowdray's last note to you and put two and two together. She said that she had something of Madeline's that she thought might interest you."

She stared at him in horror. "Do you know how that makes me feel? I could have been murdered in my bed. Who would do such a thing?" Her teeth snapped together. "What am I saying? It's what you did, isn't it?"

He leaned forward and patted her hand. "Yes, but I'm on your side. You're not alone. We're in this together." He put a finger to her lips to stay the spate of words. "The station-master knows my name, and you can bet that it won't be long before our mutual enemy knows that I'm involved, too."

He got up and lit the lamp. "I don't know about you, but I'm famished. Let's see what is here to take the edge off our appetite."

She watched as he lifted a basket done up in a checked cover from the rack above their heads. Opening the cover, he looked inside. "Cold chicken, cheese, fruitcake," he enumerated, "and—oh—a bottle of claret to wash them down." He smiled into her eyes. "Why don't you use the facilities to freshen up while I set out our meal?"

She tried not to be impressed. "You do yourself proud, don't you?" she said and sniffed.

"Oh, this isn't for me especially. We treat all our first-class passengers like this."

If she hadn't been hungry *and* desperate to use the facilities, she might have said more. Maintaining her dignity, she left the compartment. When she returned, she wasn't merely impressed; she was amazed at such luxury.

"What are you thinking?" he said softly. He handed her a glass of claret.

"I was wondering," she said, "whether I could learn to shoot a gun."

Oddly enough, her words pleased him immensely.

They went back to the beginning, from the moment Faith had found her mother's photograph in her father's trunk in Ransome's bank, to the events of that night when a band of ruffians had waited for her to leave Lady Cowdray's house. Small things she missed occurred to her, and she was inwardly damning herself for not asking her ladyship more questions.

At one point, she said, "She invited me to the next meeting of the Egyptology Society. I have a card here somewhere." She felt in her reticule and produced not only the card in question but also the photograph of her mother and the photograph that her ladyship had given her.

"This is the photograph I had to send Lady Cowdray," she said, "and this is the invitation to the Egyptology Society meeting."

He gave the invitation a cursory glance and studied the photograph of her mother. The face that stared out at him was remarkably like Faith's, but Madeline's features lacked the soft, feminine contours of her daughter's. It was possible, of course, he told himself, that he was allowing the tales Faith had related of this fearless lady to shape his thinking. He admired women like Madeline Maynard tremendously, but he preferred to do it from afar.

"It's not a very good photograph," he said, and he flipped it over to read the inscription on the back.

"No. Well, it was taken ten years ago. There have been amazing improvements in photography since then." She gave him the second photograph. "This was taken on my mother's last visit to Cairo. A few days later, she was dead."

He scrutinized the faces in the photograph and found Madeline in the front row. "Where are these people now?"

"Some of them are members of the Egyptology Society. Lady Cowdray said she would introduce me to them at their next meeting. A few of them, to use Lady Cowdray's expression, are no longer with us."

"They're dead?"

She nodded. "Or they've moved away."

"I'd like to borrow this photograph if I may."

Her reply was lost when their carriage rattled and bucked as it shot over a bridge. The sandwiches and savories on her plate did a wild dervish, then just as suddenly stopped when their carriage righted itself. A hoot from the engine had James grinning.

Faith said faintly, "I think the engineer is enjoying himself."

He slipped the photograph into his coat pocket. "I bet half the men on this train wish they were up there with him."

She smiled weakly, but the smile soon faded. "I still can't believe that I'm at the center of some devious conspiracy."

"Not a conspiracy," he corrected. "Leastways I don't think so. I'm putting my money on one villain who thought he'd got away with a capital crime—murder or something like it—and got the shock of his life when you turned up and started asking questions about Madeline Maynard."

He swallowed the dregs of his wine and looked at her over the rim of his glass. "You see what this means?"

"It means that the first thing I do is buy myself a gun and learn to use it. No. The first thing I do is get out of London! Lily is expecting me, anyway."

"And where is Lily?"

"In Brighton with her brother and his family. We go there every year."

He shook his head. "I'm not keen on your running off to Brighton, and the same goes for St. Winnifred's. These thugs will be looking for you, and those are the first places they'll look. In a few days, when no one breaks down their doors and hauls them off to prison, they'll think they're safe. I want you where I can keep a close eye on you."

She was remembering the man with the cultured voice who had pointed his gun straight at her, and she swallowed.

"Faith?"

She looked up at him. He was on his feet, returning the basket to the rack above the banquette. She watched the muscles bunch on his arms and across his broad shoulders. His hands were square and strong, strong enough to break a few heads. He was built like a wrestler. Though she was loath to admit it after the shabby way he had rejected her, she was more than willing to let him keep a close eye on her.

He sat down beside her. "Look on the bright side," he said. "With a bit of luck, we may know in a few hours who is behind the plot to harm you. All you need do is transcribe your mother's diary."

"I told you. It's not going to be that easy. It's in code."

He shrugged. "Fine. But however long it takes, I want you where I can keep an eye on you."

She shot him a glance and decided there was no hidden

threat in his words. Of course, he wasn't thinking of seducing her in some dingy hotel. He had made his sentiments as clear as crystal.

"If I can't stay at the school or join Lily in Brighton," she said, "where am I going to go?"

"My aunt, I know, would be more than happy to have you as her guest. You remember my aunt? You met her on Speech Day. Her house is in Berkeley Square."

"What's to stop those villains coming after me at your aunt's house to get Madeline's diary? I don't think two women on their own would be much of a match for them."

His mouth quirked. "I'm not so sure about that. I think you and my aunt would be a match for anyone. However, you won't be alone. I intend to move in with you. Hopefully, it won't be for long."

"Won't it look odd? Your coming to live with your aunt?"

"I'll say that I'm getting my house refurbished. Come to think of it, that will surprise no one. It hasn't been decorated in years, and most of the rooms are empty. No. No more questions. I need time to think about how we are going to proceed."

She exhaled a spurt of breath. He was doing it again, taking charge, as though he were the company chairman and she were one of the serfs. "Don't I have any say in this?"

He stretched one arm along the back of the banquette and gave her a sleepy grin. "Of course. I'm all ears. How do you think we should proceed?"

She chewed on her bottom lip and gazed out the window. "I need time to think about it."

"Fine." He looked at his watch. "There's at least an hour to go before we reach London. I'm going to catch forty winks."

Chapter 11

It was dark when they reached the house in Berkeley Square, and by the time they alighted from the hansom cab, Faith was beginning to have second thoughts. She felt like an intruder and was convinced that his aunt would be put out. James's softly spoken directive to let him do all the talking only added to her sense of awkwardness. What kept her back straight and her feet moving was the outline of her mother's diary clutched close to her bosom. Though she was out of practice, she knew how to read her father's code. That was her obsession now: to transcribe her mother's diary in hopes of finding out why someone would go to such lengths to suppress it.

Her inner reflections came to an abrupt halt when the door was opened by what appeared to be a blacksmith in livery. His blue jacket fairly molded itself to muscles as hard as boulders. He couldn't have been much older than James.

"Ah, Butcher," said James, "be kind enough to tell my aunt I'm here."

Butcher beamed. "Come in, come in. A pleasure to see you again, sir. I thought you knew. Your aunt left to visit friends in Henley, oh, on Thursday last, and on Friday, your family arrived."

"My family?" said James, and Faith detected a slight tightening of his smile.

The butler nodded. "They are in the dining room. Shall I—"

"James? Is that you?" The dining room door swung open, and a man in his late fifties emerged. He walked with the aid of a cane, and though his dark hair was turning to gray, there was no doubt in Faith's mind that she was looking at an older version of James.

"Father!" said James. "I thought you were fixed in Scotland."

They shook hands, but their greeting lacked warmth in Faith's opinion.

Others emerged from the dining room, a youngish woman in her mid-forties whose smile of welcome held a trace of anxiety, a dark-haired girl of eleven or twelve and, finally, a young man of no more than eighteen or nineteen. He was very handsome and looked as though he knew it.

James caught her hand and brought her forward. "Faith," he said, "come and meet my family." To his family, with the same strained smile, he went on, "This is Miss Faith McBride."

Before the introductions could be completed, the handsome youth straightened and took a step forward. "Faith McBride?" He chuckled. "The runaway McBride? The girl who left you standing at the altar, Brother? Well, this should make for an interesting family get-together. And here I thought it was going to be dull."

"Roderick!" interjected his father sternly, "that will do."

Faith acknowledged each person with a smile and a

slight inclination of her head. The woman with the anxious eyes was Margaret Burnett, evidently James's stepmother. The handsome youth was Roderick, a half brother, and the eleven-year-old girl, Harriet, had to be his half sister.

James had a family. The thought bounced around inside her head like a ricocheting bullet. She knew that he had a father and that there was a crumbling castle near Aberdeen. She knew his mother had died when he was only twelve. She could not say that he hadn't mentioned his family but, as far as she remembered, he'd been referring to his cousins. *James had a family.* She'd once been engaged to the man. She had made the trip to Scotland and met the woman he had eventually married. No one had mentioned a stepmother or younger siblings to her.

James's voice cut across her thoughts. "Things are never dull when you are around, Roddy. What is it this time? Gaming debts? Woman trouble? Or have you been sent down from St. Andrews yet again?"

"All three," replied Roderick airily. "We can't all be like you, Jamie, with our noses to the grindstone."

Margaret Burnett gave a nervous laugh. Ignoring this contentious byplay, she grasped Faith's free hand, the one that wasn't clutching Madeline's diary in a death grip. "Are you hungry? Have you dined? Shall I ask Butcher to bring you something to eat?"

Faith warmed to the woman at once. She wasn't polished or elegant like most women of her class. In fact, she seemed almost shabby, and Faith wondered whether it was because she wasn't interested in clothes or whether her husband kept a tight grip on the purse strings.

James's voice cut off Faith's reply. "The most damnable thing has occurred," he said, and he went on to tell his family what he'd told the stationmaster at Chalbourne, how Faith was attacked by ruffians when she left Lady

Cowdray's place, and how he, by sheer chance, had business in the same area and had managed to spirit her away. He made no mention of the diary.

When he came to the end of his story, Mr. Burnett clapped James on the shoulder. "All's well that ends well, eh, lad?"

Roderick made a loud, derisory sound, which everyone ignored.

James went on, "As you may imagine, Faith, Miss McBride, doesn't wish to return home until the police have got to the bottom of the attack on her. I gave them this address, hoping that Aunt Mariah would put us up. My place is in a shambles. Besides, it wouldn't be fitting for Faith to take up residence in a bachelor establishment. If I'd known you had taken over Aunt Mariah's house, I would have settled Faith in a hotel."

Margaret said, "A hotel? I wouldn't dream of allowing Miss McBride to go to a hotel. There is plenty of space here. I'll get the maid to make up rooms for you both."

"That won't be necessary," said James. "A hotel will do fine."

Faith saw Margaret wince, and she hastened to smooth things over. Shooting James a scorching look, she said, "What James means is that we don't want to put you to any trouble."

"Oh, it's no trouble. We'd like you to stay, wouldn't we, Colin?"

James's father nodded. "That goes without saying." He turned aside to have a word with the butler.

James looked at Faith and, more pointedly, at the parcel she clutched, and the message she received was that he wanted them to start decoding her mother's diary as soon as possible, not socialize with his family.

The silent message that she sent back was that they would

get to the diary when she was ready and not a moment before.

Smiling warmly at Margaret, she said, "I was supposed to catch the train for Brighton, but James wouldn't hear of it. The trouble is, my traveling case with all my clothes went on ahead of me. As for being hungry, I'm famished. Sandwiches with a pot of tea to go with them will do very well, thank you."

The smile returned to Margaret's eyes. "Did you get that, Butcher? And we'll be in the drawing room."

"I did, ma'am. Sandwiches and tea in the drawing room, and the upstairs maid is to get two rooms ready, one for Miss McBride and the other for Mr. James."

Margaret looked from James to Faith, as though she expected them to make their excuses and leave. When that didn't happen, she released a pent-up breath then led the way to the stairs.

Faith had taken only a fleeting impression of the house. Now she looked about her with interest. Though it was Georgian and typical of other Mayfair town houses with its beautiful proportions and cantilevered staircase, it was not decorated in the current mode. The paintings on the walls were anything but sentimental and depicted scenes of the blood and gore of long-ago battles.

James's father kept her informed as they climbed the stairs. "Stirling Bridge," he pointed out as though Faith would recognize its significance. His voice changed, softened, as he pointed to another. "Culloden," he intoned. "It should never have happened."

James's voice carried to her. "My aunt's late husband and my father are—were—passionate about Scottish history. Wait till you see the dining room."

The drawing room was more to her taste. The pictures on the walls were all of gardens, and the mantelpiece displayed silver-framed photographs, portraits of, she presumed, Mrs. Leyland's nearest and dearest. It was a comfortable room.

When they were settled, she surreptitiously studied each person in turn. Harriet had inveigled Roderick into a game of cards. The transformation in the young man was startling. His smiles and laughter were unaffected. It was obvious that his little sister adored him and just as obvious that she was in awe of James. Faith wondered about the others. Roderick was the rebel, challenging his older brother at every turn. Mr. Burnett and his wife seemed... on edge.

Mr. Burnett was explaining what had brought them all up to town. "Margaret's cousin is to be married in Henley on Saturday next."

Faith looked at James. That was the day the Egyptology Society was to meet to hear a lecture by Professor Marsh.

Mr. Burnett went on, "Your aunt is meeting us there, and after the wedding, we'll come back to Berkeley Square together. Meanwhile, we are enjoying a little holiday in town. I'm sure I wrote to you, James, the times and the dates, that sort of thing."

"You probably did." James shrugged. "Was I supposed to reply? It's not as though I know Margaret's cousin. I won't be going to the wedding."

Faith was shocked at this show of indifference, but only Margaret looked embarrassed. Faith did her bit to keep the conversation going, but when the topics of the cousin's wedding, the house and its contents, and the weather were exhausted, a long, awkward silence fell. It was a relief when the tea and sandwiches arrived.

"Roast beef," enthused Faith, trying to lighten the atmosphere. "Now that's what I call a sandwich."

That small compliment brought a brilliant smile to

Margaret's face. She pressed another sandwich on Faith, who consumed it with relish. She couldn't remember how much she'd eaten on the train, but her stomach was telling her that she was still hungry.

Conversation flagged momentarily, but when James's father posed a question that seemed totally unrelated to anything that had gone before, Faith almost choked on a mouthful of roast beef.

"So," he said, "when and where is the wedding to take place?"

"I don't remember mentioning a wedding," James replied. His tone of voice implied that he considered the subject closed.

Harriet was too young and too innocent to absorb these grown-up subtleties. Her ears pricked up. "Can I be a bridesmaid, James?" Then she looked as though she might dash for the door.

"It's 'may I,' not 'can I,'" her mother corrected. Her glance darted uneasily in James's direction.

James looked at his half sister, and his expression softened. "At my wedding," he said, "you will certainly be a bridesmaid."

Faith didn't like the sound of this, and she decided to nip it in the bud. Shooting James an arch look, she said, "James, you didn't tell me you were to be married. Who is the lucky girl?"

When everyone laughed, everyone but James, she realized they thought she was joking, and that she and James really were engaged.

Worse was to follow. Harriet clapped her hands and smiled brilliantly. "A bridesmaid at last! That will put Charlotte's light down to a peep," she cried. "She has been a bridesmaid twice already."

"My dear," remonstrated her mother, "it's the bride's

privilege to chose her attendants. No. I won't have you harass Miss McBride. When James and Faith are ready, they will tell us when they are to be married."

The look Faith shot James this time spoke volumes. *Put a stop to this,* it screamed.

His reply was a helpless shrug.

It was a relief when the butler returned, or so Faith thought, until she saw the tray with the bottle of champagne and four crystal glasses on it. As the butler dispensed the champagne, Mr. Burnett got to his feet.

"Well, well," he said, "it seems I got ahead of myself. Still, there's plenty more where this came from." He raised his glass, indicating that he was referring to the champagne. "Meanwhile, if I can't toast the happy couple, I give you Drumore."

They all stood, raised their glasses, and chorused, "Drumore."

When they were seated again, Mr. Burnett went on, "I presume, James, that when you do marry, you'll take up residence in Drumore, as is proper for my heir?"

There was a fraught moment of silence. Faith could sense the undercurrents that flowed between father and son. So, evidently, did everyone else. It was as though they'd all stopped breathing.

James seemed amused and answered easily. "Father, we have been down this road before. Drumore is not an asset as you seem to think. It's a liability. I can't afford to keep it up."

Mr. Burnett's face was suffused with color, and his voice sounded loud and harsh. "The castle has been in our family for generations. Drumore's history is Scotland's history. We have to keep it up."

To Faith, he said, "What say you, Miss McBride? Should

we donate Drumore to the nation, as James advises, or should we preserve it for future generations of Burnetts?"

She caught James's eye. He was looking vastly amused at her predicament, and that made her paste a brilliant smile on her face. To Mr. Burnett, she said, "Where there is a will, there is a way; that's what my father used to say."

Mr. Burnett beamed at her. "You'll do Drumore proud," he said.

That sinking feeling in the pit of Faith's stomach began to coil into a tight knot. This wasn't supposed to happen. She would never have inflicted herself on James's family if she'd thought for one moment that they'd get the wrong idea about James and her.

What was wrong with James? He should put a stop to it. He sat there, sphinxlike, as though impervious to what was going on around him. Was he arrogant, or was he simply insensitive to other people's feelings? Cool, distant, detached. It made her want to give him a good shaking.

The bedchamber that was assigned to Faith was at the back of the house so that, as Margaret pointed out, the comings and goings of carriages in the square would not disturb her sleep. It was a pleasant room done in shades of green and cream and smelling faintly of beeswax polish.

Relieved of James's presence, Margaret became a different person, less tense, more natural. She seemed to know just what was needed, and without fuss produced nightclothes for Faith and promised that her own things would be clean and ready for her to wear in the morning or, if she preferred, she could borrow one of Margaret's gowns.

After bidding Faith good night, she crossed to the door, hesitated a moment, then said shyly, "I'm so glad you and

James have made up your differences, Faith. You're just the kind of girl he needs. Sweet dreams."

Faith had the eerie feeling that another nail had been hammered into her coffin.

In a flurry of activity, she bustled about, seeing to her ablutions, ringing for the maid to take her garments away after she had changed into her borrowed nightclothes—a high-necked, long-sleeved flannel nightgown and woolen dressing robe—then she undid the strings of the parcel, removed Madeline's diary, and settled herself on a chair flanking the empty grate.

As she tried to decode the first page of the diary, her feelings of ill-usage drained away. All her thoughts were focused on the diary, and she wished that James would come to her so that she could talk things over with him.

She did not have long to wait. The soft tap on her door and the whispered, "Faith?" brought her head up.

"The door is open," she said softly.

James entered, still dressed in his outdoor things, and crossing to her, pulled a straight-backed chair close to hers so that they could both examine the diary.

"Sorry for the delay," he said. "I phoned a friend in Brighton who agreed to visit Lily and have your box returned by the next train."

"She'll think I'm staying on at Lady Cowdray's."

"Does it matter? You can write to her and tell her there has been a change of plan. But keep it simple. Don't go into detail. Now, what have you found out?"

She wasn't sure that it was wise to stay with his family, but she couldn't muster the energy to argue the point. It was the diary she wanted to talk about.

"What I've found out," she said, "is that this is going to be harder than I thought. The trouble is, I'm out of practice.

There's something else. Look here." She turned to the last two pages of the diary.

James knit his brows in concentration. "Numbers?" he said.

"I don't know what to make of it."

He stared at the numbers and traced them with his index finger. "It must be a code, too. These numbers must represent words."

"I wonder why she changed to another code?" She studied the numbers for a moment. "It's going to take me forever to break it."

He spoke slowly, thoughtfully. "I wouldn't be surprised if it's these last two pages our villain is after." He paused then went on, "Yes, that would explain why Madeline changed the code. There must be something here that someone is willing to go to any lengths to suppress." He frowned as he thought things through. "But who was it meant for? Who would know how to break this code?"

"I might manage it if I had enough time."

He sat back in his chair. "What do you know about codes?"

She straightened. "More than most. My father and I used to make up games with codes. It was his hobby. He told me that the War Office once offered him a job as a code breaker."

He blinked. "That's where my cousin Alex works. Maybe he can break this code or find someone to do it for us. I'll take the diary to him and—"

She snapped the diary closed and held it to her bosom. "Oh, no, you won't! I'm not letting this diary out of my sight. If your cousin can help, well and good, but he'll come to me and do it."

When he looked at her thoughtfully, she went on, "Try to understand, this is all I have left of my mother, and I'm not parting with it. I want to know what she was like, what she thought and felt. I don't want anyone else to dip into her private thoughts. It would be like eavesdropping. She was my mother," she finished feebly. "I want to know."

"Are you up to it? Families can sometimes turn out to be a colossal disappointment."

She cocked her head to the side. "Are you talking about your own family, James?"

"My family?" His brows lifted ironically. "I gave you a chance to get away from them. It was you who chose to stay."

"Because," she said, "it would have hurt Margaret's feelings. But that was before I came to see that they have the wrong idea about us, and you're not doing or saying anything to put them right."

He shrugged in that careless way she was coming to hate. "I don't know what more I can say to them. We both tried. You've seen what they're like. They get an idea in their heads, and it becomes fixed."

Her voice was becoming louder. "Well, unfix it. Speak to them. Do something."

"What difference does it make? We know we're not engaged. Let them think what they like."

She was appalled. "What is the matter with you? You've been like a block of granite since we arrived. Don't you have feelings? Don't you care about their feelings?"

He spoke to her the way he'd spoken to his brother. "Don't make judgments, Faith. You don't know what I feel for my family or what they feel for me."

"Well, I'm not stupid," she flared. "You have a house in town, don't you? Why did they come here when they could have stayed with you?"

"They've been coming to Aunt Mariah's long before I

bought my house in St. James, and my place is barely furnished. They wouldn't be comfortable there."

She was shaking her head.

"What?" he asked.

"You never mentioned your family to me; oh, I don't mean recently, I mean when we were engaged. We were going to be married, but you didn't tell me you had a brother and sister."

"Possibly because Roderick and Harriet were almost strangers to me. I was away at school when Roderick was born, then he was away at school when I left university."

He suddenly got up, put his chair back where he'd found it, and came to stand over her. "Don't get too fond of them, Faith," he said. "Remember, this is a temporary arrangement only."

"A temporary arrangement?" The inference that she might want to make it permanent, that she had hopes of snaring him as a husband, honed her temper to a razor-sharp edge. "You don't think I shall stay here? It would be too embarrassing. No. Tomorrow I shall take the train to Brighton as I always intended."

He sounded bored. "Fine. Leave the diary with me, and I'll arrange to have it decoded."

"Not on your life!" Still clutching the diary, she got to her feet so that he wouldn't be towering over her. "This diary belongs to me, and nothing will make me part with it."

He closed the gap between them till they were nose to nose and toe to toe. "Now, you listen to me, Faith McBride. I didn't risk life and limb so that you could walk off with the prize. I'm entitled to know why someone shot at me. I want to find those villains, and the diary is my best chance of doing it. So what's it to be, Faith? Will you stay with the diary or will you go off on your own to Brighton?"

She was tempted to walk out the door, but his reference to the villains set her mind off on another track. She had a vision of the man with the cultured voice chasing her through the streets of Brighton. If she met him face-to-face, she wouldn't know who he was. All she'd seen was a figure shrouded in mist.

She swallowed her pride. "I'll stay, but only until I have decoded the diary."

"Fine," he said, as though whether she stayed made no difference to him.

At the door, he turned. "I would kiss you good night, but you don't know when to stop, Miss McBride."

"What?"

The door closed before she could lambaste him with a few well-chosen words.

She locked the door and sagged against it. She was so tired, she could hardly keep her eyes open. Perhaps that was why she found it hard to decode her mother's diary. When she thought about the horrible events of the day, she was surprised that she was still standing.

After she turned down the gas lamp, she went to bed, the precious diary tucked under her pillow. In the morning, she'd find a better place to hide it.

She'd thought, hoped, that she would fall asleep right away, but her mind buzzed with a thousand impressions: Madeline, James, Lady Cowdray, Egypt.

Her mother had been quite celebrated in her own circle, but when she'd written about her travels, she'd used an assumed name. Was that so that her husband and daughter would never find her?

How could this remarkable woman have abandoned her only child? Was there something about her, Faith, that made her unlovable? Abandoned first by her mother, then by the man she loved. Was the fault in them or in her?

She was wallowing in self-pity, and that set her teeth on edge. Once she had decoded her mother's diary, she'd have a better understanding of why Madeline chose to give her up. Perhaps there were reasons beyond a daughter's ability to understand. There was no diary to help her understand the workings of James's mind. None was needed. A better prospect had come along, and that was that.

Until he'd found her in Pritchard's Bookshop. There was a mystery here she could not fathom. Why was he helping her?

Her eyelids grew heavy, and she drifted into sleep.

James's lashes lifted, and he fought to master his breathing. He'd been dreaming of Faith. His whole body was twitching. His groin was rock hard. She'd been trying to prove that she was more woman than he could handle.

He shook his head and gave a drowsy smile. *Wishful thinking, you old reprobate,* he told himself. He rolled to his side, let out a resigned sigh, and settled himself to sleep.

Chapter 12

Since the following day was Sunday, everything stopped except for the trains and Sunday worship. After attending that morning's service, everyone found something to occupy their time. James went to the station to fetch the box that he'd arranged to be sent back from Brighton, and Faith retired to her own room to write Lily a letter. So much had to be left out that she made several attempts before she was satisfied. She couldn't even tell Lily precisely when she would come down to Brighton, because she didn't know what she would find when she transcribed her mother's diary.

When the letter was written, she turned to what really interested her: the diary. It was a simple leather-bound volume with nothing to distinguish it but the faint odor of ... She wasn't sure what the odor was. She put the diary to her nose and inhaled, then promptly sneezed. Not soot. Dust? Sand? She reached for her handkerchief, held it a few inches from the open diary, and blew gently. A few grains of reddish gold sand drifted to her handkerchief and settled there.

The thought that these few grains of sand had traveled to her in the pages of her mother's diary staggered her. It was as though, after all these years of silence, her mother had reached out to touch her. She folded her handkerchief and laid it reverently on top of the escritoire.

Breathing deeply, she opened the diary and studied the first page. The definite and indefinite articles soon emerged, as well as common verbs and proper names. After that, she began to make real progress.

This was to be a record of her private thoughts, Madeline wrote on the first page. There were other notebooks she'd used to describe her various journeys, but this volume was for her eyes only. She'd written the date at the top of the page: November 1873.

Faith turned the page and plowed on. The first entry was a summary of Madeline's life after she embarked on her first expedition with like-minded ladies to the unexplored peaks of the Dolomites. There were many hardships, but Madeline's thirst for adventure was patently obvious. Faith read on.

If she'd had any doubts about what Lady Cowdray had told her, they were soon resolved. Madeline often referred to past lovers not with bitterness but with something that bordered on gratitude. They'd enjoyed their affairs, but when it was time to let go and move on, there were no hard feelings. She'd also had several offers of marriage from men of rank, but she'd laughed them off, as well she might, since she was still married to Faith's father. She wasn't a romantic. She wasn't mercenary. She just wanted to live life on her own terms.

Faith scanned the initials of Madeline's lovers, but they meant nothing to her, and she soon gave up trying to put names to them. For all she knew, they could be in code as well.

She discovered that when in London or Paris, her mother enjoyed dressing up to go to parties or the opera or the theater, but she had only one true love: Egypt. She loved its climate, its landscape, its people, but most of all, she loved its history and getting down in the dirt to scrape the sand away and find a fragment of ancient pottery or the painted floor of some ruined temple. That was when Madeline was in her element.

A picture was forming in Faith's mind. She saw a woman with many failings but whose failings were easily overlooked by the sheer passion for life that permeated every page. She tried to imagine what it would be like to have Madeline for a friend. Who could keep up with her?

Suddenly rising, she pushed back her chair and went to stand in front of the cheval mirror. She was supposed to look like her mother, but her mother radiated confidence and good humor. The reflection in the mirror showed a quiet, well-bred young woman who would never be noticed in a crowd.

How in heaven's name had her father managed to ensnare someone like Madeline? Papa was more like his daughter, quiet and understated. The one thing he'd had in common with his wife was a love for ancient history. Evidently, it wasn't enough to hold them together.

A bird in a cage. Is that how Madeline felt? Is that why she left home?

Faith stared at her reflection for a long time, trying to think herself into her mother's shoes. The thought of Egypt filled her mind, the sun beating on her face, the warmth permeating every pore. She closed her eyes. She was standing at the rail of the sailing boat that was to take them up the Nile. Pyramids, the sphinx, the Valley of the Kings— the anticipation of seeing them for the first time made her heart beat just a little faster. There were treasures to find here, tombs that had yet to be discovered. Would she be the one to find some pharaoh's lost tomb?

She opened her eyes. The young woman in the looking glass had undergone a remarkable transformation. Her eyes glowed. The corners of her lips turned up, and her cheeks were infused with color.

It took a moment for Faith to realize someone was knocking on her door.

"Faith, it's James. Are you there?"

She crossed to the door and let him in. He was carrying her box. "Come in, come in," she said, opening the door wide. "So Lily did send on my box."

"As you see." He stepped inside and closed the door with his foot. After depositing the box on the floor, he stood there staring at her, his head cocked to the side. "You look different," he said.

"Do I?" She smiled. "It must be the Egyptian sun."

She was making an effort to be pleasant after the quarrel they'd had the night before and hoped he would follow her example. If they were to be in each other's company for a while, they couldn't go around with long faces.

"I take it that means you've broken the code." He walked to the escritoire and started moving things around. "Where are your notes?"

She crossed to him and batted his hands away. "Don't touch anything!" She reached for her handkerchief and showed it to him. "Look, James. These grains of sand were on the pages of Madeline's diary. I'm sure they come from Egypt."

He looked at the handkerchief. "A holy relic, is it?"

She opened the top drawer of the escritoire and carefully stowed the handkerchief. "I didn't make notes." Her voice was tight. "I became engrossed in the diary."

"I'm all ears. What does it tell us?"

She wanted to show him the door for the snide remark he had made about a holy relic, but there was so much that she wanted to tell him that she couldn't stay angry. As she related one episode after another, she wasn't aware that her voice glowed with admiration for the intrepid Madeline Maynard. She stopped suddenly when it registered that he was watching her with an odd look on his face.

"What?" she asked.

"I thought," he said, "that you didn't want anyone to read your mother's diary. Eavesdropping, you called it. Yet, here you are, telling me the most intimate details of her life."

She was momentarily struck by his observation and had to search for an answer. "I meant that I didn't want *strangers* reading my mother's diary. You're different. We're in this together, aren't we?"

When his head began to lower to hers and it looked as though he might kiss her, she said quickly, "Do you recognize any of these initials? Can you put names to them?"

"No, but I was thinking of the photograph you gave me, the one of the group. I bet when we know the names of the people there, we'll be able to match them to some of these initials."

"Lady Cowdray knows all their names. She tried to tell me, but I couldn't take them all in. We may meet some of them on Saturday at the lecture."

She glanced at the clock and gasped. "Is that the time? It's almost time for lunch. I must have been reading the diary for the better part of two hours."

He put a restraining hand on her arm. "First, I have something for you." He dug in his pocket and produced a revolver. "This is small enough to hide in your reticule. I want you to keep it with you at all times. It's lighter than mine, and the caliber of the bullets is smaller, but it's lethal for all that. You have six shots, but you must remember to cock the hammer before each shot."

He went through the motions, demonstrating what he had told her.

When she stared at it mutely, he gave her a reassuring smile. "You may never have to use it, but just in case, it's wise to have something in reserve."

She was thinking of her mother and how fearless she was. Without a tremor, her fingers closed around the revolver's butt. "Thank you," she said. "I shall look after it as though it were a hundred pound note."

There was a brief silence. Shaking his head, he said, "That doesn't sound like you. I thought you hated guns."

"That was before someone started shooting at me. Next time, I'll be prepared." She walked him to the door. "Tell the others I'll be down for lunch in a moment, after I've tidied up."

He stopped on the threshold, and his grin flashed. Lowering his head to hers, he breathed into her mouth, "Don't fuss, Faith. I'm going to kiss you."

She'd been warned. She could have taken evasive action. That's what she meant to do. But something else was at work in her. She was laboring under her mother's influence. Madeline wasn't afraid to reach for what she wanted. And Faith wanted James. He wasn't safe; he wasn't constant. Here today, gone tomorrow. That was James. What did it matter? This time, she had no illusions, so he couldn't break her heart.

She expected heat, fire, passion. What he gave her ravished her senses and soothed every ache in her bruised heart. He seemed to know what she needed better than she knew herself.

"I think, Faith McBride," he said softly, "that you're twice the woman your mother was."

He walked away, leaving her staring after him.

Shaking her head, she crossed to the escritoire, picked up her mother's diary, and stowed it in a pillowcase, which she proceeded to hang in the wardrobe, inside her borrowed dressing gown. She thought, perhaps, that she was being a little too careful. She didn't think anyone in the house would take the diary, but Mayfair was a favorite haunt of housebreakers. To her way of thinking, any housebreaker worth his salt would take one look at her meager belongings and leave empty-handed.

After a quick look in the mirror to tidy her hair, she left her room and made for the stairs. On the landing, she came face-to-face with Roderick. They tried to pass each other but, instead, got in each other's way. Laughing, he steadied her by placing his hands around her waist.

"You're not really going to marry that old stick, are you?" he said.

She eyed him through narrowed lashes. A young man of considerable charm and grace, she decided, except in the presence of his brother. "Is he an old stick?" she asked, returning the artful smile Roderick bestowed on her.

"Come, now, Faith. May I call you Faith since we're soon to be family?" It was a rhetorical question, and he went on blithely, "You can do better than an accountant, and that's all Jamie is. Haven't you found that out yet? Debits and credits, that's all he knows." His voice lowered to a confiding whisper. "Maybe you should look for a younger man?"

She almost took offense, but something about the boy stirred her curiosity. She saw no malice in him, only mischief.

"Faith?" James's voice came from the foot of the stairs. "We're ready to eat now."

Then it came to her. Roderick liked nothing better than

to get a rise out of his elder brother, and James sounded disgruntled. Roderick had used her to gain his object.

She patted him on the arm. "When you're older, you'll understand the appeal of an older man. Meanwhile, why don't you try to make a friend of your brother? You might learn something from him."

Roderick scowled, opened his mouth to say something, thought better of it, and went thundering up the stairs.

When Faith reached the bottom of the stairs, she was met by another glowering man: James.

"What did Roderick want?" he asked abruptly.

She moved her shoulders in a careless manner. "What do young men usually want? Just a mild flirtation." She slipped in front of him and entered the dining room.

Over the next few days, Faith grew restless. She began to feel like a prisoner and that James was her jailer. She understood why he wanted to keep her out of the public eye. The police were no nearer to discovering who had waylaid them in Chalbourne, and James was trying to protect her. He'd hoped that his cousin Alex, whose finger seemed to be in many pies, would help them with the last two pages of the diary, but Alex was on some unspecified assignment, and no one at Whitehall knew when he would return. They'd come to an impasse. There was no moving forward and no going back.

Her frustration came to a head at breakfast one morning when Margaret asked her if she was up to a little outing. Margaret, it seemed, had an appointment with the celebrated dressmaker Madame Digby to collect the dress she was to wear at her cousin's wedding, and she wanted to shop for other odds and ends. Madame Digby's shop was in the Burlington Arcade, the most prestigious shopping area in Mayfair.

At the mention of shopping, Mr. Burnett opened that morning's paper and hid behind it.

"I hope you'll come with me, Faith," Margaret said. "I'm not exactly conversant in the latest fashions, though Roderick has offered his services."

Roderick was at the sideboard and made an elegant bow. "We aim to please," he said gaily.

Margaret continued, "Of course, if you're not up to it, I shall quite understand."

This was a reference to the excuse that she and James had concocted to explain why she rarely set foot outside the door, that the trauma of the attack at Chalbourne had shaken her confidence. There was some truth to it, but that was days ago, and now she was champing at the bit.

"I should like that very much, Margaret," she said.

She waited for James to try to scuttle the outing and had the words to slay him on the tip of her tongue when, after a considering silence, he said, "Why not? My shirtmaker's shop is in the arcade. I'll pay him a visit while you ladies are at the dressmaker's."

Roderick flashed Faith one of his boyishly charming smiles. "No one has ever accused my brother of being a connoisseur of ladies' fashions, but I, in my small way, am considered quite knowledgeable. If you're thinking of ordering your bride clothes, Faith, look no further than my humble self to help you with your selections."

Damn the boy! thought Faith. She was sure that he was the only member of James's family who took her at her word when she said that she and James were not engaged, but he liked nothing better than to keep the fiction alive if only to needle his brother. If she were James, she'd laugh it off, make a joke of it.

She looked across the table at James. Sure enough, he was wearing one of his famous Burnett scowls. All the Burnetts on the male side had scowling down to a fine art. Annoyed because he was making it patently obvious that the thought of marriage to her had put him in a foul temper, she assayed a light laugh.

"Thank you, Roderick, I shall remember that, and if ever I decide to marry, I may take you up on your offer."

She slanted another darting look at James. He had taken the hint and was trying to smile. A shark's smile, she thought.

The Burlington Arcade stretched for one block, from Piccadilly to the end of Burlington House. Margaret ooed and ahed at every shop window. Roderick loitered at the bootmaker's, his eyes moving slowly from one pair of exquisitely made boots to the next. Harriet went very quiet when they came to the confectioner's shop, and she mouthed a silent *Oh*.

"We're here," Margaret said, touching Faith's arm to get her attention.

Faith's eyes had been feasting on a feathered bonnet in a milliner's window. At Margaret's words, she sighed and reluctantly allowed herself to be led away.

"Where is James?" she asked Roderick.

"At the shirtmaker's."

She felt let down, which was stupid. What did she expect, a fond farewell every time he left her side? *Watch yourself, my girl,* she warned herself, *you're becoming too attached to James and his family.*

She pinned a smile to her face. "Well, what are we waiting for? Let's not forget that we're ladies, but it's every man for himself."

Laughing, they pushed into Madame Digby's salon.

* * *

James detested shopping, and all the more so when there were females involved. He'd spent only fifteen minutes at his shirtmaker's, but when he'd called in at the dressmaker's, he'd discovered that the ladies had hardly begun to shop in earnest. They'd shooed him away and told him to come back in half an hour.

So here he was, idling his way from one boring shop to another. Unlike females, he never shopped unless he had something specific in mind. He kept looking at his watch, thinking it must have stopped, but no, the big hand moved, and at long last, his time was up.

As he approached the entrance to Madame Digby's salon, Margaret and Harriet came out and joined Roderick and Faith, who were in conversation with a fair-haired young man who seemed vaguely familiar. A personable young man, James noted, with a ready smile and laugh, and well aware of his power to charm.

They all seemed to be having a jolly time. No one noticed him. The fair-haired man ruffled Harriet's hair. "What a pretty child you have here," he said. "Are you related, Faith?"

Harriet's brows came down, and that made James smile. She hated to be called a child, but worse than that was to have her hair ruffled as though she were a pet dog.

"Faith," said Harriet in a carrying voice, "is going to marry my brother, James."

At these words, the fair-haired Adonis froze as though he had turned to marble. Faith's cheeks flamed with color.

Margaret said, "Harriet, you know you are not supposed to mention it."

"Is it a secret?" Harriet asked.

All eyes turned to Faith. She fumbled for words and

finally got out, "Not exactly. It's just that...well...my uncle in Ireland has to be informed. I wouldn't marry anyone without his consent."

Adonis caught sight of James first, and the sudden look of intense dislike jogged James's memory. He was Robert Danvers, the man he'd met on Speech Day, the man who seemed to have a proprietary interest in Faith.

James came up to him and held out his hand. "Mr. Danvers, is it not? We met at Speech Day. James Burnett."

Danvers took his hand and shook it. He seemed to have recovered his composure. "Allow me to congratulate you both."

"That would be premature," James responded, "until Faith's uncle gives us his blessing."

Roderick chose that moment to poke the fire. "Faith and my brother were once engaged to be married, oh, a long time ago. Not all engagements end happily ever after, you know." He grinned at James. "This time around, we're going to make sure my brother makes it to the altar."

"Roderick!" cautioned his mother with an uncertain laugh. "You young people don't know when to stop. Here, take my parcel. Make yourself useful."

"Can we give you a lift home, Robert?" said Faith, her expression betraying only a natural pleasure in an old friend's company.

"Which way are you going?"

"To Berkeley Square," Faith replied. "We're staying at Mrs. Leyland's house. You remember James's aunt? She spoke at Speech Day."

"Yes, I remember, but I'm going the other way."

"Well, then, walk me to the carriage and tell me how your mother and father are doing."

Danvers bowed to the company in general and walked with Faith toward the Piccadilly entrance.

Roderick edged closer to James. "There's something about that fellow that I don't like," he said.

"For once, Roddy," murmured James, "we agree on something."

James was thoughtful. The fine hairs on the back of his neck were tingling. He smoothed them down as he watched Danvers smile into Faith's eyes.

"Well," said James, *"you could have knocked me over with a* feather when you told Danvers that we were practically engaged. You never mentioned an uncle in Ireland to me."

They were in a little yellow parlor in the Berkeley Square house, waiting for the gong to summon them to dinner. James was at the mantelpiece, propping himself against it with one arm. Faith was pacing.

Her voice was strained. "There is no uncle in Ireland. I didn't know what to say. I was caught off guard." She stopped pacing and glared at him. "And you were no help at all."

He shrugged his broad shoulders, setting her teeth on edge. "I tried to be vague without contradicting you. What more could I say?"

She had no answer to this, so he went on, "What did you and Danvers talk about when he walked you to the carriage?"

She sighed. "I tried to make up for the shock my words had given him, so I told him that I hoped to call on his mother in the next few days and would be pleased to receive her if she cared to call on me." She sank into a chair and looked up at him. "There's no need to hide myself away now, is there? It's four days since those villains waylaid me. They must know that I don't know anything."

He nodded. "It's the diary they wanted, anyway, and

they have no way of knowing that it's in code. They must think you've read it through and found nothing of an incriminating nature in it."

"Thank God for that."

"That doesn't mean you can lower your guard. Keep your pistol with you at all times, and be careful of Danvers."

"Robert?" she asked incredulously.

He hadn't meant to put it so baldly. "Yes, Danvers. There's something about him I cannot like. He has a proprietary interest in you."

"He's not sweet on me, if that's what you mean."

"Are you sure?"

She made a small sound of derision. "I'm a woman. Of course I'm sure."

"Mmm. Yet, when we stepped out of your classroom cupboard on Speech Day, if looks could kill, I would have died on the spot. What put that look on his face?"

A becoming blush began to stain her cheeks. She was struggling to find words. "It would be better for both of us," she said in a choked voice, "if you forgot about what happened in the cupboard."

He leaned forward and trapped her eyes in his. "You might as well tell me to forget my own name. Can you forget?" When she did not answer, he said in a husky tone, "Let's not deceive ourselves, Faith. Put us together in a locked room, and the electricity fairly crackles."

She replied with asperity. "I wouldn't depend too much on electricity, James. As I understand it, it's a newfangled invention that causes more trouble than it's worth. I prefer the tried and true." She gazed pointedly at the gas lamp on the wall.

He grinned. "I'm putting my money on electricity, and I mean that literally."

"You've invested in it?"

"Naturally. It's the coming thing."

"James?"

"Yes?"

"To get back to my mother's diary."

Regretfully, the moment of intimacy had passed. "Go on."

"Since it has not helped us so far, we have to rely on what my mother's friends can tell us, and we'll meet them on Saturday at the Egyptology Society lecture."

"I was thinking along the same lines."

"Then, it's settled. We do a little sleuthing and see what we can find out?"

He steepled his fingers and thought fleetingly of his dream. *Desert. Pyramids. A group photograph.* "Yes," he said, "it's definitely worth a try."

Chapter 13

"It's very grand, isn't it?" Faith held James's hand as he helped her alight from the hansom. They had just arrived at the Hugheses' house for the meeting of the Egyptology Society.

"It would show to better effect," James replied, "if this confounded fog would only lift."

For the last week, Faith had heard those words constantly. The whole city had become shrouded in one of those frequent and infamous London fogs that forced people to remain inside or brave the elements with a cologne-scented handkerchief pressed to their mouths. It had rained on and off for most of the day, and though the fog had thinned considerably, it still settled in pockets close to the river, and Mr. and Mrs. Hughes's house on the South Bank had extensive grounds sweeping down to the water.

"It must cost the earth to keep up a house like this." Faith's neck was craned as she looked up at the towering neo-classical building.

"It does. Places like these have outlived their usefulness. It won't be long before they are pulled down to make way for something more in keeping with the times. It's happening all over."

They were making their way up the stone steps to the front doors, along with a crush of people, all waving their invitations under the noses of two stalwart footmen in black and silver livery. James took the invitation from Faith's hand and held it up as they passed through the doors and into the house.

He pocketed the invitation. "This doesn't seem democratic," he said. "I thought that the Egyptology Society was open to one and all."

"Well, it is, but this is not the official branch of the Egyptology Society." She tried to recall Lady Cowdray's words. "I think they call themselves the 'Friends' of the Egyptology Society. Most of the people here have been to Egypt and like to get together once in a while to reminisce about old times."

"Good; then perhaps we shall learn something useful."

"Well, I'd like to know what happened to my mother's box for a start."

Though it was early evening, the gas lamps had been lit to stave off the shadows cast by the dark clouds hanging low in the sky. Everyone hoped it would rain, because the rain would chase the last of the fog away.

The hall they passed through could have been mistaken for the Egyptian section of the British Museum. Faith's eyes wandered from one treasure to another—life-size sculptures of lions, wall paintings of Egyptian hunting scenes, alabaster busts of handsome Egyptian men and women who walked the earth eons ago—and she felt as though she was walking on holy ground. She spoke to James in a husky whisper. "Mr. Hughes must have spent years collecting all these artifacts."

He shook his head and replied softly, "Mrs. Hughes's

first husband was the collector. He died many years ago, but Mr. Hughes has preserved everything just as it was when he married the widow."

They were almost level with their host and hostess in the receiving line. Beyond them, in the cavernous reception room, she saw waiters in livery dispensing champagne to a crush of guests who were dressed to the nines. Faith wasn't intimidated by the elegance of the other ladies. She knew she looked her best in a nut-brown silk dress cut in the princess line with a fitted bronze-colored jacket, meticulously tailored, with a flaring hem.

Margaret wasn't the only one who had bought a frock or two from Madame Digby. Faith had dipped into her rainy day fund and splurged on a couple of outfits for herself, and she didn't regret it, not for one minute. Of course, if it rained, it would be a different story.

Her new outfit did wonders for her confidence, so much so that she did not blush when her host and hostess effusively expressed their pleasure at receiving Madeline Maynard's daughter into their home.

"Elsie—that is, Lady Cowdray—promised you would be here," gushed Mrs. Hughes. "As you may imagine, we are all dying to meet you." She paused for breath. "You are so like your mother, it's enough to make me cry."

Those words warmed Faith's heart. "Thank you," she said.

Mrs. Hughes was of regal proportions and might have been considered handsome for a lady past her prime had she not chosen to outfit herself from her crimped hair to the hem of her flounced gown like a woman half her age. "Mutton dressed as lamb," as her old nurse would say, thought Faith, and felt a shaft of pity for the lady.

As they passed into the reception room, Faith said, "I'm afraid Madeline was quite hard on poor Sophie Hughes in her diary, but I found her quite charming."

James was almost as familiar with Madeline's diary as Faith was, since in the last few days, they'd spent many hours poring over her script. It did not seem to him that the diary was suitable reading for a lady, but he valued his skin too much to utter the damning words. Lovers came and went in Madeline's set with an almost tiresome regularity, but who those lovers were was still a mystery. None of the names they'd heard matched the initials in Madeline's diary. Not that Faith accepted that these affairs were anything more than flirtations. He did not think Faith was narrow-minded so much as innocent in the ways of the world.

But Madeline was not ingenuous. What surprised him was that Madeline had attracted a following. The characters in her diary—her "friends"—were not described in anything but scathing terms. Only Lady Cowdray remained immune. Madeline might have had many lovers, but he doubted that she had more than one real friend.

Was her death an accident? It had occurred to him that she might have been blackmailing someone who had decided to silence her, but it was a theory he was not willing to share with Faith. In her eyes, her mother was a heroic figure. She would never stoop to blackmail. The only thing they could be sure of was that someone was willing to kill to get possession of Madeline's diary.

Faith's neck was arched to give her a better view of the ceiling. "Look, James," she said in hushed tones, "there are galleries on two floors. This must be the ballroom, surely?"

He shrugged. "Ballroom, reception room, lecture hall. It's still too costly to keep up, but not half as costly as it is to keep up Drumore."

She arched a brow. "You don't have to convince me. I'm not your father."

He was looking up at the galleries.

"What is it, James? What do you see?"

He felt as though someone had walked over his grave. He looked down at Faith. "It must be the heat," he said. "I turned dizzy for a moment."

Her expression cleared. "It is rather warm in here. Let's stand beside one of the open windows."

They were sipping champagne when Faith murmured, "At last, a face I recognize. Brace yourself, James, here comes Lady Cowdray."

As the lady swooped down on them, James's first impression was of a big, black crow, but a handsome crow with brilliant eyes to match her plumage. Second impressions were kinder to the lady. The blue black gown was a dramatic foil to silvery hair that fell softly about her shoulders.

As far as he could tell, she was the only female guest who was not wearing a bonnet. She was, of course, a non-conformist—weren't they all?—and one of the few women who was much admired by Faith's mother.

"So you did come!" she exclaimed, and she embraced Faith warmly. "You may imagine how worried I was after that dreadful business outside my house. I knew, of course, that you were to spend some time in Brighton, but you did agree to attend tonight's lecture. If you had not turned up, I had decided to go to the police and report you as missing. Much good that would have done! They don't seem to care."

Faith managed to interrupt the spate of words by introducing James, but other than an indifferent "How do you do?" her ladyship paid little heed to him, and rattled on. James was amused. In his own circles, his opinions and advice were courted. Here, he was barely visible. He decided to make his presence felt.

When Lady Cowdray stopped to draw breath, he interjected, "Did the police catch the men who tried to waylay Miss McBride?" He knew that they had not but hoped they had a lead.

"No." Her ladyship's eyes narrowed on him. "What did you say your name was?"

"James Burnett."

"So you do exist! The police tried to tell me that you had foiled those villains, but I thought...Oh, well, it doesn't matter what I thought. Come along, Faith. There are a number of people who are eager to meet you."

As Faith was firmly propelled toward a throng of individuals beside the French doors leading onto the terrace, she threw James an amused look. His reply was to raise his glass in a tiny salute. It would look odd if he tried to stop her. Besides, his instincts told him that she stood in no danger. That did not mean, however, that he did not suffer a few qualms as he watched her progress.

He wandered a bit after that, taking stock of people, listening, but keeping an eye on Faith. Faith was the center of attention. People were practically fawning over her. Then why was he suspicious? Smiling too hard, trying too hard—that was the impression he was getting. They hadn't liked Madeline and were not predisposed to like her daughter. It was Lady Cowdray whose presence made the difference. She seemed a bit of a scatterbrain, but he'd bet his last farthing that her influence held sway.

He'd bet his last farthing? What made him so confident? What did he think he was—a seer?

An incompetent seer. A reluctant seer. Someone who had not bothered to test himself. He believed in his dreams, but the odd sensations that occasionally touched him were so faint that they barely registered.

When he looked at the galleries above the ballroom, he felt oddly uneasy. What was he supposed to make of that? If there was a school for seers, he would be the first to sign up for it.

On the other hand, his gift had stood him in good stead when Faith was waylaid by villains. Faith, always and only Faith. That was when his gift of second sight was most potent.

He suddenly decided to put himself to the test. Eyes on Faith as she listened politely to what their hostess was blathering about, he silently repeated the mantra he'd taught himself. *Focus. Concentrate. Infiltrate.* Sounds and sights gradually faded. There were only two people in the ballroom: Faith and himself. *Focus. Concentrate. Infiltrate.*

Turn your head, Faith, and smile at me.

His heart stood still when Faith turned her head and smiled at him. Their eyes locked. Her smile gradually faded, and she raised her brows, questioning him.

So it was true! He could infiltrate her mind.

Or it could be coincidence.

He had to find out.

She was turning away.

Faith!

She turned back to look at him.

Touch your finger to your chin.

Mesmerized, he watched as she obeyed his command. Then her brows came down and she studied him with ill-concealed suspicion. The next moment, her expression cleared. He could read her mind. *It's all in my imagination,* she was telling herself.

A masculine voice at his back said, "I see you have been deserted, too. Don't take it to heart. Miss Maynard was something of an icon. No one knew that she had a daughter. It was inevitable that Madeline's cult of admirers would want to worship at her daughter's shrine."

The gentleman who joined James was his host, Mr. Hughes. His voice was pleasantly cultured and projected an indulgent tolerance of the group of ladies who hemmed Faith in on the other side of the room. He was in his early fifties, with light brown hair just beginning to silver at the temples. He looked distinguished, jovial, and just a tad cynical around the eyes.

James said, "You are not a member of the cult?"

"Ah, no. I hardly knew Miss Maynard. We were barely acquainted when she died. It was my wife's first husband who was the Egyptologist. Sir Franklin was something of an icon, too. As you may have noticed"—he gestured in the general direction of the entrance hall and anterooms where the Egyptian artifacts were displayed— "his influence has not diminished with the passage of time."

"Ah, then your wife is the Egyptologist?"

"She is an avid Egyptologist. I am one of her converts. Sophie would never have married anyone who did not share her passion for Egypt."

James's mind was distracted by a lady on the other side of the room who did not appear to greet Faith's presence with the enthusiasm of some of the others. She seemed aloof and hostile and might have made her escape but for the strong arm of Lady Cowdray, who anchored her in place.

She was an exception to the rule, and that pricked James's interest.

"Who is that lady with the orange hair?" he asked. He

recognized her face. She was in the photograph Faith had given him.

"Ghastly, isn't it? I mean the orange hair." Hughes lifted his lorgnette and stared through the lenses. "Miss Coltrane, just as I thought. Yes. Jayne Coltrane. At one time, she and Madeline were great friends, so I've heard, but they had a falling-out. I have no idea what the quarrel was about, and neither does anyone else. They kept their differences to themselves. Ah, I see Professor Marsh is heading for the lectern, the signal for me and other like-minded Philistines to retire to my library for something more substantial than champagne. I've heard this lecture so many times, I could give it myself. Care to join us?"

James smiled fleetingly. "Some other time, perhaps. I'm under orders to be on my best behavior."

Hughes laughed. "They look innocent enough, don't they? But trust me; when the lecture is over, the barbs will start to fly. My advice to you is don't open your mouth or offer an opinion unless you really know what you're talking about." He turned to go. "The offer still stands."

James smiled and shook his head.

As Hughes ambled toward the exit, James looked across the room at the knot of people around Faith that was beginning to unwind. She seemed to glow with life. Maybe it was the autumn colors in her gown that made her seem so vibrant. He did not think that anyone at St. Winnifred's would recognize the conservative Miss McBride in the lovely, vivacious woman who held center stage.

His incipient smile died when Faith came face-to-face with a red-haired young gentleman who blocked her path. He certainly had plenty to say for himself. James's eyes shifted to Faith. She, on the other hand, seemed flustered by the encounter. Another gentleman joined the first, then another.

Plastering a smile on his face, James sauntered over. One look at him, and Faith's admirers had the good sense to melt away. With her path cleared, Faith quickly crossed to James.

"Who is that gentleman you were talking to?" he asked. His voice was pleasantly modulated. "The one with the red hair?"

Her voice was equally pleasant. "I believe he is Mrs. Hughes's nephew or second cousin. Shall we take our places? The lecture is about to begin."

He wasn't satisfied with her answer but wasn't given the chance to probe, because Faith launched into an account of some of the people she had met.

"I've managed to place faces with the initials in my mother's diary. The lady with the bright red hair? That is Jayne Coltrane, and the gentleman with her is her brother, Laurence Coltrane. According to Lady Cowdray, my mother and Jayne had a falling-out over something or other, but that was long before they went on that last expedition to Egypt."

"I wonder what they quarreled about?"

"Either no one knows, or they are being circumspect."

"Circumspect?" He raised one brow. "This mob would not thank you for calling them circumspect. They like to think they are eccentric. No, they're not circumspect, they're egotists, and I got that by listening into their conversations as I wandered around."

The annoyance in Faith's expression died away, and she sighed. "There is something in what you say, but that is not why they are unwilling to take outsiders into their confidence. And that's what we are, James, outsiders."

They found places at the edge of the back row and sat down. "Well," he said finally, "did you find out what happened to your mother's box?"

"No one seemed to think it was important. According to Lady Cowdray, boxes go missing all the time. They are left behind or left on docks and stolen. And after so many years, no one can remember who lost what or where."

He said grimly, "I'd wager that someone remembers but isn't telling. Someone here, perhaps."

Faith looked at him skeptically. "What makes you think so?"

"Have you forgotten what happened in Chalbourne? Don't let your guard down, Faith. Not for one moment."

"Hush!" A lady in a bonnet with a robin bobbing on it glared at them over her shoulder. "Can't you see that Professor Marsh is waiting for silence before he begins?"

Conversation died away, and after clearing his throat, the professor began to speak. James was prepared to be bored out of his mind, but the opposite happened. Buried beneath a mound of anecdotes was the central idea of Marsh's address, that somewhere near Luxor, in the Valley of the Kings, there were pharaohs' tombs in the cliffs waiting to be discovered. Another expedition was planned for November, if local conditions were favorable, which meant, as James understood it, if British forces kept the area clear of troublesome tribesmen.

A hum of conversation swept the audience then died away when the professor held up his hand for silence. Only one thing remained, he said, before the expedition could get under way, and that was to raise funds so that excavators who were too poor to pay their own way would have their way paid for them.

At this point, James's zeal for the project suffered a setback. He frowned down at Faith. "This is a fund-raising event, isn't it?"

She lifted her shoulders and let them drop. "I have no idea. Lady Cowdray didn't mention anything about funding the expedition when she invited me to the lecture. I'm sure no one expects you to make a donation. You're not a member of the society."

James glanced around at the other members of the audience. Necks were craned as people turned to stare at him. There was no doubt in his mind that word had gotten out that the man who had brought Madeline Maynard's daughter to the lecture had deep pockets. Bloody hell! They must think he was here to support the cause.

There was a round of applause when their host replaced the professor at the lectern.

Resigned to his fate, James folded his arms across his chest and regarded his host with a grudging respect.

Hughes was all jokes and geniality as he introduced, one by one, patrons who were leaders in their various fields and were now in a position to give back to the community in this worthwhile endeavor. As each person was named, he or she stood and was given a round of applause.

Hughes wasn't finished yet. "As you know, everyone is encouraged to donate to the cause. My steward will be on hand to receive contributions, however small. John?"

The steward was not dressed in livery but like every other gentleman who was there. He looked about fifty, but a distinguished fifty, as though he were a former soldier.

James murmured, "Diabolical! Who would dare refuse that stony-faced general anything? Hughes is scaring money out of this captive audience."

"Well, he doesn't scare me!"

"And I know," Hughes went on, "that we can count on the support of our newest, honorary member, the man who is engaged to Miss Faith McBride, whom you know better as Madeline Maynard's daughter. I mean, of course, the railway magnate, Mr. James Burnett."

"What?" blurted Faith, glaring at James.

"Don't look at me! I didn't tell anyone we were engaged."

"Then who did?"

"Didn't Harriet tell Mr. Danvers? These things have a way of getting around."

"Harriet told Robert?"

"In the Burlington Arcade. What did you tell him?"

She pressed her hand to her mouth. "Nothing."

Their conversation was interrupted by thunderous applause.

James knew when he'd been outmaneuvered and gave his host a salute, which made Hughes beam at him.

Faith whispered, "I didn't know you were an honorary member."

"Neither did I."

Her expression hardened, and she lifted her chin. "The nerve of that man! You're not the least bit interested in Egyptian antiquities! What are you going to do?"

Hughes had left the lectern and was approaching James.

James stood up. "I see I'm being invited to join the other saps in Mr. Hughes's library." He loved the fiery glint in her eyes. "Don't take on so, my pet. It's only money."

She watched him saunter toward Hughes with a nonchalant smile.

Chapter 14

✦

Not long after that, the doors to the garden room were opened, and guests cooed and gasped at the sight that met their eyes. It was dark outside now, but the garden room was lit up with Chinese lanterns hanging from every tree branch. There were tables and chairs set out informally for guests who wished to eat, and the usual complement of liveried footmen dispensing glasses of champagne and lemonade from silver trays.

Faith wasn't interested in food. She hung back and searched the sea of faces for the young man with the red hair. She still could not get over the shock of seeing him after all these years. Alastair Dobbin was the young man who had escorted her to Scotland when she'd hoped to surprise James and instead had been surprised by a visit from the girl he eventually married. Mr. Dobbin had known nothing of her troubles, though he'd known she was engaged to James.

They'd said good-bye in Edinburgh's station, and while

the train had taken him on to his home in Aberdeen, she had put up at a nearby hotel.

They'd hardly done more than greet each other tonight when James had come bearing down on them. Startled, disconcerted, she'd managed a garbled plea that Alastair should meet her on the terrace when the lecture was over, then she'd quickly intercepted James, drawing him away before he discovered her secret.

Deep down, she was aware that she was making too much of that long-ago trip to Edinburgh. At the same time, it was nobody's business but her own. She'd suffered a private humiliation. *Private.* And that was how she wanted to keep it.

There was no sign of Alastair in the garden room, so she pushed through the glass doors leading onto the terrace. One or two gentlemen were already there, trying to light their cigars. A lone woman stood out like a sore thumb. The thought prompted her to slip into the shadows then strike out along the path that meandered down to the river. When she felt she was out of sight and out of earshot, she turned aside and concealed herself in a clump of rhododendron bushes. From this vantage point, she had a good view of the terrace.

A minute went by, then another, and Faith began to wonder whether Mr. Dobbin had understood her odd request. Had she asked him to meet her on the terrace or in the gardens? The terrace was brightly lit, and it was evident to her that Alastair was not there. She looked over her shoulder. The path to the river was not so well lit.

Which way should she go? Her mind was made up when she heard the tread of leather on the path ahead. Picking up her skirts, she slipped out of the cover of the bushes and followed the sound.

"Alastair?" she whispered, then a little louder, "Alastair?"

The sound of someone moving ahead of her stopped.

She stopped, too. She had a flash of recall: Chalboume and the desperate race to escape from the villains who wanted her mother's diary.

What a fool she was to come out here alone like this! Her heart was racing, her breathing was quick and shallow. Without conscious thought, she stepped off the path and took shelter under a laburnum tree.

Eyes and ears straining, she remained frozen in place. There was little to see in front of her. Some of the lanterns had been blown out by the breeze, and though she knew that there would be boats on the river, the mist was thick at that point, and no friendly lights winked at her.

Off to her left, a twig snapped, and she stifled a panicked moan. Someone was out there, someone who was trying to conceal his movements.

Or it could be a groundsman sent to light the lanterns that the wind had blown out.

Or it could be someone from the house who had a secret tryst with a lady.

Or it could be a vagrant on the prowl for food and shelter.

Or it could be the villains who had lain in wait for her in Chalbourne.

Without making a sound, she opened her reticule and retrieved the revolver James had given her. Holding it loosely in the folds of her gown, she waited. If worse came to worst, she could let off several shots. Surely someone up at the house would hear them.

Though she had been expecting to meet up with Mr. Dobbin, she gave a start when she heard his voice.

"Miss McBride," he said, "I've been looking everywhere for you. I thought we were to meet on the terrace."

She gave a light laugh and unobtrusively slipped her revolver into her reticule. "Too many gentlemen smoking cigars."

By tacit consent, they followed the path that led to the river. Faith was racking her brain, trying to find the words to express herself without turning the Edinburgh episode into a melodrama.

She stopped under one of the lanterns and came straight to the point.

"Mr. Dobbin," she said. "Alastair, I have never told James that I was ever in Edinburgh, or Scotland, for that matter. That trip turned out to be"—she gave an artificial laugh as she searched for words—"an unmitigated disaster."

"I understand," he said, though his expression told her that he didn't understand at all.

She shrugged helplessly. "I had a change of heart at the last moment and took the next train back to London." It was the truth, or as near the truth as made no difference, so she was able to look him straight in the eye. "I was too young to marry, a silly girl of nineteen, too young to know my own mind."

His eyes crinkled at the corners. "And now you're older and wiser?"

"Something like that." She had no wish to embark on an involved explanation of her present circumstances and went on quickly, "I ran away," she said, "not only from James but from my life and friends in London. The thing is . . ."

"Yes?"

She kept her voice easy. "I don't want him to know that I was ever in Edinburgh, for reasons I cannot share with you. You're the only one who can betray my little secret. May I count on you to keep it to yourself?"

His grin faded, and his voice was oddly grave. "I won't say a word to him—"

"Thank you!"

"—but I can't promise that he won't hear of it. I

mentioned it to my aunt, seeing no harm in it, and I know she told Lady Cowdray." He was eyeing her curiously.

She felt as though someone had punched her in the stomach, but she managed to summon a smile. "You're right. What harm can there be in that? Please forget I ever mentioned it."

To her intense relief, she was spared the embarrassment of answering any questions he might have raised when great drops of rain began to fall.

"The boathouse is close by," Mr. Dobbin said. "We'll be high and dry there."

The boathouse? How far had they come? Faith looked back toward the house. The lanterns in the grounds were going out one by one, doused by the rain, but she could see the lights of the house. They seemed a long way away, and the great drops of rain were turning into a deluge.

A hand gripped her arm, and Mr. Dobbin said fiercely, "The boathouse is our best chance of getting out of this storm. Come along, Faith."

Blinded by the rain, she let him lead the way. They didn't have far to go. Mr. Dobbin opened the door, and Faith stumbled inside, tripped over something on the floor, and went sprawling. It was so dark in that small interior that she couldn't see her hand in front of her face.

"What is it?" Dobbin asked.

Faith pulled herself to her knees and felt with her hands. "A man, a vagrant, I think." Even as she said the words, she began to have her doubts. "He's terribly cold."

Alastair crouched down beside her. He, too, felt with his hands till he found the man's wrist. After a few moments, he said, "There's no pulse. He's dead, I'm afraid."

James left Hughes's study with mixed feelings. The fact that he'd been cajoled into making a substantial donation to the upcoming expedition didn't bother him in the least. What did bother him was what he had learned about the red-haired man who had approached Faith before the lecture. He was none other than the gentleman she'd gone off with after she'd left Lady Beale's employ. *Dobbin, the donkey,* he thought savagely.

Why hadn't she told him Dobbin's name when he'd asked her who the red-haired man was? Why keep it a secret?

He wandered from room to room, his eyes peeled for the sight of her saucy bonnet with its white feathers. When he failed to find it, he searched the crowd for the man with red hair. There was no sign of Dobbin, either. He was on the verge of becoming annoyed when the man who had been pointed out to him as Jayne Coltrane's brother stopped in front of him.

"You're James Burnett, are you not?" said Coltrane. "I'm Larry Coltrane. How do you do? I've just heard from our host of your generous contribution to our fund."

Larry Coltrane was much younger than his sister, a good ten years by James's reckoning, perhaps in his mid-forties. There was one thing in his favor. He didn't have red hair. In other respects, Coltrane was not the sort of man James was drawn to. He was too handsome, too urbane, and too sure of himself. At this particular moment, he was also an obstruction that James was impatient to get around so that he could find Faith.

On the other hand, this might be his only chance to put a few moot questions to Mr. Coltrane. He held out his hand. "How do you do, Mr. Coltrane. I believe you were a member of the last expedition Miss Maynard was part of?"

"I was the official photographer," Coltrane replied. "We are not all wealthy, you know. Some of us have to earn a living. I earn my living with my camera."

"Then you're not a true Egyptologist?"

"I'm afraid not."

"What about your sister?"

"Jayne?" Coltrane looked surprised. "She, Madeline, and Elsie Cowdray were the driving force behind this group. That was how it got started, with three determined women who did not wish to be treated as decorative ornaments. Trust me, Mr. Burnett, they were not afraid to dirty their hands on digs or pull their weight when things got rough."

"Yet there was, I believe, a falling-out between Madeline and your sister?"

Coltrane nodded. "They both wrote for the newspapers. I suppose you'd call it professional rivalry."

"Were you there when Madeline died?"

Coltrane nodded. "We were all devastated."

For the first time, James had the sense that Larry Coltrane's mask had slipped. He meant what he said. Madeline's death had been a terrible blow to him.

"You were in love with her," James said simply.

"I was in love with her," Coltrane replied. A moment of silence went by. "And she was not easy to love. I don't think Madeline had it in her to love anyone. It came as no surprise to me to learn that she had left her husband and daughter for adventure in Egypt. That was just like Madeline. I hope her daughter will forgive my sister's coldness. She looks so like her mother that I'm afraid Jayne said things she ought not to."

He sipped slowly before he continued. "Strange business, wasn't it, Miss McBride discovering that she was Madeline's daughter after all these years? Lady Cowdray told us that Miss McBride believed her mother had died in a boating accident?"

James replied noncommittally that that was so. There were more questions in the same vein, and it was becoming clear to him that this was why Coltrane had sought him out, not to pass on information but to ferret it out. He wanted to know how much Faith knew about her mother's secret life. James told him that Faith knew only what she'd been told by Lady Cowdray. No mention was made of Madeline's diary.

When the questions had dried up, Coltrane moved away with a nod and a smile. James watched him go, wondering what, if anything, Coltrane had to hide.

The next few minutes were spent looking for Faith. When he couldn't find her or Dobbin, he became alarmed. He was on the point of going through the doors to the terrace, when his host entered followed by a group of gentlemen.

"I had hardly time to light my cigar," Hughes said, "when the rain came down like a river in spate. Look at me. I'm wet through."

"Did you see Miss McBride?"

Hughes stopped in his tracks. "Miss McBride? No. As I said, I was only out there a few minutes. Excuse me while I change."

James pushed open the French doors as far as they would go and looked out. It took a while for his eyes to become accustomed to the dark. It wasn't dense. Shadows moved within shadows. *Where are you Faith? Where are you?*

He couldn't focus. There were too many people making too much noise. He shouldn't have wasted time talking to Larry Coltrane.

Focus. Concentrate. Infiltrate.

It had worked for him once before, when he'd entered the mind of a killer. Twice, if he counted what had happened with Faith earlier.

Focus. Concentrate. Infiltrate.

His mind went blank; then he saw her. She was moving toward him. In his mind's eye, he could see her approach the French doors, and not only her. There was a man right behind her. On that thought, he went through the French doors like an arrow from a bow.

He did not have far to go when they emerged from the shadows. His alarm died, now that he saw Faith was safe, and he was tempted to grab her by the shoulders and give her a good shaking. What stopped him was the look on her face. Her relief at seeing him would have been evident to a blind man.

"James!" she said and hiccupped, then she walked into his arms. Against his throat, she whispered, "We took shelter in the boathouse. It was awful."

It was left to Dobbin to tell him what was so awful. "There's a body—" Dobbin stopped to draw air into his lungs. "There's a body of a man in the boathouse. Miss McBride tripped over him. We had no light, so we couldn't tell who he was. All I can tell you is that he wasn't breathing."

James bit out orders as though he were instructing the navvies on one of his railways. "Dobbin, take Miss McBride back to the house. Have someone sit with her till I get back. Then tell Mr. Hughes what you have just told me. We won't send for the police just yet, not till we see what we're dealing with."

Faith made a weak protest, but Dobbin seemed to know it would be useless to argue.

As soon as their backs were turned, James drew his revolver from an inside coat pocket, grabbed a lantern that marked the path, and moved briskly toward the river.

The body was lying facedown, just inside the door. It seemed to him that whoever it was had been on the point of leaving when he was struck from behind. It looked as though he'd been bludgeoned to death with a hammer or something like it, but there was no hammer near the body.

James went down on his haunches and turned the body over. The sightless eyes that stared up at him belonged to Robert Danvers.

He sat back on his heels. Robert Danvers, he reflected now, had the habit of being on the scene whenever Faith appeared. He was a regular at St. Winnifred's. He'd been there, in her classroom, when he and Faith were locked in the cupboard. He'd been in the Burlington Arcade when Faith exited Madame Digby's.

And now the poor blighter had turned up here.

"What game were you playing?" he said under his breath. Then, brows furrowed, "Whose game were you playing?"

Chapter 15

✦

It was well after midnight before James and Faith entered the cab to take them home to Berkeley Square. They'd had to wait their turn to be interviewed by the police, then hang around for everyone else to be interviewed as well. At first, the police seemed highly suspicious of Faith and Alastair Dobbin, since they had not only found the body but also knew the murdered man. The police surgeon put a stop to that line of questioning; he could tell from the blood on the murdered man's clothes and the temperature of the body that Danvers had died at least an hour before Faith and Mr. Dobbin entered the boathouse and probably longer. It was true that Faith and Dobbin knew the murdered man, but so did many of the members of the Egyptology Society. Danvers wasn't a member, but he occasionally turned up at public lectures or other events. Though, on this occasion, no one remembered seeing him.

"What it comes down to," said James, "is that anyone could have murdered Danvers before the lecture." He thought for a moment. "Or long before that, when I think of what the police surgeon said. And who knows where everyone was at the critical time?"

A shiver passed over Faith, then another. She was still in her wet clothes, but James had draped his own coat around her to stave off her chills. "But why would anyone want to murder Robert? He was well-mannered and pleasant." She looked up at James. "I can't stop thinking about his parents, especially his mother. Robert was all she had."

"Well, she has her husband now."

She shook her head. "I suppose."

He hadn't intended to put his own questions to her until they were home and she had changed out of her wet garments, but she had opened a door, so he said simply, "You don't like Robert's father?"

"No. I do not. I don't understand why he serves on our board of governors. He certainly isn't in sympathy with the aims of the school. He is too authoritarian. I can only imagine what he is like at home."

James shrugged. "Danvers Sr. is a pillar of the banking community. Serving on boards of governors comes with the job. Some men like the prestige. Others like the opportunities it gives them to mix with other influential men."

"I shouldn't have criticized him. I really don't know Mr. Danvers. I could say the same about Robert. I mean, he only attended special events at St. Winnifred's, so I was barely acquainted with him. I can't say that I particularly liked him. I mean, I didn't particularly dislike him—" She broke off and shook her head. "None of that matters. He was a young man. His death isn't only tragic, it's heinous. I can't seem to take it in." Tears welled in her eyes. "I feel so guilty—"

"Guilty! What do you have to be guilty for?"

She sniffed. "I should have made more of an effort to get to know him, and now it's too late. I can't imagine anyone wanting to kill him. How are we going to explain it to the girls at school? They'll all be devastated. Robert was very popular with the girls."

She sucked in a breath. "Lily! I must write to Lily at once and tell her what has happened."

He grasped her hand and squeezed it. "But not tonight. You're too overwrought to put your thoughts down on paper. Wait until tomorrow."

She nodded slowly. "Yes. I'll write to Lily tomorrow, but who is going to tell the girls? Most of them have gone home for the holidays, but there are always a few who have no homes to go to. Who will tell them?"

"The police have everything in hand. They won't thank you for interfering. Remember, Faith, this is a murder investigation."

She became preoccupied with her own thoughts after that, and James did not attempt to draw her out, though he found her assessment of Danvers interesting. He was more concerned with the shivers that had now taken a firm hold of her. She was still in shock, and the effects of the minuscule brandy he had forced her to drink before the police arrived were now wearing off.

There was a porter on duty when they arrived home, but there were no lights on the upper floors as James expected. "Is the family here?" James asked the servant. "Did they make it back from the wedding with my aunt?"

"No, sir. It's not surprising; they say there's a pea soup fog all the way to Henley."

"Who says?"

"The butler, sir. Would you like to speak to him? Shall I waken him?"

"That won't be necessary." From the deathly silence in

the house, James guessed that all the servants had gone to bed, too. "But get one of the maids to help Miss McBride change out of these wet garments."

The porter eyed Faith curiously. "Caught in the rain, were you, miss?

James's voice was rough with impatience. "Just get one of the maids to see to Miss McBride. And get the lamps lit."

The porter turned smartly and hastened up the stairs.

Faith spoke in a tight little voice. "He was only trying to be polite. It was good of him to care. And now one of the maids has to be wakened from her sleep when it isn't necessary. I'm well able to look after myself."

But she wasn't able to look after herself, as was soon evident when he helped her mount the stairs. She clutched his arm convulsively. He looked at her intently and noted the colorless complexion and the way she pressed her lips together. He sensed, then, that she was reliving the moment when she had entered the boathouse and fallen headlong over Danvers's body.

"I didn't know who he was," she whispered. "I thought that he was a vagrant who had taken shelter from the rain. He was so cold. I thought if we got him a blanket, he would soon warm up."

He said something soothing, he didn't know what, then one of the maids with a coat serving as a dressing robe over her nightclothes was there to take care of Faith. He entered the room first, lit the gas lamp above the mantel, and put a match to the kindling in the grate.

To the maid he said, "Keep the fire going, and make sure Miss McBride is warm and dry. I'll be back in a little while to see that she is all right."

When the maid nodded, James said to Faith, "I'll be back in a little while; then we'll talk."

It took him no more than ten minutes to change his own

clothes, then five minutes to fetch the brandy decanter and two glasses before he was back at Faith's door. When he entered, Faith was huddled in a chair close to the fire, but there was no sign of the maid.

"I sent Millie to bed," she said. "Do you know that she has to get up at five in the morning to light the boiler? She should have been in bed hours ago but stayed up waiting for me to come home, but her eyes wouldn't stay open so…" Her voice trailed away. "I'm talking too much. Is that the result of shock?"

He crossed to her and poured brandy into one of the glasses. "It is," he said, "and this is the cure for it."

She accepted the glass and put her lips to the rim. After one choking gulp, she said tremulously, "After they separated us at the Hugheses', the police took me back to the boathouse to look at the body. I was the one who said he was Robert Danvers. I shall never forget the look on his face or the blood. It's on my gown but didn't show up right away because my gown is practically the same color as dried blood."

He was appalled. No one had told him that the police had taken her back to the boathouse. He'd already identified Danvers. There was no need for Faith to do the same. It was a trick, one of those nasty sleights of hand employed by the police to unnerve a suspect and get him or her to talk. A savage rage gripped his throat. No wonder she was in shock.

He poured himself a brandy, bolted it in one gulp, and set the decanter and his glass aside. As gently as he could manage, he said, "I'm sorry. I didn't know the police had taken you back to the boathouse."

"There's something else, something I didn't tell the police. It's probably all in my imagination anyway."

When she fell silent, he gently prompted, "What is it, Faith?"

Her shoulders lifted as she drew in a long breath. "I thought someone else was there on the path ahead of me. I thought it was Alastair until he turned aside and hid in the shrubbery. The thing is, I'm not sure. Anyway, he couldn't have killed Robert, because the doctor said that Robert had been dead for an hour at least and probably longer."

That she had been waiting for Alastair Dobbin to join her was, in the light of the night's events, a small point. That someone had followed her out or been lying in wait for her was far more serious.

He wasn't going to belabor the point. She'd been through enough for one night.

Keeping his voice easy, he said, "It was probably a groundsman. Mr. and Mrs. Hughes employ an army of servants. I suppose some of them were directed to keep the lamps lit."

"That was my thought, too." She took another choking gulp of brandy, coughed, then went on. "The lamp outside the boathouse wasn't lit. In fact, many of the lamps had gone out. That's why it was so dark."

"Don't think about it."

She went on as though she hadn't heard him. "I don't think I shall ever forget that moment. Waking or dreaming, I shall never forget it." She looked up at him with huge, fragile eyes. "It's all of a piece, isn't it? My life was uneventful until I put that advertisement in the paper. We were attacked, and now Robert is dead. If only I had not found that photograph of my mother..."

He went down on his haunches and took Faith's hand. Her skin was ice-cold, and her teeth were chattering. His dark eyes held hers. "What happened to Robert is not your fault. And it might not have had anything to do with the advertisement you placed in the paper."

"I don't believe in coincidences—leastways, not that kind of coincidence."

Neither did he, but this was not the time to discuss it. "What you need," he said gently, "is a good night's rest."

She looked at the glass of brandy in her hand and put it down. "I won't sleep." A shiver passed over her. "I don't know if I want to sleep."

He helped her to her feet. "Then don't sleep. Just go to bed."

"And where will you be?"

He pointed to the fire. "Right here, reading a book, watching over you."

She didn't remove her dressing gown but simply slipped beneath the eiderdown with a heartfelt sigh and rested her head on the pillow. Her eyes stayed wide open, and she watched him as he chose a book from the small table in front of the window.

"Charles Dickens's *Tale of Two Cities*," he said and settled himself in the chair by the fire.

He pretended to read, but his mind was completely focused on Faith. It took a long time, but finally, he felt her eyelashes grow heavy and knew the exact moment she slipped into sleep. Only then did he give up the pretense of reading. Rising, he stretched his cramped muscles and took a turn around the room. Danvers's murder wasn't the only thing that worried him. He wondered about the man who had either followed Faith into the garden or whom she had come upon by chance.

If the man who had frightened her was ahead of her on the path, then he hadn't followed her out. And if he had been lying in wait for her, then he wouldn't have been on the path. That meant that Faith had come upon him by chance.

Then what was he up to? Why skulk in the bushes?

He could come up with a score of innocent explanations, none of which satisfied him.

When Faith made a sound, he crossed to the bed. She might be sleeping, but it was not a restful sleep. Her limbs jerked from time to time, and he could hear the little sobbing breaths she took.

He remembered how Granny McEcheran used to comfort him when he was a little boy and afraid of the monsters that waited for him in his dreams. All that was needed was the weight of a warm body close to his, someone to hold on to for dear life when the monsters appeared. He could almost hear the sound of his granny's voice soothing his fears.

That was what Faith needed.

He climbed on top of the bed and stretched out beside her.

Chapter 16

"*James?*"

"I'm here. Go to sleep. I won't let anything harm you."

Those were the words his grandmother used to say. He remembered other things: how she would pat his shoulder and hold his hand. He went through the motions he remembered, but when he linked his fingers with Faith's, he felt a sudden surge of energy, like a jolt of electricity, pass between them, and he had one heart-stopping moment of clarity before he was caught in a whirlwind of brilliant light and sucked into Faith's dream...

"Thank God you're here," Faith said, clinging tightly to his hand.

They were in the Hugheses' house at the start of the evening, and all the guests had taken on a sinister appearance. They looked like vultures, though well-dressed vultures to be sure. They were crowding Faith, pecking at her, and James could sense the panic rise in her throat. That's when he flexed his newfound muscles and gave himself the aspect of a ravening wolf. The vultures retreated in disorder, and Faith let out a pent-up breath.

So this, thought James, *is how Granny got me through my nightmares.* Some grannies sang lullabies. His granny slew dragons. To each his own.

Before he could explore all the possibilities of this new twist, the scene changed. They were going through the terrace doors, and he had been displaced by a sinister, indistinct figure. There was no sign of Dobbin. Faith was bracing herself for the awful moment when she would push into the boathouse and trip over Danvers's body. Her heart was hammering against her ribs, her mind was numb with terror.

James knew what he had to do next. He had to turn her thoughts from finding Danvers's body and direct her into a safe harbor. To his utter horror, he discovered that he was woefully unprepared. He tried to drag her away, but her hand became transparent, and he could no longer grasp it. He shouted her name, but she paid no attention. Her mind was fixed on Robert Danvers's sightless eyes. Her hand was on the door, ready to push it open.

As he hesitated, wondering what to do next, the unthinkable happened, and he and Faith were sucked into his worst nightmare.

The big, wrought-iron gates of the ruined mansion loomed out of the fog, then the house, like a ghost of its former self. He could hear the crunch of his boots on gravel as he pushed between the gates. Water dripped from the trees, and the earth, warmed by the heat of the sun, converted the rain into a fine, lacy mist.

He'd had this dream so many times he knew it by heart. He entered the marble foyer with its cantilevered staircase rising to the floors above. He knew that Faith was here somewhere in fear of her life. Someone was waiting for her in the shadows, someone with hatred in his heart and murder on his mind.

His own heart beat a frantic path to his throat. Blood thundered in his ears. He tried to clear his mind of the panic that held him frozen. There was a way to find Faith and keep her safe. That was why he'd been given this premonition. The future could be changed.

A terrible scream rent his mind and he knew he was too late.

He wasn't too late. He wasn't too late. The future could be changed. The litany rang inside his head as he began to run. "Faith," he yelled. "Faith!"

One long corridor turned into another long corridor, then another. This wasn't a house, it was a labyrinth. Faith was here somewhere. He had to find her. "Faith!" he shouted. "Faith!"

A small sound reached him. A woman's moan. Something. He was reaching for her, reaching...

The labyrinth disintegrated before his eyes, and the mist came in like a whirlwind. "No!" he yelled. "No!"

He was shaking. Heart pounding, throat tight with fear, he opened his eyes. Faith was kneeling on the bed. Her cheeks were wet with tears, her hands were on his shoulders, shaking him awake.

The ugly pictures in her mind faded a little when she saw that he was awake. "I couldn't find you," she said. "I thought I had lost you."

He was still gasping for air as though he really had sprinted up and down all those corridors looking for her. "It was the same for me," he got out. His hands cupped her face. "I'm all right. Don't take on so. It was only a dream."

She set the palm of her hand against his cheek. His skin

was warm to her touch. Their eyes met and held, then she slowly lowered her head and brushed her lips against his. The kiss was whisper-soft and comforting, but it could not blot out the raw emotions that threatened to break her.

"It seemed so real," she whimpered.

"I know. For me, too."

Faith's shoulders began to heave as snatches of the nightmare came back to her. When she struggled to draw air into her lungs, James spoke soft, soothing words in her ear, and his hand swept up her back then stroked her hair. She pressed closer to the warm shield of his body and kissed his throat.

Pulling back a little to see his face, she said hoarsely, "I was in this wreck of a house. There was a maze of corridors. I was trying to find you, but you kept moving away."

"I was there, too. I was having the same dream."

He didn't tell her that her dream was a foretaste of what was to come. She wasn't nearly ready to hear that. All that mattered was the knowledge that she was safe.

But for how long? a small inner voice demanded.

Until I change the future! he answered fiercely.

The possibility of failure haunted him still, and his arms tightened around Faith's slight frame as though he could shelter her from all harm by absorbing her into himself. For a man who took appalling risks in the world of business and could win or lose a fortune without turning a hair, when it came to the person who mattered most to him, he was a monumental coward.

"Faith," he said, and he kissed her with a desperation he could not control.

Faith felt his tremors and instinctively tried to soothe his fears, as he'd soothed hers. His nearness and strength helped to keep the horror at bay, but her emotions were still tearing her apart. All the heartache that she'd suffered in the past was as nothing to what she'd experienced when she'd thought she had lost him. It didn't matter how many times she told herself it was only a bad dream. It didn't feel like a dream but more like a memory.

She wasn't going to look back. She wasn't going to look ahead. Her mother had written much the same thing in her memoirs. All anyone could count on was the present moment.

Brave words, but she couldn't stop her teeth from chattering as reaction to the nightmare tightened its grip on her once more. Then there was Robert Danvers. Would she ever forget the sight of his bleached complexion when the policeman held up his lantern so that she could identify the body? What if it had been James's face she saw? How could she bear it?

As another shudder ran over her, she burrowed closer to his warmth. He groaned and pushed himself off the bed. She sat up and reached for him, but he took a step back and combed his fingers through his hair.

"Don't you know anything about men, Faith?" he demanded harshly. "I can't stay in bed with you like this. I'm desperate to make love with you."

The intensity of his words made her heart begin to thud in slow, painful strokes. "You promised to stay with me."

He muttered an oath. "You know what will happen if I stay."

She realized with a shock that that was exactly what she wanted. The thought circled in her mind and sank into the deepest reaches of her psyche.

He was looking at her as though his life depended on her next words. A slow smile warmed her lips. Holding out her hand, she said, "Well, I can't say I haven't been warned."

They dispensed with their clothes as though they were on fire, then rolled together on the bed. The words they spoke were hardly coherent, but they didn't need words. They didn't need gentleness or tenderness or a practiced finesse. They needed to feel the pulse of life quickening inside them. They needed to keep the shadows at bay. Their coming together was swift and fierce and profound. At the end, she felt a quick, tearing sensation, but she was too steeped in wonder to care. She cried out on a crest of shattering pleasure and slowly collapsed against him.

When James had recovered his breath, he rose on one elbow and looked down at Faith. "My God!" he said. "What was I thinking? Did I hurt you?" He answered himself testily, "Of course I hurt you. This was your first time."

Faith was still trying to catch her breath. On a shaken laugh, she wheezed out, "Did you hurt me? I didn't have time to think about it. You came at me like a rampaging bull."

"And you came at me like a runaway train."

The picture that formed in her mind pleased her enormously. It made her feel that she had left Miss McBride, schoolteacher, moping on the railway platform, while she had taken off, at full speed, on an adventurous journey.

"I *was* like a runaway train, wasn't I?"

She couldn't hold the image. A blessed inertia was stealing over her, making rational thought impossible. With a little sigh, she closed her eyes and nestled closer to James.

He heard the smugness in her voice and heaved a sigh of relief. He'd never considered himself the world's greatest lover, but he'd never sunk to the level of a callow youth since... well...since he was a callow youth. It had never occurred to him to go slow with her and initiate her with all the skill of which he was capable. He'd been gripped by a confusion of emotions that clouded his thinking. He'd felt helpless to keep her safe against an enemy he did not know, and he'd tried, in some obscurely primitive way, to convince himself that nothing could touch her without going through him first.

If only it could be that easy.

He felt the familiar fear tighten his throat. He was only a mortal man, and he might be no match for the forces he sensed were ranged against them. Where was the enemy? Who?

He was thinking clearly now, and as each thought turned in his mind, he examined it closely. He didn't understand how Robert Danvers fitted into the puzzle, but all his instincts told him that Danvers was a key player. He thought of the thugs who had attacked Faith right after she was given her mother's diary by Lady Cowdray. Alastair Dobbin also needed to be explained. Why had Faith gone off with him, on her own, in a darkened garden, when there had already been one attack on her? What was so important that she would take such a risk?

There were other things that were equally pressing, such as, where did Faith and he go from here? Now it was his turn to be smug. Faith wasn't a high flyer. She wasn't cut out for an affair or to be a man's mistress. And she wouldn't have given herself to him unless she was committed. They'd had their problems in the past, but compared to the danger they faced now, those problems seemed trivial.

They had to talk, had to clear the air and put the pieces of the puzzle together. He was a seer, for God's sake, and he'd been forewarned. That ought to count for something.

The room was warm, but her skin was cold to his touch. After pulling up the covers, he tried to wake her by shaking her gently.

"Faith?" he said. "We must talk."

She came awake slowly. Her dark lashes fluttered then lifted, and she looked up at him. Her eyes warmed when they focused on his face, then she stretched like a languorous cat. "I'm listening," she said.

He was captivated by the change in her. Her eyes were

love-sleepy, and her skin glowed. The plait of hair at her back was beginning to come undone, making a soft halo around her face. There was more to her than beauty, though, in his eyes, she was more beautiful than any woman had a right to be. Everything about her surpassed anything he had ever found in another woman, not because she was extraordinary but because she was so right for him.

And she had thrown it all away.

The words that came out of his mouth were not the words he had intended to say. "My God, Faith! All these wasted years between us! I know I'm not a faithful letter writer, but I thought you understood." His lips flattened, and he shook his head. "I promised myself I wouldn't regurgitate ancient history, but I thought I knew you. I thought you knew me. I thought we trusted one another. And now, tonight, you went haring off with that... that freckle-faced fribble, the one you ran away with before. Were you trying to make me jealous of Dobbin? Is there something going on between you two?"

She levered herself up till they were eye to eye. His tone of voice, his expression, were not what she expected from a man who, not long before, had become her lover. Then the meaning of his words registered, and she bristled with indignation. "You hypocrite!" She stopped, expelled a breath, and went on in a more controlled tone, "You married Fiona, didn't you? A rich man's daughter? You always intended to marry her, even when you were seeing me! You needed her father's money to bail you out of your troubles. Well, I did the honorable thing; I faded out of the picture to make things easy for you."

He was bewildered. "I married Fiona because I couldn't have you, and I didn't care who I married. Yes, she was a rich man's daughter. Yes, her father invested in my company, but that was long after you had run off with your pet donkey!"

"My pet donkey? That is despicable!"

When she flung out of bed, he threw up his hands in a placating gesture. "I'm sorry. That was uncalled for. I know well enough that there's nothing between you and Dobbin, nor ever was. And do you know how I know, Faith? Because I know you."

She had slipped into her dressing robe and was belting it tightly. "Is that supposed to be an apology? Because if it is, you can stuff it up your—" She stopped to loosen the belt, which was now digging into her.

"Yes?" he goaded.

"Nose!" she retorted.

"Spoken like a true lady!"

Teeth gritted, she got out, "Not only have you insulted me, you have also insulted Alastair." Hands on hips, she raked him with her eyes. "Alastair is a gentleman to the tips of his fingers. I did not run off with him, as you put it. We traveled together on a train. When I reached my destination, he continued on to his parents' home."

"His parents' home?" He frowned and hauled himself up to sit with his back propped against the pillows. "And where might that be?"

"Scotland!"

She'd known it would come to this, ever since Alastair had told her that others knew about the train trip to Scotland. She was cursing herself now for keeping it a secret. Having once suppressed her foolish escapade, it seemed easier not to mention it at all. She no longer had a choice. If she did not tell James, he might hear of it from someone else. Better by far that he should hear of it from her.

"Scotland?"

"Yes," she said. "They live in Aberdeen. Alastair was to spend a few days with them before taking the boat to Orkney. There are ancient dwellings there that he wanted to explore."

His eyes were fixed on hers and seemed to be puzzled rather than annoyed. "Where did you part company?"

"In Edinburgh," she said tightly. "I registered at a hotel close to the station and sent a note to you to say that— surprise, surprise—I had arrived in town."

"I never received your note!"

"I know." Her voice had developed a tremor, so she cleared her throat. "It was intercepted by Lady Fiona Shand. You remember Lady Fiona? She was the daughter of the business acquaintance you were staying with."

"My erstwhile wife," he muttered, "as you know very well."

"Quite." She paused to get command of her voice. "She lost no time in appearing at my door to put me right about the man I thought I was engaged to."

She'd lived through that scene a thousand times, and it came back to her now with crushing effect. To cover the embarrassing tears that were stinging her eyes, she walked to one of the windows and looked out. There was nothing to see, but she could hear the rain running in rivulets from the roof and thought, absently, that the rain would clear the fog.

It wasn't Lady Fiona's beautiful form and features, or the elegance of her expensive garments that Faith remembered best. It was her undisguised amusement. She'd mistaken Faith for her own lady's maid, or so she said, and from that moment on she adopted a patronizing air. By the time she had left, Faith's confidence was shot to pieces. All she wanted was to leave Edinburgh before anyone knew what a fool she had made of herself.

"Fiona! I might have guessed. Why didn't you tell me?"

"She said that it was better if you never knew. And I had my pride. I agreed with her."

She turned to face him. He had begun to dress and was

stuffing his shirt into the waistband of his trousers. Cold rage had hardened his features to flint.

His voice was rough with the force of his fury. "And you believed that conniving bitch before you would believe me? Ask me about Fiona, and I'll tell you what she was like."

"I don't want to know."

"No. You'd rather believe the worst of me. There were others who had faith in me, but apparently not the woman who claims the name for her own."

"You're a fine one to talk of faith!" Her bitterness, held in check for so long, spilled over. "You never once mentioned her in the few terse notes you wrote to me. You were gone for three months, and all I ever received was your itinerary. It was like reading a railway timetable: 'Tomorrow in Aberdeen, and Perth after that.' I got more information from the gossip columns in the London papers. That's where I first read of you and Lady Fiona."

"So," he said savagely, "you thought you'd surprise me in Edinburgh and—what, Faith? Catch me in flagrante delicto with Fiona?"

"Don't be crude! I wanted to see you, judge for myself whether there was any truth to the rumors."

"And you took Fiona's word over mine?"

"You married her," she said vehemently.

"And came to regret it before the ink was dry on our marriage papers!" He took a step toward her, then another. "She wanted me, and I suppose I was flattered. After all, you had left me without a word of explanation. I looked for you for months, but it became patently clear that you did not want to be found."

"I thought it was for the best." She folded her arms across her breasts. Her voice was husky with the emotion she was trying to suppress. "I never wanted you to know about my trip to Scotland. That was why I arranged to meet

Alastair on the terrace. I wanted to talk to him privately, to ask him not to mention that I had ever traveled to Edinburgh. But I was too late."

She cleared her throat. "It was pride on my part, I suppose. I didn't want anyone to pity me."

She backed up a step when he closed the distance between them. He didn't smile nearly often enough to suit her, but when he did, he had a lopsided grin that could melt the hardest heart. The grin he offered her was a travesty of the one she loved. It was painful to watch.

"What happened between us," he said, "was in a different lifetime. Isn't it time to put the past behind us and start over?"

"Start over?" Her eyes flicked uneasily to the bed then back to his face. "We're different people now."

"Faith," he said, shaking his head, "if I could change the past, I would. But I can't. This quarrel serves no purpose. We've got to work together to find out what happened to Danvers. Then there's your mother's diary. If we're constantly at each other's throats, we won't get to the bottom of that mystery, either. Can't we call a truce and go on from there?"

She didn't know why she was fighting him. A short while ago, they'd become lovers. But James had resurrected the past and all the desolation she remembered from that other time had flooded back with a vengeance.

What had happened to her resolve to live for the moment? It came to her again, that awful nightmare and the emotion that crippled her when she'd thought James was lost to her forever.

He didn't speak; he didn't smile. He cupped her face in both hands and gave her a searching look. "It's over," he said. "I'm all right, and so are you." Then he pressed his lips to hers.

Chapter 17

Calmly, deliberately, he held her steady with one hand pressed to the small of her back, then he used his other hand to cup her breast. As he fingered the crest, she gave a little gasp. He swallowed the sound and did it again.

When she pulled back slightly, she was breathing hard. She'd wanted the feel of his arms around her, but she'd expected him to comfort her. The intent look in his eyes told her that James had other ideas.

"We're going to slow down," he said. "I'm going to show you how it's supposed to be."

"You mean..." Her brows puckered. "I didn't do it right the first time?"

He winced. God, he was never any good with words. "No, *I* didn't do it right. I suppose I lost my head. My only excuse is that I've waited eight long years for you." He winced again. Was there no end to his stupidity? This is what had caused their spat just moments ago. He tried again. "What I mean to say, Faith—"

She stopped his words by pressing her fingers to his lips. "I don't need excuses; I don't want protestations of love. What happened tonight with Robert, well, we're both off balance. That won't last." She swallowed. "I hope to God it won't last." Her thoughts drifted to her dream, and she shuddered. "It's enough for me if I can forget, at least for tonight."

The nightmare shouldn't affect her like this, she thought dimly. It was only a dream, wasn't it? Then why did she still feel bereft, as though she'd truly lost James?

She must have voiced what she was thinking, because he cradled her in his arms and began to rock her. Against her hair, he murmured, "Forget about the dream, Faith. Forget about labyrinths and corridors. I won't get lost. I won't let you get lost."

He meant what he said. It was *his* dream not hers. Next time they came to the gates barring entrance to that derelict house, he would lock them and throw away the key.

Even as the thought occurred to him, he knew that he was doomed to enter that house and try to rescue Faith. That was how this premonition worked.

He didn't want to think about premonitions, or the past, or what might await them on the morrow. He hadn't liked the sound of her voice telling him that they were two different people now. He wasn't different, not in the things that mattered, and he didn't think Faith had changed in any significant way, either.

That wasn't entirely true. Distrust and misunderstanding had taken their toll. But the magnetism that had drawn them together was still there. It wasn't lust. That could be easily satisfied. All he knew was that when Faith walked into a room, the world seemed a brighter place.

He wanted that brightness for himself, not only for today but for all their tomorrows.

Brows beetled, he focused on Faith the way he focused on every aspect of his trains. She found his scrutiny a bit unnerving, but she stood perfectly still as he fluffed out her hair and combed it with his fingers to fall in waves to her shoulders. Neither spoke, though there was a slight hiatus in their breathing. Satisfied with the disarray of her hair, he touched his fingers to the slope of her cheekbones, the lobes of her ears, sliding his hands down to her shoulders, where his fingers toyed with the collar of her robe.

"What is it about you?" he murmured as if to himself.

From the moment he'd met her in Lady Beale's ballroom, he'd been struck by how different she was from the debutantes who vied for masculine attention. They were like Fiona. It wasn't a particular man they wanted but the material things they would come into if they could only lead a suitable candidate to the altar. Faith knew her place as a paid companion and had not given him a second glance.

Naturally, he'd been intrigued. He hadn't singled her out. That would have been too obvious, but he'd created opportunities to get to know her better, and the more he talked to her, the more he came to admire and like her.

There was a softness to Faith he'd found appealing, maybe because he'd never taken to the artificial characters he'd encountered in society. She was, however, too trusting for her own good. She accepted people at face value and never questioned their sincerity or their motives.

She had kept him at a distance because, he supposed, she believed that there was no future for a paid companion and a man of his substance. That was what society thought, and society was an ass. He couldn't say his intentions were honorable, because at that point he hadn't had any intentions toward Faith. He admired her and liked her, and he enjoyed her company.

That was how things stood before he caught her under

the mistletoe. He'd almost burned to ashes in the raw emotions that one kiss had provoked. After that, he couldn't get her out of his mind.

"First love," she quipped, when the silence became unbearable. The intensity of his stare was making her breath catch.

He'd forgotten the question evidently, so she elaborated, "The poets have written about it since the beginning of time. One always remembers one's first love."

He gave her the grin that could melt her heart. "You know I don't read poetry."

"Yes, I remember." Her tone was dry. "Poetry to you is a railway timetable."

"No, poetry to me is you, Faith. I don't always understand you, but I know..." His voice trailed to a halt. What he left unsaid was that the world would be a darker place without her. His world would be darker.

His hands cupped her shoulders, clenched and trembled. She saw the change in him and held her breath. A moment before, they'd been playing with words. Now his features were set in harsh lines, his mouth was flat and hard. She gasped when he suddenly scooped her into his arms and stalked with her to the bed. She scooted up to the headboard and hugged her knees. She wasn't afraid of him, but she could see that he wasn't himself.

"James, what's wrong?" she asked softly.

He lowered himself to the bed. "What's wrong is..." He pulled back and looked down at her. He'd been hovering at the edge of that awful nightmare again, but he didn't want to remind her of it, so he said instead, "What's wrong is that I want to make this good for you, but I want you so damn much that I'm afraid my control may not be equal to my good intentions."

His words arrested her. What could be more passionate

than the way they'd come together so short a time ago? An ache started in her breasts and moved lower. Heat shimmered over her skin.

He'd told her only a small part of the truth. That he wanted her went without saying, but it was fear that was driving him. She was so small and defenseless and no match for the monster that lurked in the ruined mansion of his dream. He wanted to bind her to him so that she would never run from him again. Her life depended on it…and so did his sanity.

When he joined her on the bed, that intent look was back in his eyes. For a moment, a fraction of a moment, she felt a shiver of alarm. He seemed like a stranger. Then he whispered her name, and her fear was forgotten as anticipation for the moment he would put his hands on her tightened every muscle. The moment came, and she moaned from the sudden rise in pleasure.

He opened the edge of her dressing robe and bore her into the mattress with the press of his weight. His mouth covered hers in a lingering, wet kiss, then dipped lower, brushing with tantalizing languor her throat, her shoulders, before hovering over one painfully tight breast. He prolonged the torture, using the tip of his tongue to lave one distended nipple, then the other. When he finally took her into his mouth and sucked hard, she heaved up to give him freer access to her body. Like a sprig of ivy, she clung to him, winding her limbs around his hard length. It wasn't enough for her. She wanted to know him as intimately as he knew her. She wanted bare skin against bare skin.

He smiled when he felt her hands trying to strip his garments from him. She needed help, and he quickly peeled out of his trousers and shirt before joining her on the bed again. He was going to take her with all the skill he should have used before. He wanted to make this perfect for her.

He might have succeeded in his noble objective if Faith had not started to buck and arch beneath him. He could feel her soft breasts rubbing against his chest, feel her hands clutching at the muscles that bunched in his arms. And those keening cries she made at the back of her throat made his ears ring with the pounding of his blood.

She could feel his control begin to slip, and it thrilled her in some deeply primitive way that she only half understood. She had never imagined she had such power over him. What made her bold was the knowledge that she had only to say the word, and he would stop. He would be angry, or sulky, or curse fluently, but she never doubted that she had the power to make him stop.

She didn't want him to stop. She'd discovered something about herself that filled her with awe. She was a deeply passionate woman. What was it about this man, she wondered, that made him different? Many men had stolen kisses from her. It was one of the perils of her employment as a companion. But no man's kisses had had the power to touch her as James's kisses had. Now she was as wild to have him as he was to take her.

Shamelessly, wantonly, she guided his sex to the entrance to her body. "Now," she said, her voice husky.

It was all he wanted to hear. Pushing her knees high, he drove into her.

She thought she was prepared for the shock of his possession, but she couldn't help sucking in a sharp breath. She didn't know that her nails were digging into his shoulders.

"I hurt you," he said in a shaken voice, and he made to withdraw.

Her arms tightened convulsively around him. "Don't you dare leave me, James Burnett."

When she lifted her hips to draw him deeper, a muffled groan tore from his throat. "Easy," he said, "easy."

But she didn't want easy. She began to move.

Every muscle in his body tensed. He tried to hold on to his control, but she'd taken it away from him. Rhythmically, rapidly they moved together till they lay shuddering and spent in each other's arms.

It was a long time before either of them moved. James turned his head to look at the clock. It was the middle of the night, and he was perfectly sure that his family would not travel in the dark. They would have put up at some comfortable hotel and would probably set out at first light. That gave him plenty of time to talk to Faith. Somehow, he had to find the words to put her on her guard without making her more frightened than she already was.

He was sorely tempted to kiss the pout from her mouth, but prudence won out. One kiss would lead to another, and they would never get around to having that talk. He swung out of bed, and as he began to pull on his garments, he studied her as she slept. One hand was tucked under her cheek. Her hair was spread about her pillow like a curtain of fine lace. As he watched, she sighed and rolled onto her back. From the folds of the eiderdown, one pink-crested breast peeked up at him. God only knew what had happened to her dressing robe.

There was an odd tightness in his throat. It seemed so right, so natural to be here with her like this. He wanted to wake up to her first thing every morning. He wanted to hear her voice long into the night. They should have had a troop of children by now, or at least one or two.

The old resentment began to stir, and he quickly crushed it. He hadn't known about Fiona, but Faith was right; he wasn't blameless, either. She had written long, newsy letters to him, which he had thoroughly enjoyed. His only excuse for neglecting her was that he'd been mired to his neck in sensitive negotiations that were too complex to explain in a letter.

They couldn't change the past, but they could start over. In fact, they didn't have much choice. Even now, she could be pregnant with his child.

He toyed with the idea of pointing out this truth and decided against it. Faith had enough to contend with right now. Let her come to it herself. She must see that marriage was the only solution for them.

She seemed to be sleeping peacefully, so he took the chair by the fire, which was now reduced to a heap of glowing cinders, and after making himself comfortable, he steepled his fingers and concentrated on the most worrisome aspect of the whole business: Robert Danvers's murder.

After coming at it from all angles, the only thing he was certain of was that Danvers had been recruited to do someone else's dirty work. Either he had failed to do what he was supposed to do, or he had become expendable.

A memory came sharply into focus. He'd sensed, when he was going through the responses to Faith's advertisement, that he had missed something important. Had Danvers arrived before him? It made sense. Then he'd told his superior the time and place of Faith's appointment with Lady Cowdray, and his superior had set thugs on her.

It was all speculation. What he needed was hard evidence or a dash of his granny's insight.

He got up and stretched his cramped muscles. A movement in the bed caught his eye. Faith had pulled herself to a sitting position and had dragged the eiderdown up to her chin.

"Not another bad dream?" he asked, crossing to her.

"No, just the usual." She patted the bed, inviting him to sit.

"What's the usual?" He sat beside her and took her hand.

She shrugged. "I'm standing in front of my class the first day of school, and they are all looking at me expectantly. The only thing is, I can't find my notes, so I don't know what to say. The headmistress is there, and I feel awful." She stopped and gave a halfhearted laugh. "It's not the same caliber of nightmare that I had earlier. But I think you know that."

When she shivered, he put his arms around her.

"What happened, James?" she asked. "Why was I in that wreck of a house? Why were you there? It wasn't only my dream, was it? It was yours as well. We were there together."

"Now, what makes you say that?"

"Don't try to smile your way out of this! I knew it was your dream, too, because...I don't know...something you said? Yes. Now I remember. You mentioned being lost in a labyrinth. Well, that's my dream, too. I'm running through a maze of corridors, trying to find you."

She squeezed his hand, and her eyes searched his. "Tell me what's going on."

He sighed. He shrugged. He shook his head. He knew one thing: he wasn't going to scare her out of her wits by talking of premonitions and changing the future, so he gave her a slightly distorted version of the truth.

"Someone wants to hurt me," he said, "and I dream about it. I think I told you once that my grandmother was a witch, and I inherited some of her powers? You thought I was joking. Well, this is how her gift works. I dream about the future so that I'll be prepared to defend myself when I come face-to-face with the person who wishes me harm."

"He doesn't wish to harm only you, James." She leaned forward as if to make her point. "He is after me, too. I was in the dream, remember?"

"But it was my dream, not yours."

"A dream that we shared. How many people do you know who share their dreams?"

He was surprised that she accepted his reference to his psychic powers without question. He'd expected her to reject that part of his account and substitute something more mundane. It was what he would have done in her place.

"You don't think that sounds far-fetched? I mean, that I have second sight?"

She answered him seriously. "Of course it sounds far-fetched, but I'm part Irish. I know there are things in this world that defy explanation. Besides, in the dream, I knew you had special powers, but you weren't using them. Is it true? Can you divine the future? Or was it just part of the dream?"

"It's true, up to a point. I can't tell who the villain is or what the end of the dream will be."

They went back and forth, recounting different parts of the dream as they occurred to them. At one point, she suggested that they should try to sleep their way into the dream again.

"Don't you see, James, it will give us a chance to look around, take impressions, and maybe see the villain's face."

He made a violent motion with one hand. "You can forget about that! Haven't you heard of people dying in their sleep when they were in the peak of health? It does happen."

There was a long silence as she considered his words, then she said slowly, "Is this dream going to become real? Is there a house like the one we dreamed about? Are we going to be lost in a maze of corridors?"

He made light of it. "Hopefully, no. But just remember,

if you find yourself in a derelict building, waking or sleeping, call my name, whisper it, or just think it, and I'll come running. I mean that, Faith." The look on her face prompted him to add, "It was a dream, just a horrible nightmare to warn me of danger. Now, let it go, and think about something else."

"I don't want to go to sleep."

"I don't blame you. Would you like a book to read?"

She shook her head. "I don't think I could read Dickens, and that's all there is to read here."

"There is your mother's diary."

"I suppose." She didn't sound very enthusiastic. "Are you going back to your own room?"

"No. I'm going to sit right here and read *A Tale of Two Cities.*" And he was going to make quite sure that he didn't fall asleep clutching her hand. He wasn't going to drag her into that hell again.

"What about your family? What are they going to think if they find us here together?"

"I don't think they will be home before it's light, but even if they are, I'm sure they'll understand why I didn't want to leave you alone, not after what happened at the Hugheses' house tonight. I'm going to turn up the lights and leave the door wide open. Now, where do you keep your mother's diary?"

Her slow, tremulous smile became a broad grin. "Thank you. It's locked in the wardrobe"—he was at the wardrobe before she had finished speaking—"but it's hidden in the folds of Margaret's dressing robe. I keep the key in the top drawer of my escritoire."

She looked baffled when he opened the wardrobe without the key.

"The lock has been forced," he said. He began to shake out all her clothes. "There's no diary here."

She scooped her dressing robe off the floor and shrugged into it as she quickly crossed to the wardrobe. Then she, too, shook out every garment.

"Someone has taken it," she said faintly. "Who could have done such a thing?"

"Who else but Robert Danvers?"

"Robert stole the diary? But why?"

"Because someone either asked him to or paid him to do it. Sadly, he paid with his life."

She drew in a long breath as she thought this through. "Wouldn't someone have seen him if he'd broken into the house? The servants? One of us?"

"Not if he chose his moment with care."

Without thinking, she sank onto the upright chair beside the writing table. "The Burlington Arcade!" she exclaimed with feeling. "What a fool you must think me."

"What about the Burlington Arcade?"

"When he walked me to the carriage, I practically told him when the house would be empty. We were trying to arrange a time when he could bring his mother to see me. Of course, she didn't come. I thought the fog had kept her at home."

"When did you last look over your mother's diary?"

"Yesterday. I made a few notes—not that it got me any-where. That blasted code still has me stumped."

He edged one hip onto the flat of the desk and narrowed his gaze on her face. "Danvers knew the house would be empty this evening. He must have stolen the diary when we left for the Hugheses' house." He paused as a picture formed inside his mind. "He would invent some pretext for getting inside the house, something that wouldn't arouse the servants' suspicions. Then he'd go through the bed-chambers one by one until he found yours. Once he had the diary, he would lose no time in handing it over to the man who killed him. And that man must have been at the lecture this evening. Yes, I see it now. They arranged to meet at the boathouse to make the transfer."

She suppressed a shudder. "What could be so damning in that diary to cause these horrible events?"

"That's what we're going to find out."

Her shoulders slumped. "That's easy to say, but how?"

He tipped her chin up with one finger. "You can begin by telling me exactly what Mr. Danvers said to you when you met in the Burlington Arcade. Leave nothing out."

Chapter 18

The family arrived home before noon the following morning and, as expected, James's aunt was with them. Faith was glad of the distraction. Her mind kept veering from the murder of Robert Danvers to what had happened afterward when she and James arrived home. Murder, dreams, nightmares, and a wondrous night of pleasure: it was all too much to get her mind around. Then Aunt Mariah breezed into the house, filling it with her own special energy.

After a late luncheon in the garden room, Harriet went off to play while the others sat around the table, drinking tea and coffee. Up to this point, the conversation had revolved around the wedding just past, but when there was a lull in the conversation, James seized the moment and told his family in as few words as possible that Robert Danvers, the son of the banker, had been brutally murdered the night before at a house on the South Bank, and that Faith had discovered the body.

The silence that followed these stark words was absolute.

They might not have known Danvers Jr., but his father was a well-known figure in the commercial world. As suddenly as the silence had fallen, it shattered as everyone burst into speech. Bit by bit, the story was told. James did most of the talking, with Faith filling in details as they occurred to her.

Speculation was rife about who might have committed such a heinous crime. It was a vagrant, a jealous lover, a wronged husband. There was no end of suspects, but all of them were nameless, faceless strangers. No one at the table could conceive of it being someone they knew.

"You haven't said anything, Roderick," said James. "You knew Danvers, didn't you?"

"Knew him?"

"You told me once that you didn't much care for him."

Roderick leaned back in his chair, balancing it on two legs. "I knew him slightly, but he never acknowledged the acquaintance. He was a lot older than me, so that may explain it. But you're right, I didn't care for him. He had too much money to play with and was too obvious with it." He shrugged. "If I were a policeman, I'd be looking for someone who knew that Danvers always carried a wad of notes on him."

A thought occurred to James, but before he could voice it, Margaret rushed in: "What do you mean, he had too much money to play with? Are you back at your old tricks, Roderick? Are you gaming at cards and betting on horses?"

Roderick noted the frown on his brother's brow, and his lips curled in a world-weary smile. "What else is there for a young man to do in this thriving metropolis? I go where my friends go."

Margaret flashed a look of appeal at her husband, but the only help she got from that quarter was an indifferent shrug.

Faith smoothed out her napkin as she tried to control her indignation. By her lights, Mr. Burnett was an appalling parent and even worse as a husband. She didn't think he should give Roderick a public dressing down, because she didn't think the boy was half as wicked as he made himself out to be. What Roderick needed was a little fatherly interest, a masculine mentor whom he could respect and look up to. She might not know much about boys, but she did understand young girls. At St. Winnifred's, they'd had their share of rebels and never gave up on them.

It was left to Aunt Mariah to defuse what was turning into an unpleasant scene. "Of course Roderick goes where his friends go, and quite right, too. I never met the man yet who did not indulge in a few follies when he was a boy. He'll grow out of them." She looked pointedly at James.

He acknowledged the hit with a slight inclination of his head. "Quite," he said. "The real trouble will start when Roderick becomes interested in girls."

"Who says I'm not?" drawled Roderick.

Margaret's look of dismay had everyone chuckling.

At this point, Aunt Mariah diplomatically led the conversation away from young men and their follies to what they had been discussing earlier. "Poor Mr. Danvers. What could have induced him to meet someone in a boathouse? He must have had an appointment with someone from the house."

"That narrows it down to a hundred suspects," said James dryly.

"Nonsense!" replied his aunt. "He didn't know all the people at the house, did he? No, this was someone he knew and trusted."

"Perhaps," said Mr. Burnett, "this acquaintance wanted to borrow money, and when Mr. Danvers refused to oblige, they quarreled, and he killed him."

James reached for the coffeepot and poured himself a fresh cup. They were edging closer to his own theory but not close enough. His family knew nothing of Madeline Maynard and her diary or that he suspected Danvers had stolen it. It wasn't a suspicion; he was sure of it, and now he knew how it was done.

He'd questioned the butler and learned that just after he and Faith had left for the meeting of the Egyptology Society, a young detective had come to the door claiming that the police were searching the area for a thief who appeared to have entered the back lane and slipped into a neighbor's garden. It was his duty, the detective said, to search the premises. The butler and servants were told, for their own safety, to remain belowstairs until he had completed his task. They had complied, leaving the imposter free to roam the house at will.

And he was an imposter. As soon as he got the story from Butcher, James had made enquiries that very morning at the local police station. No one had been assigned to search the houses in Berkeley Square.

Clever, clever Danvers, but not clever enough, or he would not have mistaken the character of his partner.

He was jarred from his speculations by a question that had been put directly to him. "I'm sorry," he said, looking at his aunt, "I didn't quite catch that."

"I said that I presume you and Faith will be going to the funeral?"

"The funeral?" He looked at Faith.

"Yes," she said, answering the question in his eyes. "I'm sure that my friend, Lily, will want to be there. I'll write to her today to let her know what has happened."

"And I shall come, too," said Aunt Mariah. She looked at their blank faces and went on to explain herself. "I bank with Mr. Danvers Sr., so we have a nodding acquaintance, and I did meet young Mr. Danvers on Speech Day." She lifted her shoulders in a tiny shrug. "All right, I'm curious. Have you considered that the murderer might be there? We old ladies must take our excitement where we can find it."

"Is that wise?" asked her brother, who had one eye on the clock. "Murderers don't like people looking over their shoulder."

"I shall be a model of decorum. Besides, James and Roderick will be there to watch over Faith and me."

"What?" Roderick had been leaning back in his chair again, but he was so startled by his aunt's comment that the chair fell forward, almost unbalancing him. "But I hardly knew the man. Why can't you go, Father?"

Mr. Burnett shook his head vigorously. "Not my cup of tea. No, I'm sure my presence isn't necessary." As though to cut off further debate, he got up. "Will you look at the time? I've arranged to meet Major Howie and a few friends at my club. It's his sixtieth birthday, you know, and we are laying on a splendid celebration for him." To his wife, he said, "Don't wait up for me, my dear. I shall be home very late."

"Pity," said Aunt Mariah in a cheerful voice. "What about tomorrow night? Will you be engaged then as well?"

Mr. Burnett looked nonplussed, but only for moment. He snapped his fingers. "I'd almost forgotten. Card party. Sorry. I can't get out of it."

"No matter," replied his sister in the same cheerful voice. "But you'll miss a treat I have in store for all of you." She looked from one person to another. "Before I left for Henley, I reserved a box at the Savoy Theatre. Yes, Gilbert and Sullivan are putting on a performance of *The Mikado*. They say it's brilliant." She chuckled. "You'll love it, James. The place is completely lit by electricity."

She gave them a moment or two to grasp her words, then excusing herself, she left the table.

"No, don't go. I want to talk to you, Roderick," said James.

As the others filed out of the garden room, James reached for the silver cigarette case on the table. When he opened it, he found it empty. "Can you spare one of yours?" he asked his brother.

Roderick eyed him curiously. "I don't smoke. The weed gives me asthma."

That was something James had forgotten. Torn between embarrassment and guilt, he said, "We haven't exactly been the best of brothers, have we? My fault, I know, but I do worry about you."

Roderick's reply was the skeptical lift of one eyebrow.

James plowed on. "What I should have said was that I have your best interests at heart."

"Well, that's a first. I'm nineteen years old, and you've never regarded me as more than a pesky gadfly. No. I exaggerate. You gave the impression that you weren't aware of my existence. Oh, don't get your tongue in knots trying to explain your indifference. I understand. You had your railways to build, and I'm only your half brother."

"You're nineteen? I thought you were eighteen."

Roderick rolled his eyes.

James's remorse began to waver. "Look here," he said, "if you've been racking up gambling debts or losing money on horses, I want to know about it."

Roderick folded his arms across his chest and grinned. "Don't say you'll bail me out? Why, Jamie, I'm touched."

James inwardly allowed that his concern for his brother's welfare had been thin at the best of times, but that was because the boy had a father. *Their* father was Roddy's guardian and trustee. He had no real authority here. Even as the thought occurred to him, he felt a ripple of annoyance. He controlled the purse strings, more or less, and that gave him some say in how things were run. His father was useless, worse than useless. Without his intervention, Colin Burnett would spend every spare penny on keeping up a castle that soaked up money like a sponge did water.

James knew what Faith would say, that his brother needed a masculine mentor to confide in and look up to, but James did not feel comfortable stepping into that role, and he was damn sure that Roderick wouldn't let him. They were practically strangers. He hadn't deliberately neglected the boy. They hardly saw one another and had simply drifted apart.

He looked at Roderick and saw something of himself at the same age. They'd both been packed off to school at eight, had infrequent visits from their parents, with only servants and occasionally Granny McEcheran and Aunt Mariah to look after them in the holidays. No wonder they'd become resentful and difficult. The difference between them was that he had stopped rebelling when he'd developed a passion for trains. He wondered whether Roddy had any interests besides the obvious ones. He agreed with his aunt up to a point. A boy should be allowed a few follies. What he feared was that his brother might be getting in over his head.

He tried again. "Look, Roddy—!"

"No, you look, big brother!" Roderick abruptly stood and brushed the sleeve of his jacket as though brushing off a restraining hand. "I don't want your charity, and I don't want you telling me what to do. Frankly, you've left it too late to play the role of the elder brother. So, if I want to gamble, wench, or drink myself silly—keep out of my way."

James snapped back his chair and got up. He was simmering. No. He was boiling, and the germ of truth in his brother's words only exacerbated his tempter. But, damn it all, he was the mainstay of this family, and though he didn't expect to be loved for it, he did demand a little respect.

Through his teeth, he got out, "I'd advise you to mind your tongue, or I'll teach you a lesson you'll not soon forget."

Roderick let out a hoot of laughter. "I should warn you, brother dear, that I was the champion wrestler of my year before I was expelled."

James sneered. "Wrestling little boys is one thing. You're not man enough to take me on."

The amusement was wiped from Roderick's face, but it was not replaced by caution, far from it. His chin jutted, his nostrils flared, and his eyes flashed with grim determination. The resemblance between James and his younger sibling had never been more obvious.

In one deft move, Roderick shrugged out of his jacket and tossed it aside. James did the same. In a gesture that was meant to provoke, Roderick curled his index finger and beckoned to James.

"Thigibh an so, bodach!" he said. *Come here, old man.*

"Lord preserve us! The boy knows a little Gaelic." James crouched down in a wrestler's stance. *"Eisol, bhala-ich."* He'd exhausted the little Gaelic he knew but went on regardless. *"Nach ist thu."*

A frown puckered Roderick's brow. "What does that mean?"

"Come and get me, little boy."

The words were hardly out of James's mouth when Roderick charged, and they went tumbling to the carpeted floor in a tangle of arms and legs. The delicate porcelain crockery on the table rattled alarmingly, but neither paid any heed to that. They grunted, they heaved, as each strove to get a lock that would disable the other.

They broke apart, jumped to their feet, and came at each other again. This time, not only did they bring down the delicate crockery, but they also crashed into a chair, which cracked then crumpled like a broken matchstick. James had the advantage of weight, but Roderick was proving to be as slippery as an eel. James couldn't hold him in a lock, so he grabbed a fistful of hair and dragged his brother's head back to expose his throat. What he was going to do next, he had no idea. In a real fight, he would have chopped Roderick's throat, but he didn't want to injure his brother, merely teach him a lesson.

Roderick did not labor under such scruples. With tremendous force, he swung his elbow back, right into the soft part of James's belly. James gasped, he choked, but he didn't let go. Through a red mist of pain and rage, he pounded Roderick's face into a cushion that had fallen on the floor. He was going to smother the bastard.

The door to the garden room suddenly crashed open, and Aunt Mariah, followed closely by Faith and Margaret, charged into the room. Margaret had had the foresight to bring a broom. She didn't wait for the two adversaries to catch their breath. Like an enraged Fury, she went at them, beating them both about the head with her broom, screeching oaths that would later make her blush when she recalled them. Meantime, Faith had grabbed James by the shirttails and was pulling with all her might. Aunt Mariah had Roderick by the collar.

What shamed the brothers into giving up the fight was not the brute force of the ladies but the tears of a child. Harriet came fearfully into the room, saw the chaos, and immediately burst into tears.

The men got sheepishly to their feet.

"It was a game," said Roderick. "Only a game."

Harriet ran into his arms and glared up at James.

"Tell her, James," said Roderick.

He obliged. "It was a wrestling match. Roderick was giving me a few pointers. You didn't think we were in earnest, did you?"

Aunt Mariah looked at the broken shards of her prize crockery and the smashed Hepplewhite chair, and she snorted in the manner of an English Thoroughbred.

"A game?" said Harriet dubiously.

Roderick smiled down at her. "Silly chit! Don't you know that James and I are the best of friends?" He looked at James and held out his hand. "We're the best of friends. See, Harriet?"

James clasped the proffered hand and shook it. "The best of friends," he said.

Harriet relaxed. Her tears dried, and she said in a coaxing voice, "May I go to the theater with you, Mama? Do say yes. I love Gilbert and Sullivan. Please? *Please?*"

They left the room as if nothing untoward had occurred, though the ladies' smiles were a little stiff. No one wanted to shatter the illusions of a child.

Going to the theater so soon after a young man was murdered did not seem right to Faith. On the other hand, she needed something to distract her from constantly reliving that moment in the boathouse when she'd tripped over Danvers's body. Then there was James to think about, and how they'd come together like a sudden electrical storm. So much was weighing on her mind that she was sure she would not enjoy the performance.

She was wrong. The Savoy Theatre on the Strand was beyond anything Faith could have imagined. The building was only four years old, palatial, with a stage that could have rivaled the amphitheaters of ancient Rome. Lights blazed from every level, but surpassing everything by far was the performance itself. Gilbert and Sullivan certainly knew how to please the crowd. She found her toes tapping in time to the music. She laughed, she clapped, she even hummed along with the rollicking choruses. When finally the lights went up, and it was time to go, she felt light-headed, as though she had tossed off a bottle of champagne.

The foyer was crowded with patrons who were now eager to be first in line to get to their carriages, with James and Roderick leading the pack. There was a good deal of pushing and elbowing. Someone trod on the hem of Faith's gown, one of the new gowns she'd ordered from Madame Digby. She felt it tear, and though it cost her to appear unaffected, she managed to pin a smile on her face as she turned to look at the person who had committed the crime.

It was Mr. Hughes of the Egyptology Society. Far from apologizing, he looked right through her as though he did not recognize her and was unaware of the damage he had done. Faith opened her mouth, but before she could say his name, Aunt Mariah gripped her arm and pulled her away.

"Not now, Faith!" she said in a forceful undertone. "You cannot recognize a gentleman when he is with his fancy piece."

Faith's jaw dropped. "His fancy piece? You mean his mistress?"

"That's exactly what I mean." Aunt Mariah shook her head. "It's his wife I feel sorry for. This is bound to get back to her. I wouldn't be surprised if some of her friends are here tonight and will lose no time in apprising her of what her faithless husband is up to. As though poor Sophie needs to be told!"

Faith said, "Why doesn't she leave him or throw him out? I mean, this is the eighteen eighties. A man doesn't control a woman's property like he once did. And Mrs. Hughes was left well off, wasn't she?"

"The wisdom of youth is so refreshing," observed Aunt Mariah with a faint smile. "Because, I suppose, she loves him. Yes, I know, it's pitiful, but some women are slaves to love. Sophie Hughes is one of them. But there is more to it than that. She would pay a price, too. Separated or divorced women are still social pariahs. Sophie would lose her friends, and she wouldn't be invited anywhere."

Margaret and Harriet came level with them at that moment, so the conversation was dropped. Harriet's face was shining with the thrill of the performance, and her words tripped over each other in her excitement.

"Wasn't that the most marvelous operetta you've ever heard? It was so funny! When I grow up, I want to go on the stage and..."

Faith listened with half an ear. Her eyes were trailing the couple who were making for the exit, Mr. Hughes and his fancy piece. Though Hughes was a handsome man, he looked old enough to be the lady's father. And she *did* look like a lady—not a quiet, well-bred lady but an animated fashion plate with a flirtatious smile.

Faith was affronted on behalf of the betrayed wife. Mrs. Hughes had been kindness itself when Faith waited her turn to be interviewed by the police after she'd found Danvers's body. She'd offered her a fresh set of clothes. She'd sat with her and held her hand. Her soothing presence had gone a long way to prevent Faith from going to pieces. She deserved better than this from her faithless husband.

Something else occurred to Faith: the depressing picture of a woman past her prime dressing in the style of a debutante. Mutton dressed as lamb. Was Sophie Hughes trying to look younger to compete with the lady her husband had taken up with? Did she love her husband? Aunt Mariah could well be right about that, but she was wrong about Mrs. Hughes's friends. They did not conform to society's rules. Her mother's memoirs could attest to that. They would not turn their backs on a friend just because she had divorced her husband. They wouldn't care one way or another.

By the time they got home, the pleasant buzz in Faith's head had evaporated. All the same, as they climbed the stairs to their beds, she kept up her end discussing that night's performance. Harriet was in her element. Both her brothers were laughing and joking together, and both insisted on escorting their little sister to her room.

Faith wondered how long this new civility between James and Roderick would last.

Chapter 19

"Why, Millie, it's perfect."

Faith was in her bedroom, examining the frock she had worn to the lecture, when Margaret and Aunt Mariah breezed into the room. She looked up and held out the dress so that they could see the skirt.

"Millie is a miracle worker," she said. "Look, there's not a mark on it." She couldn't bring herself to say the word *blood*. "How did you do it, Millie?"

The maid colored and beamed. "I tried everything, miss, but I think it was the spirits of wine that did the trick."

Aunt Mariah took charge. "Yes, Millie is a wonder, which is why I pay her a fortune so that she won't be lured away from me."

Millie giggled and allowed herself to be shooed from the room.

Two pairs of eyes were then trained upon Faith.

"What?" she asked.

"Your secret is out," declared Aunt Mariah severely.

Margaret came forward and gave Faith a hug. "We met Mrs. Hughes on Bond Street, and she told us that it's common knowledge that you and James are engaged. Of course, we couldn't deny it, but it did come as a bit of a surprise. We thought it was a secret and that you were waiting to hear from your uncle in Ireland before you announced your engagement."

Faith sank slowly onto the bed. She was remembering Mr. Hughes at the lectern and how he had branded James publicly as the man who was engaged to marry Madeline Maynard's daughter.

She looked at Margaret and saw nothing but pleasure in her eyes. Aunt Mariah's stare was more penetrating. Her eyes might have faded with age, but her shrewd intelligence had not dimmed one bit.

How, Faith asked herself, had she got herself into this mess? And how could she defend a course of action that now seemed indefensible?

It wasn't a course of action. It was a course of inaction. She should have told James's family straight out from the very beginning that she and James were not engaged.

But that was what she had done. So where had she gone wrong?

"It's like this," she said. "James and I made such a debacle of things when we got engaged all those years ago, that this time we want to be very sure before we commit ourselves. All we need is a little time to get to know each other again."

Margaret, ever the peacemaker, said, "That sounds sensible, doesn't it, Mariah?"

Gradually, Aunt Mariah's hard stare softened, and the beginning of a smile touched her lips. "Very sensible," she agreed, "but don't wait too long before you make up your mind. It wouldn't be fair to James or to us. You see, Faith, we're beginning to think of you as one of the family. It would be a terrible wrench if you were to leave us."

When the ladies left, Faith stared into space, thinking, thinking, thinking.

She bided her time and waited until just before bedtime before she went in search of James. He was in the library, looking through photographs of trains.

He looked up with a smile. "I was just thinking how we could add a passageway to our trains so that it would be possible to get from one end of the train to the other when it's moving." He stopped when he saw her face. "What is it, Faith? What has happened?"

She took the chair closest to his. "Margaret and Aunt Mariah met Mrs. Hughes on Bond Street," she began, and she went on to tell him how it was becoming common knowledge that they were engaged to be married. "It was Mr. Hughes's announcement from the lectern that did it. I'm sorry, James. I didn't know how to answer Aunt Mariah, so I let her think that all we needed was a little time before we decided, well, whether we could make a go of it this time around."

She looked at him expectantly. Though she would hardly admit it to herself, she was hoping he would say something profound.

He looked at the photographs in his hands and set them aside. "No harm done," he said. "I think you handled it really well."

That was all he had to say? The only thing that was profound was her sense of letdown, and that made her angry with herself. What had she expected—a declaration of undying love? He was obsessed with trains. Even now, surrounded by books, he chose to look at photographs of trains. No woman could compete with that.

He was looking at her warily, as though he expected— what? Tears? A temper tantrum? She forced herself to sound pleasant when what she wanted was to find a dark corner where she could mope in private. "I didn't handle it. I postponed the inevitable."

He frowned. "What does that mean?"

"You must see," she said, "that I can't stay here. We're deceiving your family, and that is so wrong. Aunt Mariah and Margaret, I'm sure, will soon start planning our wedding. We can't build up their hopes only to dash them. The sooner I leave, the better."

"Leave? Have you forgotten about those villains who attacked you?"

"I'm in the clear now, aren't I? We're both in the clear. Whoever killed Robert must have the diary or he has destroyed it, so we don't have to keep looking over our shoulders all the time."

His eyes narrowed on her. "What difference does that make?"

She let out a long, impatient sigh. "You're not usually so obtuse. The villain must know that I'm no longer a threat to him, so I can take up the threads of my own life."

He gave a disbelieving laugh. "And do what? Go back to St. Winnifred's?"

Anger shot through her, and her breathing quickened. "There's nothing wrong with St. Winnifred's, but I haven't decided what I want to do. I have a little money of my own. I can get by until something else comes along."

"I know what it is," he said. "You want to be like those women you've put on a pedestal: your mother and all her like-minded friends."

When she got up, he got up as well. "You hypocrite!" she flung at him. "It's all right for a man to be ambitious, but let a woman try to make something of her life, and all she gets from you is scorn. You should admire them, James. You have so much in common."

He stood there glaring at her for a long moment. Finally, he heaved a sigh. "You can't leave yet." He spoke over the protest she tried to make. "The danger isn't over, and it won't be over until we live through the nightmare I dragged you into. I told you. I'm a seer. I see into the future, and I know that you and I are going to be in that derelict house with a cold-blooded killer hot on our trail."

"What?" she was bewildered.

"The dream we shared? That's in our future, Faith. We're going to live through it, so we can't go our separate ways."

She sank back in her chair and looked up at him with wide, questioning eyes. "You said that it was only a dream."

"I know. I didn't want to frighten you out of your wits. What with Danvers's murder and everything else, I thought you had enough to contend with."

She couldn't take it in. All she could do was shake her head.

He went on. "That's the reason I tracked you down. I knew you were in danger." She looked puzzled, so he elaborated. "I knew you were in danger before I met you in Pritchard's Bookshop. I was given a mission. I was sent to save your life."

"My life? You told me it was only a dream to warn you of danger."

"No. That's where it will end, but until then, I'm going to make damn sure that no one hurts you or maims you."

She linked her fingers and sat with her head bowed as

her mind grappled with all the implications of what he'd just told her. When she thought she had herself well in hand, she looked up with a cool smile. "I thought there must be more to it than you told me. What was it you said? That your only purpose in seeking me out was so that we could put the past to rest."

"I meant that, too. But I couldn't tell you the whole truth at that point. What was I to say, that I'd had a premonition and would do everything in my power to keep you safe? You would have laughed yourself silly and shown me the door."

She gave a low chuckle and twitched her skirts. "I see your dilemma. I suppose I should be flattered. You pursued me with the same tenacity that you always employ in the pursuit of your goals. But James, was it really necessary to take me to bed?"

His contrite expression was quickly changing to one of annoyance. "I thought that was what we both wanted."

Her reasonable tone was rapidly edging toward irate. "What *I* wanted? I didn't stand a chance against you. You play to win, and it doesn't matter who gets hurt in the process."

She jumped to her feet and made to pass him. When he reached for her, she gave him a hard shove and sent him staggering back on his heels. It felt so good that she shoved him again. All her anger and disappointed hopes surged in a wave, and words tumbled from her lips in a torrent.

"Now you listen to me, James Burnett. I don't want to become your mission in life. Do you understand? Whether you had come into my life again or not, I intended to find out what happened to my mother. I've been glad of your help, more than glad, but I'm quite capable of taking care of myself."

"I understand. Just make sure you understand me." His

voice was hard, his eyes were blazing. "Until this damnable affair is put to rest, you'll do as I say. I'll not have you turning up bludgeoned to death like Robert Danvers. I'd blame myself, and I refuse to have your death on my conscience."

His reference to Danvers made her flinch.

"Yes," he said. "I'd rather have you frightened than have to identify your broken body." He ended hoarsely, "It could have been you in that damn boathouse."

When she started to shake, he captured her wrist. "Faith," he said thickly, "we shouldn't be quarreling like this. Let me take you to bed. When we make love, things have a way of sorting themselves out. Come to bed with me, Faith. It's what we both want, isn't it?"

That was when she punched him on the shoulder with her balled fist. When he released her, she danced out of his reach. "You! You!" She was having trouble finding words scathing enough to express her feelings.

James kept a wary eye on her as he rubbed his shoulder. "There was no need to hit me," he said moodily.

Bosom quivering, her voice low and intense, she choked out, "Ah, but I wanted to get your attention. I wanted to make sure that this time *you* would listen to *me*. You don't have to take me to bed to make me compliant. You don't have to frighten me into doing what you want. You've made your point. I won't strike out on my own just yet." She pointed a shaking finger at him. "But no more of your unprincipled tricks. I won't go to bed with you." She marched to the door and flung it wide. "And stay out of my dreams."

Surprise held him motionless, then he went running after her. "Faith! It wasn't a trick. You can't believe that."

He stopped when his brother filled the doorway. Roderick looked as though he'd just returned home from a long night of debauchery. When he saw James, he propped himself against the doorframe and leered suggestively.

"Does this mean the wedding is off? Jamie, Jamie," he shook his head, "you may know how to run a business, but you know damn little about women. Would you like me to give you a few pointers?"

James had had enough. He slammed the door in Roderick's face and stomped to the table where he'd left the train photographs. He stared at them absently for a moment or two, and then, with one vicious swipe, he sent them scattering to the floor.

Chapter 20

*Faith wore her darkest dress to the funeral service, a bottle-*green crepe that was far too hot for the summer months but was suitable for the occasion, and with the black accessories she'd borrowed from Margaret, who had decided to stay home and nurse a cold, she hoped she would not look out of place. James kept his hand on her elbow as she entered the carriage, and that made her feel a little better.

They had set aside their differences in order to solve the mystery of who had killed Robert and why. James believed that the more they knew before the dream became reality, the better prepared they would be. She didn't know what she believed. In her saner moments, she was willing to allow that she'd had a frightful nightmare that was similar to James's nightmare. On the other hand, she couldn't explain away how James seemed to be there whenever she needed him. What was not in doubt was that James took his premonition seriously. Better safe than sorry, until James was proved wrong, seemed a reasonable compromise.

They went directly to the church for the service, then to the graveside for the burial. It was a somber occasion, but Faith found it all the more somber because Robert Danvers's life had been cut short before he'd reached his prime. That he had betrayed her trust and almost certainly stolen Madeline's diary did not lessen the horror of his death. Someone had willfully and deliberately bludgeoned him to death, someone here, perhaps, someone whose outward appearance gave no indication of the evil that festered inside.

She could not keep her eyes from straying among the mourners. The Egyptology Society was well represented, because, she supposed, Robert's body had been found on the premises where they were meeting. Sophie Hughes was clothed from head to toe in severe black and, strangely enough, looked quite elegant. Their eyes met, and they exchanged a quick smile. It was amazing, thought Faith, how much Sophie Hughes had improved since the older woman had shown her a little kindness the night Robert was murdered. She didn't look like mutton dressed as lamb. She looked like a woman who would bloom very nicely if only her husband would pay her a little attention.

Her gaze shifted to take in Mr. Hughes. Her opinion of him was *handsome is as handsome does*. He wasn't smiling, and Faith wondered whether that was because of the seriousness of the occasion or because his wife had found out about his latest indiscretion and was making him pay for it. Alastair Dobbin stood a little apart from his uncle, silent and unsmiling. They hadn't spoken since the night they'd discovered Robert's body. That was the last thing she wanted to talk about. The experience was still to raw, too vivid, to examine in minute detail.

Her gaze shifted to Larry Coltrane. He seemed ... withdrawn, almost sad. His sister, on the other hand, looked bored. Jayne Coltrane had made no concession to funeral conventions. She wore a peacock-blue suit with a matching hat that covered her ghastly hair.

Faith winced as the thought occurred to her. This was a solemn occasion. She should be listening to the vicar's words, not judging people and finding them wanting. Maybe someone here was thinking the same about her.

She looked across the grave to where the chief mourners were standing. Mrs. Danvers's face was convulsed with grief. She was leaning heavily on her husband's arm. He, too, looked grief-stricken. Robert Danvers was an only child. Faith could not begin to imagine what his parents must be suffering. It all seemed so senseless and wicked. Her thoughts came full circle. Was it possible that Robert's murderer was one of the mourners at his funeral?

Mr. Danvers's house was in Knightsbridge, and though it was within walking distance of the church, all the mourners bundled into their carriages for the short drive to where a funeral luncheon would be laid out for them.

Though it was a spacious house, as big as Aunt Mariah's, the number of mourners made it seem smaller. James knew many of the couples because the husbands belonged to the same clubs as he, or he knew them through business. It was inevitable that he would stop to talk with one then another. Faith played her part with aplomb and was highly amused, so she told herself, at how the wives ogled not only her but James as well. Particularly James. She should have expected it. His looks weren't as groomed as Larry Coltrane's, but they were far more potent.

As they moved away, he bent his head to hers. "You've been staring at me as though I were a prize piece of horse-flesh you were hoping to buy."

"The thought may have crossed my mind," she replied.

He grinned. "And what did you decide?"

She gave him a straight look. "It wouldn't be worth my while. Horses are always looking for greener pastures."

Their eyes clashed and held. Faith swallowed her next breath. They'd set aside their differences, but her resentment still simmered just below the surface. She was his mission, he'd told her. It made her feel like a charity case.

She tore her gaze from his and exhaled a shallow breath. "Shall we mingle?" she said.

At one point, James excused himself to have a word with Larry Coltrane. Roderick was supposed to stay with her, but they became separated in the crush. From the corner of her eye, she saw James's aunt in conversation with Mrs. Danvers, and she began to weave her way toward them when she was stopped by a touch on her arm.

"Faith," said Lady Cowdray, "I thought I saw you at the graveside. This crush is intolerable. I can't hear myself think. Let's go into the dining room. There are only servants there now, setting things out."

Faith was glad to escape the heat of so many bodies in a confined space. The dark green crepe was making her skin itch. In the dining room, a few of the mourners had wandered in and were helping themselves to the lavish baked meats and sandwiches that were laid out on a table that could have seated twenty people. But this was not a sit-down luncheon, and Faith felt awkward balancing a small plate in one hand and a glass of wine in the other. How were people expected to eat? She put down the glass of wine.

Lady Cowdray, on the other hand, accepted a glass of wine and ignored the food. "I meant to ask you," she said, "at the lecture the other night, how you were getting on with Madeline's diary. But...well...events overtook us, and the thought was driven out of my mind."

"I'm afraid it's much harder to decode than I thought it would be. Have you told anyone about my mother's diary or that you passed it on to me?"

The question seemed to startle Lady Cowdray. "No one at all. As I told you when I gave it to you, Madeline knew too much for her own good, or she pretended to. I didn't want anyone to be embarrassed by what she might have written."

"Yet you gave the diary to me."

Her ladyship smiled. "But not before I had a chance to take your measure. Within five minutes of meeting you, I knew you were the right person to take charge of the diary. All the same," she heaved a sigh, "I sometimes wonder if I should have destroyed it when I had the chance."

This last remark started a chain of connected thoughts in Faith's mind. She said slowly, "Tell me the truth, Lady Cowdray. Why didn't you find someone to decode Madeline's diary? Why did you hold on to it all these years?"

Lady Cowdray said, "I told you—" She stopped suddenly, gave Faith a strained smile, and started over. "You're right. I could have found someone to decode the diary, but I was afraid that he might not be discreet. You see, Faith, I had a love affair, oh, a long time ago, with a man who had a lot to lose if it became known that I was once his mistress. He died some years ago, but his widow died only six months ago. She can't be hurt if my affair with her husband comes to light now."

"Why didn't you destroy the diary?"

"I don't know. I can't explain it except to say that it was Madeline's."

Faith understood the sentiment. Her loss was greater. It

was the nearest she had come to knowing her mother. Now she had lost her again.

She said quietly and truthfully, "There is nothing spiteful or shocking in the few pages I have managed to decode. In fact, they're rather amusing."

"What is amusing?" Jayne Coltrane, unseen, had joined them and was helping herself to a glass of wine. "Well?"

Faith felt her spine stiffen. She did not like this dour-faced woman, not because of anything she had done to Faith, but because she'd made disparaging remarks about Madeline. "Oh, it was a private joke," she responded, forcing a smile, "and not worth repeating."

Those unsmiling lips turned down at the corners. "How very like your mother you are."

"Thank you." Faith did not force a smile this time.

"Just be careful, Miss McBride, that you don't make as many enemies."

"Really, Jayne!" Lady Cowdray protested.

Faith was furious. "What does that mean?"

"It means, Miss McBride, that your mother was a cheat and a troublemaker. She didn't care whom she hurt. You should know that better than anyone. She abandoned you and your father, did she not? I did not know that she had a husband and a daughter until you suddenly appeared out of nowhere. Madeline Maynard was an unscrupulous wretch who would do or say anything to get her own way."

Faith was still fumbling for words to annihilate Miss Coltrane, when the lady smiled triumphantly and moved away.

Lady Cowdray made soothing sounds as she patted Faith's arm. "Jayne was always jealous of your mother," she said. "They both wrote for the newspapers, you see, but Madeline's pieces sold for more money, and that galled Jayne."

Faith made some innocuous reply, but on another level, she was trying to dredge up a cutting rejoinder to Jayne Coltrane's wounding diatribe. Not that it mattered. Jayne Coltrane was well out of earshot.

More people wandered into the dining room, talking across each other, milling around the table, so she and Lady Cowdray moved away to give them room. By and by, Lady Cowdray excused herself and went to speak to a friend, leaving Faith to wander from one knot of people to another, looking for a face she knew, but no one seemed to notice her. James, she noted, was in conversation with Larry Coltrane. The next time she looked, he was with Alastair Dobbin. She was beginning to feel awkward, when she recognized a young woman who seemed as lost as she.

"Lily!"

She'd raised her voice to get her friend's attention, and several people turned to stare. Faith cared nothing for that. She hadn't seen Lily since the day she'd gone to Chalbourne to meet Lady Cowdray, and she'd missed their late night tête-à-têtes. Besides this, the scene with Jayne Coltrane had left her shaken, and Lily's friendly presence was exactly what she needed to soothe her nerves.

A young girl stepped from behind Lily, and Faith recognized Dora Winslet, but not the Dora whom Faith remembered. She looked ill. Perhaps it was the unrelieved black mourning clothes that drained her face of color, or perhaps it was the trauma of the untimely death of a young man she knew and liked that gave her that pinched look. What Faith could not understand was why Lily had allowed a St. Winnifred's girl of seventeen years to attend the funeral of someone she was not related to.

Dora nodded in answer to something Lily said, then she went to the table and began to fill a small plate with savories. Lily came on. She started off with a smile on her face, but by the time she fell into Faith's arms, her cheeks were wet with tears. The sight of Lily's tears dissolved a hard knot of resentment against Robert Danvers that Faith wasn't aware, till that moment, had lodged deep inside her. The two girls clung together for long minutes without saying a word.

When they broke apart, Lily said unsteadily, "When I read your letter, I was shocked. I can't even imagine what you must have suffered, finding his body like that."

Faith tried to suppress the pictures that were beginning to form in her mind. "I think," she said, "it was the lowest point of my life. If he had died naturally, or because of an accident, I could have accepted it. But murder!"

Lily produced a handkerchief and blew her nose. "I feel so guilty," she said. "I wish I had tried to get to know him better. I wish I hadn't made fun of him. I'm such a nasty-minded person. I don't like myself at all."

"The same thoughts have been going through my head. I should have been nicer to him, and now it's too late."

After dabbing at her cheeks, Lily said, "You have nothing to regret. I was the one with the acid tongue. You were always nice to Robert."

Faith shook her head. "Not always." She meant not always in the privacy of her own mind.

Lily's gaze was wandering over the crush of people. "James Burnett," she said, and turned her eyes on Faith. "He's here. Is it true, Faith? Are you engaged to marry him?"

Faith was glad to drop the subject of Robert's murder. "Everybody tells me that I am," she said, "so it must be true. However, you don't see a ring on my finger, do you?"

A smile twitched at the corners of Lily's mouth. "I knew it couldn't be true. You're too sensible to be taken in by a bounder like Burnett. He's a wastrel, that one."

Oddly, Faith did not like to hear those words coming from another person. If anyone was going to tear James Burnett's character to shreds, it would be she and no one else. Besides, she told herself, she could hardly allow someone to heap scorn upon the man who had saved her life. He wasn't all bad.

"Things are not always what they seem," she said. "I know he is not an easy man to get to know, but—"

"Not easy to get to know? I can read him like a book." People were turning to stare, so Faith grasped Lily's wrist and pulled her through the doors and into the garden. Undaunted, Lily went on, "Actions speak louder than words, Faith, and I say that his actions toward you were shoddy. Don't tell me you're in love with him, because I won't believe you. Is it his money? Or does the prospect of remaining a spinster frighten you?"

"Lily," Faith interjected forcefully, "I didn't say that I was engaged to him. That's what people are saying, but it's only gossip."

"Then tell me this. Why are you staying with his family? And don't try to put me off with that fiction about having to stay in London to help the police with their investigation. You could just as easily stay at St. Winnifred's."

Faith was taken aback. Lily was her best friend. She'd told her the truth, but Lily didn't believe her. She was beginning to sense that some mischievous spirit was working against her.

"Oh, Lily," she said, "not you, too."

Lily looked intently into Faith's eyes. After a moment, she said slowly, "Now I don't know what to believe."

"Trust me, Lily. I've told you the truth. Now, let's find Dora. What on earth persuaded you to bring her here?"

Lily looked as though she wanted to say more, but evidently Faith's closed expression warned her that it was time to change the subject. "She insisted," she said, "because Robert had always been kind to her, and she thought it was the decent thing to do. I tried to dissuade her, but that only upset her more." Lily shrugged. "We're the only ones representing the school. Nearly everyone else is on holiday. So, I thought—why not?"

They entered the dining room and came face-to-face with Dora. The plate she was holding was shaking. Her eyes looked fever-bright.

Faith put out a hand to steady the girl, but Dora flinched away. "Are you all right?" Faith asked. "You don't look well, Dora. I think the strain of the service has been too much for you."

"You do look unwell," said Lily, peering into the younger girl's face. She put a comforting arm around Dora's waist. "You look as though you're running a fever. Come along, Dora, it's home to bed for you."

Dora did not budge. Eyes trained on Faith, she said, "You killed him, didn't you? You murdered Robert. It had to be you. You met him at the boathouse. Everyone knows you were there. You were jealous because he loved me and not you. That's it, isn't it?"

People turned to stare. Faith stood frozen in place, her mind reeling under the verbal attack. Lily and Dora were talking across her, but she wasn't listening. All she was aware of was the hurt and hatred that blazed from Dora's eyes.

She came to herself with a start when James suddenly appeared at her side. Roderick was with him. Lily was leading Dora away and clucking like an angry hen.

James said, "What happened, Faith? What did the girl say to you?" When she did not reply, he squeezed her hand to get her attention. "What did Dora Winslet say to you?" he repeated.

"She said that," she blinked slowly, "she said that everyone thinks that I killed Robert. She said that he loved her and that I was jealous." She shook her head. "I think she truly believes it."

"Don't think about it now. We'll talk about it later. Roderick, take Faith to our aunt. And tell Aunt Mariah it's time to go."

"Where will you be?"

"I want a word with Miss Winslet, and I want to make sure that she gets home safely. Gather our little group and meet me outside."

Faith felt herself coloring as she and Roderick began to make their way out of the dining room. The guarded stares, the whispers, the backs that were suddenly turned on her made her writhe with mortification. It was only when Roderick whispered in her ear to keep her chin up that she managed to give the appearance of a woman with nothing to hide.

Only one person did not clear a path for them: Jayne Coltrane. Her eyes were hard; her smile verged on gleeful. "Well, well," she said, "are you still amused, Miss McBride? Are you still laughing up your sleeve at some private joke? It would seem that the joke is on you."

Though her voice was shaking, Faith forced herself to speak. "Murder is not a laughing matter, Miss Coltrane, and especially not the murder of a friend. Robert Danvers was my friend. Now, if you will excuse, me, I want to express my condolences to the family before I leave."

Jayne Coltrane was not finished yet. "That tragic demeanor fools no one," she began and got no further.

Roderick moved closer to Faith, putting himself squarely in front of the irate woman. What he might have done next was not put to the test, for Jayne Coltrane's wrist was suddenly grasped by the lady at her side, Sophie Hughes.

"I think," said Mrs. Hughes in an arctic voice, "that you have been making too free with the wine, Jayne."

Miss Coltrane tried to wrest herself from a grip that was evidently as immovable as a vise. "Sophie—" She winced as the grip tightened.

"My apologies, Miss McBride." Mrs. Hughes's smile was fleeting. Her gaze was fixed on Miss Coltrane. "Come along, Jayne. You're making a spectacle of yourself, and that reflects badly on your friends. If you go on like this, you'll find yourself ostracized."

The words were well-taken, and Jayne Coltrane allowed herself to be led away. Faith breathed in deeply, then slowly exhaled.

Roderick slanted Faith an amused look. "Methinks I heard a threat in Mrs. Hughes's parting shot," he said. "*Ostracized* has a nasty ring to it, doesn't it?"

He was giving her time to come to herself, and Faith was grateful for his thoughtfulness. She mustered a smile. "Just what did you intend to do when you stepped in front of me, knock the woman down?"

"Oh, it wouldn't have come to that." He held up a glass of red wine. "I lifted this from a waiter's tray. One more word out of that harpy would have ended in an unfortunate accident to the lady's gown."

Faith giggled, though it was a nervous giggle. She was excruciatingly aware that she was the focus of the whispers she heard all around her. It was only to be expected. She'd been involved in two frightful scenes, one with Dora Winslet and the other with Jayne Coltrane.

Roderick deposited his undrunk glass of wine on a passing waiter's tray. "Come along, Faith," he said. "His Highness said that I was to take you to Aunt Mariah, and that is what I shall do."

"Since when have you followed James's orders?"

He grimaced. "Since he made mincemeat out of me during our impromptu wrestling match."

Faith inclined her head to get a better look at James's brother. It came to her then that she had begun to warm to this difficult young man over the course of their short acquaintance. He seemed like a younger version of James, except that when James was not present, Roderick's manners were easier, and he smiled more often. If he had a particle of James's ambition, he would go far.

He caught her staring, and his brows rose.

"I was thinking," she said, "that you're more like James than you know."

He put a hand on his heart. "You really know how to wound a fellow, don't you?"

She was gripped by a sudden conviction. "You admire him, don't you?"

Those eloquent brows jiggled. "Who, James?" He sounded incredulous.

She nodded.

"Now, what would make you say such a thing?"

She touched a hand to her head and grinned. "I think I may be psychic."

James returned at that moment. He sounded exasperated. "Your friend, Lily," he said, "wouldn't allow me to say one word to the girl. She bundled her into a hansom, and that was that." He looked at Faith, and his voice gentled. "This has been quite a trial for you, hasn't it? Let's find Aunt Mariah and pay our respects to the family, then we'll be free to go."

Lady Cowdray had the same idea. She was waiting in line ahead of them. That jogged Faith's memory, and she told James about the conversation she'd had with her ladyship that explained why she had held on to the diary for so many years without attempting to have it transcribed.

"I think that shows real character," Faith concluded. "She didn't want to hurt the feelings of her lover's wife."

"Don't get to like her too much," James warned. "No one is in the clear yet."

He was thinking of Dora Winslet.

Chapter 21

✺

On the short drive back to the house, Faith tried to appear as though nothing had happened and, as far as Aunt Mariah was concerned, nothing much had. All Faith had told her was that one of her pupils had taken ill and had to go back to the school.

Sunk in silence, Faith listened with half an ear to the conversation that went on around her. She was thinking that as funerals went, this one would be indelibly stamped on her mind. It equaled any operetta by Gilbert and Sullivan, only Gilbert and Sullivan made her laugh. This melodrama made her shudder.

Something Aunt Mariah said registered, and Faith looked up. "Did you say that Robert's rooms were ransacked?"

Aunt Mariah nodded. "That's what his mother told me. His father went there to clear out his things and found the place in a shambles."

"When was this?"

"The day before yesterday. There was nothing missing

as far as Mr. Danvers could tell, but he sent for the police anyway."

Faith looked at James. He nodded then said, "I heard the story from Alastair Dobbin. According to him, the police seem to think that Robert had something of value the thief wanted, something he hoped to get when he lured Robert to the boathouse. When he didn't get it, he killed Robert and turned his attention to Robert's rooms on Rider Street."

Roderick said, "He always had plenty of money on him, at least whenever I happened to meet him."

"And we all know where that was," James muttered darkly.

Roderick gave him one of his challenging smiles.

Aunt Mariah kept to what most interested her. "Mrs. Danvers did not mention money, but she wouldn't, would she?"

"Why do you say that?" Faith asked.

"It would raise too many questions, such as where did he get it. We all know he didn't get it from his father. Old Danvers is a tight-fisted miser."

Roderick said, "Well, he didn't get it at cards or betting on horses." He looked at James, but this time there was no baiting in his expression. "I know he lost heavily at the gaming tables, but he always paid off his debts."

"Maybe," said Aunt Mariah, "he was selling off the family plate or his mother's jewels."

James and Faith exchanged a quick look. They both had the same thought. Maybe someone was paying him for services rendered.

On arriving home, the first thing Faith did after changing her clothes was check on Margaret. She found her by following the sound of girlish laughter to the yellow parlor. Harriet was with her, and they were huddled over a small table, playing cards. They both looked up at Faith's entrance, and a guilty flush ran under Margaret's skin.

"Feeling better?" Faith asked.

It was only when Faith smiled that Margaret stopped looking guilty. She lifted her shoulders in a tiny shrug. "As you see, I've had a miraculous recovery." They both laughed. "Won't you join us?"

"Yes, do!" Harriet pleaded. "Mama is hopeless at cards."

Faith felt it would be churlish to refuse when she had newly arrived. Besides, her emotions were in turmoil, and the one thing she had discovered about Margaret was that she was a restful, comforting presence.

"Thank you," Faith said, "I would like that," and she drew a chair up to the table.

Harriet began to deal. "I should warn you," she told Faith, "that I play to win, so don't hold back because I'm a child."

The resemblance between Harriet and James when he was intent on getting his own way struck Faith forcibly: a calculating expression about the eyes, unsmiling lips, and the air of a cat ready to pounce.

"I wouldn't dream of it," Faith said sweetly, and she meant it. She'd be damned if she would let this child intimidate her. One Burnett was more than enough.

Margaret did not play, but as the game progressed, she asked Faith about the funeral service. Faith touched on it lightly, mindful of Harriet's tender years. As time passed, Faith found the stiffness in her muscles relaxing. The small talk, Harriet's evident pleasure at having a worthy opponent to play against, the laughter and chuckles were just what she needed to compensate for the ugliness of the hour she had spent in the Danverses' house.

It was Margaret who set the tone, Margaret who steered the conversation away from awkward or painful subjects. She drew Faith out on her life as a teacher at St. Winnifred's, and Faith was sure that she did it deliberately. She looked at Margaret with a new respect.

At fist acquaintance, she'd summed Margaret up as the self-effacing wife of a man who had married beneath him. She was coming to see that Margaret was his superior. Had she not been saddled with a troop of handsome, strongminded relations, Margaret would have shown to better effect. They were all Burnetts, all the same. Only she and Margaret stood in the shadow of these larger-than-life characters.

Thoughts of her own mother tried to intrude, but she pushed them away. Just for a little while, she didn't want to think of the past or the future. She needed all her powers of concentration to beat this beastly little Burnett who, naturally, was winning every hand!

This was how James found them after he'd changed out of his mourning clothes and come looking for Faith. They were unaware of his entrance, so he stayed where he was, just inside the door, reluctant to make his presence known. It seemed a shame to spoil this pretty picture of domesticity, and he wasn't sure of his welcome. No one ever said anything, but a look would come into Margaret's eyes, as though he were an invalid who had to be cozened, and Harriet would either glare or grimace if she didn't get her own way.

As for Faith, she must know that they had a lot to discuss after what they'd learned at Danvers's funeral. Things were beginning to click into place, except for the face of the murderer. They had to talk.

He wished he knew what she was thinking. There was a way to find out. All he need do was try to open his mind to hers. The problem with that was she would be furious if he succeeded. No. They had to talk face-to-face.

She was dealing the cards. Her fingers were as deft and sure as those of an inveterate gambler, but his mind wasn't on gambling. He remembered how those hands had moved over his naked body, bringing him to the peak of pleasure. Better by far, however, was the pleasure he had brought to her. She'd been stunned by the power of her release. What he could not understand was why she was holding him off. They'd found each other again. What did it matter how it had come about?

He swallowed a sigh. He had no time to waste on debating the rights and wrongs of ancient history. He had an errand to run. It was more than an errand. This was important. Faith and that face-to-face talk would have to wait. Perhaps it was better this way. If she knew what he was up to, she'd want to go with him.

Unseen, he turned on his heel and left them.

Sweet Jesus, Faith, I'm drowning out here. Come down and open the door. I know you can hear me. Wake up and open the door.

James's voice. She refused to listen. She didn't like his tone of voice. Besides, she was upset with him. She much preferred her dream. She was with her mother at the top of the Great Pyramid, and Madeline was pointing out all the places of interest they would visit during their stay in Egypt. Mother and daughter. Faith loved the sound of those words.

Her mother smiled into her eyes. She opened her mouth to speak, but it was James's voice Faith heard. *Open the bloody door, Faith, before someone mistakes me for a housebreaker and sends for the police.*

Her eyes flew open. It was only a dream, wasn't it? That scoundrel couldn't invade her mind at will, could he? He was a seer. What in Hades was a seer, anyway?

Open the bloody door!

It wasn't a dream. He really had invaded her mind. Coldly furious, she pushed back the bedcovers and got up. It took her a moment to light the lamp and another moment to don her robe, then she marched out of her room and down the stairs to the front door.

Even had he not invaded her mind, she would have been furious with him. She had not seen him since they'd arrived home from Robert Danvers's funeral. There was so much she'd wanted to talk over with him, but he'd left the house without a word of explanation, only a message passed on by the butler that he would not be home for dinner. She didn't know whether Roderick had returned home, but everyone else had gone to bed, including the servants. What she should do is go back to bed and leave him to his own devices. People should know that there were consequences to their actions.

Lord above! She was beginning to sound like her father.

The first words out of her mouth when she opened the door were, "I suppose you think it's all right to force your way into a person's mind just because you're a seer?"

"I didn't know if it would work, and I don't think it would have if you hadn't been receptive to me."

"Receptive to you?" She had to unclench her teeth. "You spoiled a perfectly wonderful dream." Her next words were equally unsympathetic. "You look like a drowned rat."

"That's because I've been out in the rain for half the night."

The lamp in the vestibule was still burning, and she had a clear view of his face when he stepped over the threshold.

He looked deathly pale, and water dripped from his hat in a steady stream.

"James," she gasped. "What happened to you?"

He tossed his hat on a chair. "I was attacked by house-breakers," he said and grimaced when he tried to take a step. "And no, I didn't report it to the police, because I didn't want to answer any awkward questions."

"Where was this?" Since he was having difficulty walking, she supported him with an arm around his waist.

"I'll tell you when I catch my breath. No, don't hold on to me. You'll only get your own clothes wet as well."

"As though I care about that."

Outwardly, she was composed, but inwardly she was alarmed. Blood smeared his neckcloth, and the flesh around his left eye was swollen.

It was a slow, laborious business, but they finally made it to his bedchamber. She was all for sending for the doctor, but James wouldn't hear of it. "I'm not seriously hurt, just a few scrapes and bruises." He frowned. "What dream?"

"What?"

"You said that I had spoiled a perfectly wonderful dream when I roused you to open the door."

"Well, I wasn't dreaming about you, Mr. Vanity, so don't let it go to your head. If you must know, I was dreaming about Egypt and my mother and her friends."

"Oh." His frown slowly melted. "That reminds me. There was something I meant to tell you. I know who took the group photograph. Coltrane told me that it was Basil Hughes. Seems that dear Larry was always on the wrong side of the camera, and he gave in to his sister's request to have *his* photograph taken for a change."

"Is it important?"

"Not as far as I can see."

She lit the lamp and closed the door. He sat down on the edge of the bed.

"Don't you want to know what I've been up to?"

His wheedling smile had no effect on her. She was still a little angry with him. "After I've taken a look at these scrapes and bruises. Let's get your coat off."

He grumbled; he cursed.

"Stop complaining," she told him. "I thought you'd be glad to have me undress you."

He peered up at her with his good eye. "You're saying that because you think you're safe, but if I thought for one moment that that was a serious offer..." He let his words hang.

She decided to change the subject. "Tell me what happened."

"I thought not. Ah, well."

As he began to speak, she removed his coat and neck-cloth, then opened his shirt. When she spread the edges, her fingers trembled. That's when he stopped speaking.

Their eyes met. "Think of me as Florence Nightingale," she said.

"Florence Nightingale! Old Iron Drawers? Now that is beyond me."

Exasperated, she said, "Enough of this. I want to know where you were and what happened."

A smile spread across his face. "I went out to St. Winnifred's to speak to Dora. And Faith, she gave me your mother's diary."

Dumbfounded, she sank onto the bed beside him. She spoke slowly and carefully as though she might have mistaken his meaning. "You went out to St. Winnifred's to see Dora, and she gave you my mother's diary?"

He nodded. "Roderick has it, but he'll bring it to you tomorrow as soon as he gets back."

"Roderick? Dora?" She shook her head. "Why? How?"

"Think about it, Faith, and I'm sure you'll figure it out. We have a lot to talk over, but first I want to get out of these wet clothes."

There was a dressing room just off his bedchamber. He was gone for only a minute or two, and when he returned he was wearing a maroon dressing robe.

"Well," he said. "Have you figured it out?"

"More or less. Danvers stole the diary, and he gave it to Dora to keep for him because he knew he could trust her. After all, she was head over heels in love with him." Her tone was as corrosive as acid. "I suppose he didn't hand it over to his employer, because he hoped to raise the price?"

"According to Dora, the money from the diary was for their elopement. Unfortunately, Danvers got greedy and paid the price for his greed."

"He wouldn't have eloped with her! She's too young. He was using her!" Now she was sorry that she'd ever felt that she had wronged him.

"I know, but you can't tell Dora that. She won't believe you."

"Poor Dora. Does she know who his partner is?"

"She says not, and I believe her."

"I suppose you terrified her into telling you all you wanted to know?"

In contrast to her heated tone, his was mild. "What would you have had me do? Pat her on the head and tell her that she was a good little girl?" His voice changed color, became harsh. "I told her the truth, that whoever had that diary stood in mortal danger of meeting the same fate as Robert Danvers. And how right I was. Look what happened to me tonight."

He took one of her hands. "Don't make excuses for her, Faith. She deserved a tongue-lashing and a lot more besides. Yes, Danvers engineered it so that she would fall in love with him, but she chose to help him. I think he tried the same tactic on you but gave you up as a lost cause. Dora was your stalker. She watched you all the time. You wouldn't have been aware of her because she was, you might say, part of the scenery."

When she was silent, he went on, "I knew that someone had been through the replies to your advertisement. Who better than Dora to slip into your room and look for them? She admitted that she told Danvers the time and place of your interview with Lady Cowdray. Whether he arranged for the attack on you or whether his employer did hardly matters. They're all guilty."

She breathed deeply as her mind grappled with all he had told her. "Tell me what happened tonight," she said. "Tell me how Roderick comes into it."

He nodded as though she had conceded a point. "After Dora's outburst at the funeral, I knew I had to move quickly. Not many people would have known who she was, and I was hoping that would give her some protection until I'd had a chance to speak to her. But every time I thought of her, the fine hairs on my neck began to rise. I knew time was running out. Someone else at the funeral may have heard her outburst and put two and two together."

Her hand fluttered to her throat. "You mean that Robert would have confided in her, perhaps have told her where the diary was hidden?"

"That's exactly what I mean. I had hoped to speak to you before I left, but—well, I was afraid you would persuade me to take you with me—"

"Of course I would have gone with you!" She jerked her hand out of his clasp. "This was my business! I should have been involved!"

"So I asked Roderick to go with me."

Her brows climbed to her hairline.

He shrugged. "I know we haven't been the best of friends, but he is my brother. He was there. And I'm glad I had the foresight to take him with me." He chuckled. "He's a better fighter than I am. Fearless, too." His voice warmed as he related the sequence of events. "We got there first, so I had my chance to terrorize your little lamb into submission and get the diary. Now, don't glower, Faith. It doesn't suit you. Your friend Lily was there, too, and she was more angry with Dora than I was. I got the diary and gave it to Roderick for safekeeping. Lily and Dora packed a suitcase with a few things, and Roderick spirited them away in a hansom to that new hotel on Regent Street. That was all he was supposed to do, take care of Lily and Dora and the diary, but once they were settled, he came back for me. But I'm getting ahead of myself. With Dora out of the way, I hunkered down in some shrubbery and waited for events to unfold.

"That's when the rain started. Anyway, with this being the holidays, there were few teachers or girls about, and no one wandering around the grounds. It made it easier to spot an intruder."

She was aghast, then livid. "Do you mean to tell me that you had a chance to get out of there without a fight, and you stayed anyway?"

He looked toward the door. "Keep your voice down. Yes, I stayed and with good reason. I wanted to find out if anyone would come for Dora. I wanted to beat the truth out of him and discover who he was working for."

She said tautly, "But that's not how things worked out, is it?"

He gave a rueful grin. "Not exactly. I wasn't expecting two of them."

She snorted. "Some seer you are! So what happened?"

"To cut a long story short, while I was on top of one, the other came at me from behind and cracked my head with something hard. I was stunned but not out of it. That's when Roderick came charging in. The thugs took to their heels. Roderick dropped me off here, then went back to the hotel to watch over Lily and Dora. Tomorrow morning, he's going to escort them by train to Margaret's cousin in Cambridge. They'll be safe there." He allowed her to reflect for a moment then said gently, "Maybe you should think of going with them."

His suggestion earned him a baleful stare. "Maybe I should go with them? What about my mother? Do you think I can forget about her? I don't want strangers to act for me. I can't explain what I feel. All I can tell you is that I'm beginning to think that she didn't die accidentally. It's beginning to make sense." She paused as she tried to recall what Lady Cowdray had told her. "Madeline met someone not long before she died, someone she recognized but who did not recognize her. Shortly after, Madeline died from an overdose of laudanum, and her diary mysteriously wound up in Lady Cowdray's luggage. What did she know that could get her killed? What did she write in her diary that would make someone go to such lengths to get hold of it?" She shook her head. "I'm Madeline's daughter. I won't let this go till I know what truly happened all those years ago. Of course I want to be part of it."

When he sighed, she jumped up and stalked to the window. Below her was the deserted square with its patch of gardens and trees. Gaslight glazed the foliage in pale silver. It looked profoundly peaceful and a far cry from the tumult of her own emotions.

She'd been dreaming about her mother when James broke into her mind. Mother and daughter. She'd liked the sound of those words. But Madeline hadn't been a real mother to her. Her father was the one who had been there for her in sickness and in health, when she was happy and sad. But he had lied to her, and she found that hard to forgive. She could have written to her mother. They could have formed some sort of bond, however tenuous. Her father had taken that away from her.

Maybe it was all wishful thinking on her part. Maybe it was Madeline who hadn't wanted to know the daughter she had left behind. It didn't matter. Right or wrong, she had to know who the enemy was and bring him to justice.

That day would come, according to James, when she found herself in a derelict house with a cantilevered staircase.

"I can't go with Lily and Dora," she said. "I have an appointment with destiny. We're supposed to be together at the end, aren't we?"

No response.

She turned to look at him. He had stretched out on the bed and appeared to have fallen asleep. "James?"

He stirred and put out a hand to her, but his eyes remained closed.

She crossed to him, drew the quilt over him, and put her hand in his.

"I don't want Florence Nightingale," he murmured. "I want you and no one else."

When he tugged on her hand, she sat down on the bed. There were raw scrapes on his knuckles and welts on his face. He looked like a fallen gladiator.

An odd little ache started in the vicinity of her heart and spread out to encompass her whole body. Her knees felt weak, her fingers trembled, and her throat tightened unbearably. This gladiator had fallen in service to her, and his only reward was the sharp edge of her tongue. She should be ashamed of herself.

She sniffed and stretched out beside him. Eyes heavy with sleep, she nestled closer.

She wakened from her dream to discover that she had taken hold of his hands and was pressing kisses to the ragged abrasions on his knuckles. Beneath her fingertips, she could feel his pulse beating erratically. Catching her breath, she tilted her head to look at him and found herself trapped in his wary stare.

"Tell me I'm not dreaming," he said.

It was then that she became aware that at some point during the night she had slipped beneath the quilt, and his rock-hard body was pressed close to hers. "Yes, I mean, no," she answered brilliantly.

The wariness left his eyes. "What are you doing, Faith?"

"Kissing the pain away." This explanation seemed inadequate, so she elaborated. "It's what my father used to do when I scraped my knees as a child."

"No, don't stop. There are scrapes on my face, too. I can feel them. Aren't you going to kiss the pain away?"

"It was a dream."

"We're not dreaming now."

"Obviously not."

"That's all I wanted to hear."

There was no hesitation on his part as he lowered his head and took her lips in a ravishingly sweet kiss, no hesitation as he separated the edges of her robe and took possession of her breasts. He heard the sudden catch in her breathing, felt the quick kick of her heart, but she didn't push him away. Instead, she skimmed her hands over his shoulders and twined her arms around his neck. He kissed her again and again, and the passion he tasted on her lips made him hungry for more.

He was so hard, he wanted to take her there and then. He knew he wouldn't, he shouldn't. It was more than lust that was driving him. He wanted to take her to bed again and again to convince her, in the age-old way of the human race, that she belonged to him.

He tore his lips from hers. She didn't stop him when he stripped her of her nightclothes and tossed them away. He did the same with his own clothes. They came together, bare skin against bare skin, but he wasn't finished yet. He wanted to stroke and pleasure her soft woman's body until she was as ready for him as he was for her.

He rubbed his thumb over the peak of one breast, and her little cry of pleasure made his blood pound. He replaced his thumb with his tongue and lips and sucked strongly. Her back came off the bed, and she gave a little keening cry. When he did it again, she pushed herself free of him.

He was so short of breath that he could hardly get the words out. "Don't tell me you don't want this, because I won't believe you."

"Idiot!" She was as short of breath as he. "I'm here with you because I want to be. You don't have to seduce me or rush me into anything. I won't change my mind." She rested her forehead against his. "I make my own decisions. So shall we start over? But this time, I want to be one of the players."

She was right. He hadn't wanted to give her time to think in case she changed her mind. All this twaddle about taking a woman to bed to convince her that she belonged to him was just that—so much twaddle. She was her own person. She went where she wanted to go.

And that's what tied his stomach in knots.

He had rivals, but they weren't made of flesh and blood. Her head was filled with the glamour and pathos of the mother she had never known, her intrepid mother and her like-minded friends. He didn't know how he could fight it, but he knew he was going to try.

"Fine. Start playing," he said.

She was no longer a novice, and she knew how and where to touch him to make him writhe. But this was more than pleasuring the senses. This was a woman asserting her right to be a full and equal partner in a ritual that was as old as time. She took his breath away.

Slowly, she began a trail of wet kisses from his lips to his groin. He had to grit his teeth against pleasure so intense it was almost a pain. Sweat broke out on his brow when she blew a warm stream of air across his tightly muscled stomach. Her caresses grew bolder, till he could not think beyond a haze of desire that seemed to permeate every pore. Then her fingers found his rigid arousal, and his control shattered. When he tumbled her on the bed and reared over her, she let out a squeal that turned into a laugh. He laughed, too, but their laughter turned to hoarse moans when his fingers slid into the slickness of her sex. Her gasping cries of pleasure made him frantic to take her.

With one swift thrust, he locked his body to hers. She wrapped her arms and legs around him. The crisis came upon them like a lightning storm. Incoherent lovers' words spilled from their lips. At the end, there was no need for words. There was only the driving need to become one.

Later, much later, with his hands linked behind his neck, James smiled up at the ceiling. "That was special," he said. "I mean, it was good for me. Was it good for you?"

She was snuggled against him, eyes closed, and her breath tickled his armpit. "It was wondrous," she said.

He wanted more from her than that. After all, she had invaded his every waking and sleeping moment. He'd long since come to know that she was the only woman for him.

Though he was too faint-hearted, too afraid of rejection to say the words first, he wanted a declaration from her.

"How was it wondrous?" he prompted.

"Mmm? Well, it was like standing at the top of the Great Pyramid and looking out on all sides. It's a humbling experience."

She drifted off to sleep, leaving James to mull over her answer. The Great Pyramid. He wasn't sure that he liked the sound of that.

He turned into her and winced at the sudden pain that shot through his right shoulder. There were other aches and pains that were making themselves felt, all from his encounter with the thugs who had been sent to get the diary from Dora.

He'd made mad, passionate love to Faith and hadn't felt a twinge. That's what came of being totally focused on only one thing. Her power to make him forget pain was awe inspiring.

Another pain shot through him, and he sucked in a breath. Even in sleep, Faith heard him. She patted him as a mother would pat a crying baby and made comforting cooing sounds.

He fell asleep with a smile on his face.

Chapter 22

✴

On the third day after Danvers's funeral, when James came down for breakfast, he found Roderick in the breakfast room. The salvers had been removed from the sideboard, but there was a pot of coffee on the table and the usual complement of crockery and cutlery to go with it. James told the waiting footman that all he wanted that morning was coffee and a small bowl of porridge with cream.

He kept his expression pleasant, because the footman was watching, but he was ready to explode. Roderick was supposed to have returned to London two days ago, but the young jackanapes had taken his own sweet time about it.

As soon as the footman left, Roderick spoke. "You look as though you've been through a mangle. Have you considered putting a beefsteak on that black eye?"

"Thank you. I'll bear that in mind next time we're involved in a free-for-all."

James pulled out a straight-backed chair and gingerly lowered himself onto it. Every muscle in his body felt as though it had petrified. It wouldn't last. As soon as he got moving, the stiffness would go. Roderick, on the other hand, looked as lithe and nimble as an acrobat. There wasn't a scratch on him, though he had been in the thick of the scrimmage, too. It was deflating to discover that he could hardly keep up with this youngster.

"I assume," James said, "that you got Dora and Lily safely away on the Cambridge train?"

Roderick's brows rose at James's harsh tone. "As I wrote to you in my express."

"As you wrote to me!" James refrained from grinding his teeth together with great difficulty. "I expected you to return on the next train out of Cambridge and report to me in person."

"Why? Everything went as planned. I delivered Faith's friends to my cousins. I only stayed on because I met some of my own friends. And I sent the diary home with my express."

"Did it ever occur to you that I would be worried about you?"

Roderick's jaw dropped. "Frankly, no. You've never worried about me before."

"Well, times change!" James roared.

A silence fell. Finally, Roderick reached for the coffee-pot and held it up. "Coffee?" he asked politely.

"Thank you." James watched as Roderick poured coffee into his cup.

Another silence went by. "So, where do we go from here?" Roderick asked. He topped up his own coffee.

"I don't know. It would be helpful if we could decode the diary."

"What do you hope it will tell you?"

"Why Danvers was killed, of course, and who is behind his murder."

James had taken Roderick into his confidence, up to a point. His brother now knew that the diary belonged to Faith's mother and that, since the diary had surfaced, a killer was out to suppress it. What he hadn't told his brother was that he possessed the gift of foresight. He wanted to be taken seriously, not have his sanity called into question.

Roderick said, "I dipped into the diary on the train to pass the time, and it seemed pretty tame stuff to me. The Maynard woman possessed an acid humor, highly satirical really, but there is nothing there worth killing for, not as far as I can see."

James was about to say that people had been killed for less when Roderick's words finally penetrated. "You decoded the diary?" He was astonished. Codes to him were as incomprehensible as the hieroglyphics on the Rosetta Stone. "I'd no idea you were so talented."

Roderick blushed. "It's not that hard a code to crack, except for the last few pages. I could not make head nor tail of those."

"I don't suppose you could. If anyone can decode them, it will be Alex, but he's off on one of his diplomatic missions, and no one knows when he will return."

Roderick shook his head. "Alex won't crack the code, not unless he has the proper tools."

There was a silence, then James said, "Well, don't stop there. Don't keep me in suspense. What tools will Alex need?"

Roderick was obviously relishing this reversal of roles, thought James. He'd lived in the shadow of his elder brother, but now that his elder brother needed his help, old quarrels were forgotten. They were collaborators and, James decided, he liked the feeling.

Elbows on the table, Roderick edged toward James. "The tools are two copies of the exact same edition of a book, one copy for the person who sends the message and the other for the person who receives it. In fact, it's called 'the two book system' and was invented by an Englishman called Scovell during the Spanish Campaign. This is how it works."

He went on to talk of page numbers and columns, all of which was well above James's head. Finally Roderick said, "Questions?"

James tried to look intelligent. "Would you mind repeating the part about how the code works?"

Roderick obliged, and this time the system began to take shape in James's mind. "Two people sending messages to one another," he mused. "Does this mean Madeline was sending a coded message to someone who had the means to decode it?"

"It would seem so."

"It sounds simple, too simple."

"Ah, but that's the beauty of it." Roderick plucked a grape from a bowl of fruit in the center of the table and popped it into his mouth. "Scovell's code was never broken, you know, and that gave the British a tremendous advantage."

"What sort of book are we talking about?"

"It could be anything: a novel, a dictionary, or even a poem. But both parties to the message must use the exact same text."

James was impressed. "How do you know so much about codes?"

Roderick shrugged. "Mathematics: that's what I'm good at. Codes are pure mathematics. I like to play with numbers."

James sat back in his chair. He was thinking that the more he learned about his brother, the more he realized how little he knew him.

Roderick watched him for a moment before interrupting

his thoughts. "I'm good at cards, too, though I know you'll find that hard to believe. I know I misled you, but that was because you always seemed to expect the worst of me, and I couldn't help playing up to you."

James's thoughts chased each other at lightning speed. "What about your gaming debts?"

"There weren't any." Roderick cleared his throat. "Any money I made—and it wasn't much—went to Mother and Harriet. Occasionally, I paid off Father's debts. He isn't good with numbers, unfortunately."

Roderick raised his cup to his lips and gazed at James over the rim. He looked, thought James, like a schoolboy who had been caught out by the headmaster in some heinous mischief.

A schoolmaster! Is that how he appeared to his younger brother? How had that come about? And why hadn't he applied to him, James, to pay off their father's debts?

He was sunk in thought when Roderick cleared his throat again. "James?"

"Yes?"

"Do you know what text Faith's mother used?"

"No, but Faith may know." James scraped back his chair. "I'll go and ask."

"She's not here. They all went off together: Faith, Aunt Mariah, Harriet, and my mother."

"What?" James's cup rattled as he put it down.

Roderick frowned. "I thought you knew, or I would have told you right away. It was arranged days ago. They're having luncheon at Verry's on Regent Street, then they're going on to Burlington House to take in an exhibition of watercolors. After that, I think they're going to do a little shopping in the Burlington Arcade."

James looked at the clock. It was well past noon. He'd overslept, but it had never occurred to him that there was need for haste. He'd taken it for granted that Faith wouldn't go anywhere without discussing it with him first.

Roderick seemed to grasp his unease. "Do you think those louts whom we fought off will try to harm her?"

"I don't know."

"But why would they? It's the diary they want, and she isn't likely to have it on her. If they do anything, they'll come here."

"You're probably right." James braced his hands on the table and heaved himself to his feet. "All the same, I'd feel easier if I were there, you know, just in case."

"For the love of God!" Roderick got up as well. "You're in no fit state to fight your way out of a soap bubble. I'll go. You'd better alert the servants to keep a close guard on the house."

He strode for the door.

"Roddy!" James called out.

"Yes?"

"Thank you. For everything."

"Don't mention it."

It was the customary response, a mark of civility that signified nothing. On this occasion, however, Roderick's shy smile and unguarded expression drove another nail into James's already overburdened conscience. Why had he never made the attempt to get to know this boy?

After Roderick left, the porridge arrived, but James did not pick up his spoon right away. He was thinking of Faith, wondering if he ought to go to her. He thought for a moment and decided that he was overreacting. Three days had passed since he'd taken the diary from the Winslet girl. The killer must know that Faith didn't know anything, or he would be in custody right now. Roderick was right. It was the diary the killer wanted.

He dipped his spoon into his bowl and found that his

porridge had the consistency of wet cement. His stomach heaved. Pushing his bowl away, he got up and went in search of Butcher to alert him to the possibility that there were housebreakers in the area, and he should take every precaution to keep them out.

He made straight for Faith's room to get the diary and other personal effects. After that, he retired to his own room and spread everything out on the table in front of the window.

There was little enough to go through. Her father's papers were tied together with a piece of string. He set them aside. What he was left with was the diary, the replies to Faith's advertisement, the photograph of her mother, and the group photograph taken in the courtyard of the Grand Hotel. He'd studied them many times. Nothing seemed to point him in any one direction.

He'd discovered that when he kept moving, the stiffness in his joints and limbs became easier to manage. It was when he sat down that he turned into a block of wood. That being the case, he took a few turns around the room, then stopped in front of the long cheval mirror. His own reflection stared back at him, and it was not a pretty sight. The swelling under his eye had subsided, but the purple bruise was running to yellow. He pulled back his lips. At least he still had all his teeth.

"Well, Granny," he said, "where do I go from here?" There was no response, nor did he expect one. "You don't need to give me a name. A face would be helpful." Only his own ravaged face stared back at him. He went back to the table, and the first thing his eyes alighted on was the photograph of Faith's mother. He held it up to the light.

Not for the first time, he thought that the resemblance

between Faith and her mother was uncanny. All the same, he would have known who was who at a glance. He'd met replicas of Madeline Maynard in the boardrooms of commercial and financial institutions, but those were all men who were driven to succeed. He was one of them. The same kind of resolve shone in Madeline's eyes. He did not object to a woman with ambition. The girls who would graduate from St. Winnifred's were a case in point. They would bring in a new era. Alex would applaud. He would get used to it eventually, but what he would never get used to was a selfish wretch who deserted her own daughter without a backward glance.

He thought of Dora Winslet and felt a pang of regret. There was always one bad apple in the barrel. On the other hand, if she learned from her mistakes, she might well turn out to be the first female member of Parliament.

Madeline's diary lay tantalizingly within reach but beyond his powers to decode, not because he hadn't grasped the essentials of Scovell's code, but because he didn't have the text to break it.

He looked at the diary more closely, then brushed his fingers over the leather cover. It was cracked in places, but the gold-leaf lettering denoting the owner was still legible. Madeline Maynard.

He took a step back, his brows beetled in concentration. He'd seen a book very like this in Faith's room at St. Winnifred's when he'd gone through her things. The book was a commentary on Herodotus's histories, and the author was her father. She was very proud of that book.

His aches and pains were forgotten as he made his way to Faith's room once again. He found what he wanted, in plain sight, among the books she kept on her bedside table. Not a twitch or twinge entered his conscience as he returned to his own room, pulled a chair up to his writing table, and set to work.

Within two minutes, he knew that he was on the right track. "Page number, column, words or letters from the top," he muttered in sequence as his fingers traced over first one book then the other. He jotted down each letter as he deciphered it. After twenty minutes, he stopped, exultant over his success. He read the words he'd deciphered back to himself.

Dearest Malcolm,
   If anything happens to me, take a close look at
Basil Hughes. His real name is Arthur Toombs...

Though there was a lot more to decode, he stopped right there. Faith had told him that on Madeline's last night, she'd told Lady Cowdray that she'd recognized or thought she'd recognized an acquaintance. She'd seemed out of sorts.

It had to be Basil Hughes. Everything was coming together.

Toombs. Toombs. The name meant something to him. He got up, crossed to the table where he'd laid out Faith's effects, and picked up the replies to her advertisement. Apart from Lady Cowdray's letter, they were all asking for money.

He found the one he wanted. It was signed by Liza Begg of Greek Street in Soho.

I think my aunt, Mrs. Bertha Toombs, God rest
her soul, once knew Madeline Maynard. If there is
money left to my aunt, it should come to me.

                    Yours sincerely, I'm sure
                    Miss Liza Begg

The hair on the back of his neck was beginning to rise. Basil Hughes was Arthur Toombs. What relation was he to Bertha Toombs?

He cleared the table, returned the articles to Faith's room, then called for a footman to find him a hansom cab to take him to Greek Street.

The exhibition of English watercolors at Burlington House did not hold Harriet's attention for long. She wanted to flit from painting to painting in double quick time so that they could all go shopping next door in the Burlington Arcade.

Faith didn't blame the child for being restless. She was, after all, only eleven. She was becoming restless herself. She kept looking at her watch, hoping it was time it move on. Not that she was particularly interested in the shops in the Burlington Arcade. It was the outing itself that had appealed to her, something to take her mind off the havoc that had blasted her quiet, staid existence to pieces in the last little while.

It wasn't finished yet, James had told her, but his dream was about a derelict house with a cantilevered staircase. There were no derelict houses here nor in the Burlington Arcade. What was there to fear?

Truth to tell, she was rather pleased with herself. She'd been drifting, allowing others—James most of all—to take charge of her life and make decisions for her. It was time she took charge of her own life. This little outing was a step in the right direction.

They'd been staring at the same watercolor for a full five minutes. She stifled a yawn. When Harriet began to mutter under her breath, Faith was struck by a sudden inspiration.

"Why don't I take Harriet to the arcade?" she said. "We can meet there at Madame Digby's after you're finished here."

Harriet clapped her hands. "Then I can choose the material for my flower girl's dress."

Faith held her peace. No good trying to correct Harriet. They all believed what they wanted to believe.

Margaret was reluctant. "Oh, no, Faith, that would not be fair to you. I should be the one to take Harriet out. You stay and enjoy yourself."

"It's no trouble," Faith protested.

Harriet was more vociferous. She wanted Faith, and only Faith would do. The argument was settled by Aunt Mariah.

"You worry too much, Margaret. Leave the child alone. Faith is a teacher. She knows how to manage mischievous children."

Faith reflected on Aunt Mariah's words as they crossed the courtyard into Piccadilly, made a sharp right, and entered the Burlington Arcade. She was wondering how much mischief one small girl could get into in the arcade. There was no traffic to navigate, only strollers like themselves who were admiring the wares in the shop windows.

Dora Winslet suddenly came to mind, prompting Faith to tell Harriet to take her hand.

She could not think of Dora with an easy heart. James was right. What that girl had done was far more serious than mischief-making. She'd conspired with Robert Danvers to steal Madeline's diary. Dora had told him about her appointment with Lady Cowdray without a thought for whom she might be putting in danger. And for what? For love? And though she must know now that Robert had used her for his own ends, she still professed her love for him.

That was not love. That was willful blindness.

The thought brought James to mind. Their irregular situation—or did she mean relationship?—had to be resolved one way or another. She was sure, hoped, that she meant more to him than a casual fling.

Or was that willful blindness on her part?

She was his mission. Her jaw clenched, and her eyes began to heat. The devil she was! It was humiliating to be thought of in those terms. Not only was the man hopeless at writing letters, he was useless at putting words together, except in the throes of making love, and what woman could believe what a man said to her then?

Why wouldn't he say the right words?

Jackass!

Harriet tugged on her hand. "Faith," she said, so softly that Faith had to lower her head to hear, "there's a man following us. No, don't look back. You can see him in the shop windows."

Heart thumping, Faith said, "How can you be sure that he is following us?"

"He stops when we stop and pretends that he is interested in the goods that are displayed. He's looking at dolls. Even I don't look at dolls anymore."

Harriet's anxious eyes stared up at Faith. "Do you think he is a pickpocket?"

To allay Harriet's fears, Faith said, "There's a beadle in this arcade who is trained to help people. We're going to find the beadle and tell him about the man you think is following us."

"What's a beadle?"

"He's a sort of policeman."

Faith told herself that the poor gentleman who was behind them was probably as innocent as a lamb. Besides, the real danger would not come until she entered the derelict house. But she could be hurt. She could be maimed. Isn't that why James was there to rescue her when she went to see Lady Cowdray?

What if James wasn't a seer? What if it was all in his imagination?

She patted her reticule. She had her revolver with her. She wasn't helpless.

They stopped to admire the display of ladies' hats in a milliner's window. The glass reflected the shoppers nearby. As naturally as she could manage, Faith angled her head this way and that to get a better look at the pedestrians. Then she saw him, and her heart skipped a beat. She knew him, but she didn't remember how or where she knew him. He was a well-set-up man, fiftyish, with a powerful physique and austere features that looked to be carved from stone. Most telling of all, however, was the abrasion across one cheek.

She watched as he turned his head in her direction, then he lifted his fingers to touch the brim of his silk top hat. He could be signaling to someone up ahead, someone who had entered the arcade from the Burlington Gardens end.

She mustn't let her imagination run away with her. Supposing he was one of the villains James and Roderick had encountered at St. Winnifred's, how could he have known that she would come here today? Who had told him? How had he found out? From Margaret? Aunt Mariah? One of the maids?

It wasn't a secret. If he'd wanted to find out what engagements she had, it would not be difficult.

When their eyes met in an unwary glance, both looked quickly away. Every nerve in Faith's body tightened unbearably. She took a breath. "Listen to me, Harriet," she said. "I'm going to take you to Madame Digby's so that you can choose the material for your dress."

There were no whoops of delight from Harriet. She seemed to sense Faith's alarm. "Where will you be, Faith?"

"I'm going to find the beadle and tell him about the man

who is following us. No, don't talk. Just listen. We may not have much time. Tell Madame Digby that you are to stay with her until either I or your mother comes to fetch you. Whatever you do, don't leave Madame Digby's."

Harriet's lips quivered. "Faith—"

"No! No argument, no questions. Be a brave girl."

The harshly spoken words silenced Harriet. Faith dared not soften toward the girl. It was one thing to be the target of some demented killer and quite another to involve an innocent child.

"Don't look back, just walk on," she said.

A jumble of thoughts revolved in her mind. She could scream at the top of her lungs and cry "Murder," but she couldn't be sure that anyone would rush to her aid. Most people would freeze or start asking questions and by that time it might be too late. This killer was tenacious. This killer had silenced Robert Danvers and possibly her mother as well. Now he was intent on silencing her. But the man who was gaining on them could not be the principal actor in this drama. He was an underling. The principal had to be a member of her mother's last expedition.

So how did she know the man who was following them? It came to her then. He was Basil Hughes's steward, the man who had collected donations for the next expedition to Egypt.

Her knees were knocking together by the time they arrived at Madame Digby's shop. She was only half aware of the well-dressed patrons who were passing her in the arcade. All her senses were focused on the man who was following them. When they stopped, he stopped.

"Harriet," Faith said, "remember what I told you?"

Harriet nodded.

Faith waited a moment. Ladies were approaching the shop. "Now!" she said in a forceful undertone.

Harriet seemed to understand what was required of her. She inserted herself into the group of ladies as though she were with them, and she disappeared into the shop.

Faith let out a quick breath. She wasn't brave. She wasn't the least bit heroic. Left to herself, she would have run like a hare, but she had Harriet to think of now. The steward could not pursue both her and Harriet, and she was wagering that she was his quarry, not the girl.

Steeling herself to appear natural and unaware of the steward's presence, she strolled down the length of the arcade, all the while her eyes searching for the uniformed beadle or a possible accomplice of the steward. What she couldn't understand was what they meant to do with her. Kill her? Abduct her? Beat her to teach her a lesson? And why were they holding off?

They wanted the diary, she thought bitterly. All this for Madeline's diary, and she still did not know what secrets were hidden in its pages.

She was almost at the end of the arcade when she saw the beadle in his dark uniform and hat trimmed with gold braid. He wouldn't be armed, but she was. The thought made her reach into her reticule and withdraw her revolver. Hiding it in the folds of her coat, she made her way toward him.

He was a young man, and that surprised her. She thought a beadle would be older, more experienced. "Yes, miss," he said, his brows faintly rising. "How may I help you?"

She was shaking so violently she could hardly get the words out. "Officer," she said, and stopped when his gaze flicked momentarily to a point beyond her shoulder before coming to rest on her face again.

Like an animal of the wild, her instincts took over. She brought up the gun, but she was too late. An arm like a vise locked her from behind, and a cloth soaked in a sweetly cloying substance was pressed to her nose and mouth. The revolver slipped from her fingers, and she sagged against the man who was holding her.

"Make way for the lady," she heard the beadle shouting. "Make way."

The smothering cloth was removed from her face, and she was swept into someone's arms.

"The lady has fainted," the beadle cried. "Make way! Make way!"

The last thing she remembered before she lost consciousness was someone hoisting her into a hansom cab.

Chapter 23

"Hell and damnation! I hate this waiting!"

James dragged his fingers through his hair and began to pace. He and Roderick were in his aunt's library in Berkeley Square, waiting for the appointed hour to arrive for the exchange to be made: Faith for Madeline's diary.

After visiting Miss Begg, he'd arrived home to find the house in an uproar. Faith had been abducted by two men in the Burlington Arcade, Harriet told him. She made an excellent witness. Faith had known someone was stalking her and had ordered Harriet to remain with Madame Digby. But Harriet had never been known to meekly follow orders—thank God!—and she'd witnessed the whole thing, so she'd told Roderick when he came racing into the arcade with Aunt Mariah and Margaret at his heels.

The scoundrels had subdued Faith in broad daylight with a rag soaked in ether. James suspected it was ether, because one of the beadles was subdued in the same way before his coat and hat were stripped from him. These villains were not afraid to take risks. They'd left the note, addressed to him, pinned to the beadle's waistcoat. Thankfully, Roderick had had the presence of mind to tear it open and read it, otherwise he might have called in the police.

James picked up the note and scanned the few lines on it. The sum of it was that there would be dire consequences for Faith if the police were called in, and that the exchange would be made at eleven o'clock that night on the north side of Westminster Bridge. *Be there alone. Bring the diary.*

His eyes flicked to Roderick. His brother was frowning in concentration, tracing columns and assiduously writing down letters as he tried to decode Madeline's last message to her husband. It didn't seem important now. Even without the diary, he could prove motive. Miss Begg had given him more than enough for that. But he still could not prove that Basil Hughes had murdered Madeline or Danvers. If it came down to it, he might have to take the law into his own hands. The only thing that mattered now was keeping Faith alive.

Faith, he silently called to her. *Where are you?* He called to her again and again. Ether, he knew, was a powerful narcotic. Was she still suffering its effects, or were they sedating her with something else?

His throat tightened in fear. *Faith! Wake up! Fight it!*

*She came to herself on a moan of pain. Her head was ach*ing; her stomach was heaving. She knew she was going to be sick. Dragging herself up, she blinked rapidly, trying to take in her surroundings. At first, she thought she was dreaming. This wasn't her bright and airy bedroom in Berkeley Square. This was a dank and dusty wine cellar. The only light came from a gas lamp at the top of the rickety stairs, and her bed was no more than a pallet stuffed with straw.

As she tried to rise to her feet, a wave of dizziness swept through her. She waited a moment then tried again. She was clinging to one of the racks when the door at the top of the stairs opened. The man she knew only as the beadle poked his head in, but he did not descend the steps.

"I thought I heard something," he said.

His cheerful tone of voice made her want to spit. "I'm going to be sick," she said. "And I have to use the facilities."

"My, my, we are genteel, ain't we, Your Highness? There's an old lavatory down that way." He pointed to the darkest area of the cellar, a darkness that seemed to Faith to go on forever. "But I can't promise you'll want to drink the water. Come to think of it, I can't promise that there will be any water. This place is due to be demolished." He half turned away and spoke over his shoulder. "Oh, by the way, there is no way out except through this door, so don't get any ideas."

He shut the door with a snap, and she heard the key turn in the lock.

Memories were coming back to her. She'd heard that voice before, when she'd left Lady Cowdray's house in Chalbourne. He was one of the men who had come upon her at the waterfall.

Or maybe she was confused.

Her mind was hazy, her reactions were blunted, and objects were wavering as though she were half blind. How much ether had she inhaled? She was lucky to be alive.

The last thought spurred her to make her feet move. Lurching from one stack of wine bottles to another, she finally reached the far wall. There was no door on the lavatory, but she could just make out a sink and a thronelike water closet. He was wrong about the water. It gushed from the tap but smelled so vile she could not bear to splash it on her face.

Having taken care of her most basic needs, she came out to the light, supported herself by leaning against the wall, and tried to put her thoughts in order. She didn't know why she was here or what they meant to do with her, but it seemed prudent to make herself scarce.

A bubble of panicked laughter caught in her throat. There was no way out except through that locked door, and if she didn't get out soon, she would die of thirst.

Wine. She could drink the wine.

It took her five minutes to discover that every bottle was empty. She should have realized that the people who had lived here were not going to leave anything of value behind. She tried to moisten her lips, but her tongue felt like old leather, and she couldn't summon the spit. Tears of frustration stung her eyes. The angrier she got, the more her head cleared. A plan began to take shape. It wasn't a very good plan, but it was better than doing nothing. She couldn't simply stand there like a tethered goat, waiting for the tiger to pounce.

She reached for an empty wine bottle and carried it, one slow step at a time, to the top of the stairs. After reducing the gaslight to a peep, she set the bottle down on its side on the top stair. Satisfied that everything was in readiness, she descended the stairs, picked up another wine bottle, and threw it with as much strength as she could muster against the stone wall, where it shattered with a gratifying crash. Then she began to scream. She screamed and screamed and screamed.

She heard the thunder of running feet, then the door was flung open. She screamed again. Cursing fluently, her captor started down, lost his balance when he stepped on the wine bottle, then pitched headfirst down the stairs. At the bottom, he made a feeble effort to rise, then collapsed in a heap. Faith did not wait to see more. Hand over hand, she hauled herself up the stairs, flung herself through the doorway, shut the door, and turned the key in the lock.

She took a step back and stared at the door. She'd done it! She'd actually done it! Her success made her heady. But it was momentary. Two men had abducted her. Where was the other one?

Trying to stay alert, she groped her way to a door, pushed through it, and came to a stop. Her abductor had told her that the house was due to be demolished, and it looked as though workmen had already begun the process. There was a cantilevered staircase that lurched alarmingly away from the supporting wall.

A cantilevered staircase. A derelict house. Images were flashing one after another inside her head. She'd been here before. A killer was after her. She had to get away.

The gas lamp flickered and went out. Her eyes flew wildly from one grotesque shape to another. That was all she could see: shapes. All her other senses became acute. She could hear someone breathing. Then she smelled it, the sickly sweet aroma of ether.

Her feet moved the moment before he charged her. She bounded through the front door and with a sob of pure terror flung herself into the cover of darkness.

She did not go very far. Though she could see lights in the distance, the darkness was made all the more eerie by a mist that clung to her face like a flimsy veil. Behind her she could hear the movements of her abductor—the steward, she supposed—who was thrashing at the shrubbery in an effort to flush her out.

He was coming closer.

Biting down on her lip to stifle a whimper, she inched her way forward. The shapes of bushes and trees slowly emerged from the fog. Beneath her feet, gravel crunched, and she knew she was on the approach to the house.

Suddenly, out of the mist loomed the great wrought-iron entrance gates. She sucked in a breath and stared, then cautiously pushed through them.

Then she remembered everything.

James, her mind screamed, *I'm in your nightmare!*

He answered her at once. *Listen to me, Faith. You must tell me where you are.*

She sobbed the words aloud. "I don't know."

The voice in her head was urgent and commanded her attention. *Look around you. Describe what you see.*

She looked around her. *I'm beside the river. I think I see lights winking from boats. There's a street. I'm on a street. And there's a signpost.*

What does it say?

She peered up at the sign. *Belvedere Street.* Her head whipped around when she heard a twig crack. Her pursuer had caught up to her. *Run.*

Faith! The Hugheses' house is on Belvedere Street! Don't go near it. Hide. I'll find you.

No response. "I've lost her."

Roderick looked up from his notes. "What did you say?"

"I said that I know where she is, and there isn't going to be an exchange. I've known from the beginning how it will end."

"How can you possibly know?"

"Because I've lived through this night many times. Get your coat, and make sure you're armed."

"But—but..."

"I'll explain everything on the way to the Hugheses' house."

"But..."

"Move your arse, Roddy! We don't have much time."

* * *

She didn't know how long she had been stumbling from the cover of one tree to another, but she knew she could not go on much longer. Breathing was difficult, there was a stitch in her side, and the mist had penetrated her clothes, making her skin cold and clammy.

At the next clump of dense shrubbery, she crouched down and listened. She could hear his muted steps. He was gaining on her. She let out a whimper of pure animal terror. She had to move. He'd seen her! He was coming for her!

Starting to her feet, she ran like a hare, unmindful of the stitch in her side or the bushes that tore at her clothes and exposed skin. There was no attempt to hide from him now. She could hear him crashing through the shrubbery, but she refused to give up. She was running the race of her life.

Suddenly the trees thinned, and a house, ablaze with lights, loomed in front of her. If she was running like a hare before, now her feet moved like lightning. She was outdistancing him! Sobbing with relief, she gave a last burst of speed and raced across a terrace. Light spilled out from a French door. She burst into the room and fell to her knees. A lady came toward her.

Crouched over, Faith gasped out, "You must help me. There's man chasing me. I think he wants to kill me."

Hardly had she said the words when the man who was chasing her stepped though the French door. He spoke to the other woman.

He, too, was gasping for breath. "I'm sorry, ma'am. She got away from us. If I'd known she was making for here, I would have taken my time."

"No harm done, John. You might say Fate guided her steps."

They both chuckled.

Faith's head jerked up, and she looked into the cold stare of Sophie Hughes. "You!" she whispered, doubting what her eyes and ears were telling her. Mrs. Hughes was her friend.

No one answered her. The steward grabbed her by the shoulders and dumped her unceremoniously in a chair. Faith was too stunned to struggle or protest.

The steward said, "I should go back to the old Briggs place to make sure Roper is all right." He withdrew Faith's revolver from his pocket. "Do you know how to use this?"

"Do I know how to use a revolver?" Mrs. Hughes laughed. "My dear John, one does not travel in Egypt unless one knows how to use a gun. Give it here."

The steward smiled. "Lock the doors," he said, "we don't want any of the servants wandering in."

As he left, Mrs. Hughes locked both doors, but she did not take her eyes off Faith.

Faith's wits were becoming sharper by the minute. *James*, her mind cried out.

Faith! At last. Don't shut me out. Keep your mind open. Let me hear what you're thinking.

I'm with Mrs. Hughes in a room off the terrace. She's the villain, James, and her steward is outside in the grounds. Be careful! She has my gun! They're both armed.

Keep her talking. Delay her. I'm on the Westminster Bridge. Don't give up. I'm inside your mind now, and I'll know every word you say or think.

He knew where she was and knew that Mrs. Hughes was a villain. Hope soared. Keep her talking. Delay her. "What are you going to do with me?"

A faint smile touched the corners of Sophie Hughes's mouth. "We have arranged an exchange: you for Madeline's diary."

"Who is we? You and your husband? Or you and the steward?"

Mrs. Hughes brought up the revolver, and her knuckles showed white as her fingers tightened on it. "My steward and I shall do whatever is necessary to protect my husband."

"*Your* steward?"

"John Arden was my late father's steward and is completely loyal to me."

Sudden comprehension exploded behind Faith's eyes, and she blurted out, "He was the man who was watching me when I went out to meet Alastair in the garden the night of the lecture. He was going to kill me."

Mrs. Hughes gave a titter of laughter. "So, you haven't worked everything out. No. You were quite safe then. You interrupted John when he went back to the boathouse after it was dark to move Danvers's body. I didn't want him found on my property, you see."

Faith said slowly, "Your husband isn't a part of this, is he? You were the one who murdered my mother. Madeline recognized your husband, didn't she? She knew his secret and tried to warn you, but you wouldn't listen. You were afraid that she would reveal his secret in her memoirs, and you couldn't allow it. Yes, that's how it must have been."

You're shutting me out, Faith! You're shutting me out!

She was too caught up in grief and horror to hear James's warning. "You drugged her. She must have suspected that she was drugged, and she hid her diary. It was premeditated. You wanted her to die so that she would be silenced forever. Then you looked for her diary. Is that why her box went missing? Did you steal it, hoping to find her diary in it?"

Sophie Hughes gave a superior smile, but she remained silent.

Goaded, Faith went on, "But the diary wasn't there, was it? All these years, what you must have suffered, not knowing when it would turn up! Well, look at you. You're an old woman before your time. No wonder your husband strays to other women."

The transformation in Mrs. Hughes was dramatic. Her eyes bulged, her lips twisted, baring her teeth, and rage flashed in her eyes. "Basil loves me. He always has, and he always will. I won't let anything or anyone come between us."

Faith could not keep the sneer from her voice. "You sound like a love-struck schoolgirl. Dora Winslet could take lessons from you. That is not love. That's a delusion. If your husband loves you, where is he now?"

The older woman's face was a mask of disdain. "He is a man, Miss McBride. He doesn't give me an account of every minute of every day. He has his clubs to go to."

"And his women? Oh, it's no secret. But you know about them, don't you? Are you sure you're not more afraid of the scandal to yourself than you are of your husband's downfall? You'll be a laughingstock."

The older woman's face flushed an angry red. "My husband is a real man. Those women are mere distractions. They mean nothing to him."

Faith was running out of things to say. "Danvers," she said, with no idea of what she would say next. With a facility that surprised, her, the words flowed naturally. "Is that where your husband met Danvers, at his clubs? Did Danvers owe him money? Is that how you lured him into your game?"

"What an inquisitive person you are!" Mrs. Hughes gave a creditable laugh. "Guilty as charged. If poor Robert had not become greedy, he would be alive today. He deserved to die."

Faith shook her head. "If you could only hear yourself.

He was greedy, so you murdered him? What about me? What are you going to do with me? James won't give you the diary if you kill me. And it's possible that I've decoded the diary. What will you do, then?"

"Why do you think I'm keeping you alive?" Her voice turned vicious. "But once the exchange is made, you'll both die."

The threat cleared Faith's mind as nothing else could. *James?*

Get ready to run, Faith. I'm going to distract her. When I do, run like hell.

The crack of a pistol shot exploded outside on the terrace.

"John!" Mrs. Hughes ran to the French door.

In one heave, Faith was out of the chair and took off in the opposite direction. Her fingers had never moved faster to unlock the door, then she went tearing into the hall. A shot whizzed past her ear and became embedded in the wall ahead. Ducking, weaving from side to side, she bolted up the cantilevered staircase. Servants in nightclothes came out to look down over the banister. Two shots in quick succession had them scurrying for cover.

When she came to the first landing, she hesitated. She didn't know which way to go. The stairs were lit from a chandelier high above, and though the light had been turned down, it was bright enough to give her position away. On her right was a long, dark corridor with a light at the end. Holding her breath, in fear and trembling, she plunged into the sheltering dark.

Faith, where are you?

In a corridor, a long, dark corridor. Oh God, it's just like our nightmare.

Don't panic!

Easy for you to say!

She had to stop to catch her breath and screamed when a vase on a tall pedestal shattered, and fragments of porcelain went flying. Fine dust settled on her hair. Another shot exploded over her head.

James, she's getting closer!

Listen to me, Faith. There's a gallery on the next floor up, don't you remember? It overlooks the room where we heard the lecture. Go to the gallery.

Where will you be?

I'll be waiting for you.

Though she could hear steps behind her, she did not look back. Blind instinct gave her an agility she had not known she possessed. She raced down the corridor and up the next flight of stairs, then came out on the gallery. There was no sight nor sound of James.

She turned back to look along the corridor. A shadowy figure began to close the distance between them, Faith knew it was Mrs. Hughes. She knew this was where it would end. She didn't have the strength to go on. For every inch Mrs. Hughes advanced, she retreated. She wasn't conceding defeat. Her mind was crystal clear. There was no panic. She would disable the other woman or...or...She braced herself as Mrs. Hughes raised the revolver, then her breath caught when a voice spoke out of the darkness: James's voice.

"Mrs. Hughes, you're under arrest for the murder of Madeline Maynard."

Sophie Hughes whirled around and pulled the trigger. Faith heard James gasp as the bullet struck him. She was frozen in shock. Then the Hughes woman turned the gun on Faith. Nothing happened when she pulled the trigger except a click on an empty chamber.

Faith's eyes searched the dark corridor. "James?" she quavered. "I can't see you."

"Give me a moment." His voice sounded strained. "That bullet gave me quite a nick. Just stay where you are. The police should be here at any moment. I sent Roderick to get them. He took Arden with him, trussed like a turkey for safety's sake."

At these words, Mrs. Hughes lunged for Faith with the ferocity of a cornered wildcat. She was pulling her to the banister, shoving her against it, trying to push her over. Faith found herself fighting for her life. She heard James groaning as he dragged himself to his feet, but all her wits and energies were focused on keeping her feet on the ground. She heaved, she bucked, she bit and scratched. The other woman was stronger and heavier. She was lifting Faith off her feet, bending her over the banister. They were both going to go over.

"You'll never publish your mother's memoirs," Mrs. Hughes ground out between clenched teeth. "You'll never disgrace my husband."

James distracted the Hughes woman when he started forward. With a mighty shove, Faith pushed out of those strong arms. For a heart-stopping instant, Sophie Hughes flapped her arms like a bird taking flight, then she slowly toppled into the void. Her bloodcurdling scream could be heard through the whole house.

The next few hours passed in a blur for Faith. Roderick arrived with two policemen who took their statements then let them go. They got James home and sent for the doctor, who proceeded to remove a bullet from his shoulder. The whole house, it seemed, buzzed with people, all crowded into James's bedchamber. Faith couldn't get over the difference in them. They were Burnetts. They didn't show their softer feelings, yet here they were, all ashen-faced and trembling and choking up with tears, and hugging each other as though James was at death's door, when the doctor insisted that his patient wasn't in any danger. She came in for a few hugs, too.

Finally, in sheer frustration, the doctor ordered everyone out. They were all reluctant to leave, but the doctor became a tyrant and insisted he was only thinking of his patient. Before she got to her own door, she was intercepted by Roderick.

"Faith," he said softly, as though he might waken the whole house if he raised his voice, "James has broken the code to the last two pages of your mother's diary."

It took her several seconds to comprehend his meaning. "James broke the code?"

He nodded. In his hands he had her mother's diary and another book that she recognized instantly as her father's commentary on Herodotus.

"Look," he said, "this may not be the right time to explain how it works. You've been through enough for one night. What I really wanted to say is that, with your permission, I'll decode it for you and give you a complete transcript after you've had good night's rest."

Suddenly, sleep was the furthest thing from her mind. "No. That is, I think I should be the one to transcribe my mother's last message. Will you show me how to do it?"

"Of course. I thought that's what you would say."

"Let's go to my room."

His provocative grin that was almost a leer did not offend her. "Faith," he said, "what would James say if he could hear you now?"

It was the first time she had smiled in an age.

Chapter 24

Grand Hotel
Cairo
November 1875

Dearest Malcolm,

*If anything happens to me, take a close look at Basil
Hughes. His real name is Arthur Toombs, and he is
married to Bertha Toombs, who keeps the board-
inghouse on Greek Street where I stay when I'm in
London. I know this because she keeps a wedding
photograph of Hughes-Toombs on her mantelpiece.
He left home about ten years ago and has not been
seen nor heard from since. Poor Bertha thinks he
was murdered by footpads and his body thrown
into the river. I always had my doubts. Missing,
presumed dead, I believe, is how the police put it.
  Imagine my shock when he arrived in Cairo*

a week ago to join Sophie, whom he married in England before the expedition got under way. Sophie is ecstatic. I was taken aback. He has changed his name and has elevated himself from bookkeeper to a successful man of business. I recognized him from his photograph, but he would not have recognized me, since we had never met. I noticed something curious. Mr. Hughes is extremely shy of having his photograph taken. I wonder why.

At first, I was amused. You know me. I don't believe in interfering in the lives of other people. Sophie is old enough and wise enough, I reasoned, to see through someone like the oily Mr. Hughes. I must be softening in my old age. This is our last night in Cairo, and tomorrow we part ways until the next expedition gets under way. I was feeling sentimental, something, and not like myself at all. At any rate, I decided to save Sophie from the mercenary Mr. Hughes. She is a very wealthy widow.

I should have adhered to my philosophy never to interfere in other people's lives. There was a ghastly scene. She accused me of wanting Hughes for myself. I, in turn, told her that if she doesn't go to the police, I will. Bigamy is a criminal offense.

Of course, I would do no such thing. That was just temper on my part, but later, I got to thinking that if she tells Hughes that I know who he is, well, who knows what he might do?

Frankly, I don't think I have anything to fear, but on the odd chance that I'm wrong, I shall hide this notebook in Lady Cowdray's room. I know Elsie will pass it on to you if anything happens to me. Apart from our solicitor, Mr. Anderson, she is the only person who knows of your existence.

You may be wondering why all my notes are in code. Put it down to professional prudence. This is how I earn my living, writing about the people I have met and the places I have visited. Plagiarism exists even among scholars and writers. It happened to me once. Her name is Jayne Coltrane. She still can't see that what she did—publish one of my pieces under her own name—is outright robbery. After that episode, I made my notes in code. Tonight, I'm using our special code. Am I overreacting?

I'm feeling sentimental again, probably the result of the glass or two of champagne I drank before I came upstairs. We are having the usual last-night party before we set off for home tomorrow. I should not have had that second glass of champagne. My brain feels woolly.

I have to say that I have no regrets about the choice I made to follow my own star. I was never cut out to be a wife and mother. You know it, too. I thank you, Malcolm, most sincerely, for honoring my deci-sion. As you are fond of saying, there are conse-quences to the choices we make, and I think I have paid my dues. Yes, I've wondered about the daughter I left behind, and wonder whether she takes after her mother. I've kept to our bargain. You wanted a clean break, and I think it was for the best. I have never once tried to see our daughter or correspond with her.

I should go downstairs and make my peace with Sophie. I still treasure your commentary on Herodo-tus. I have visited many of the places he mentions in his histories. That was the destiny I chose. I hope you have been as happy with your choice.

Madeline

Faith put her pen down, closed her father's commentary on Herodotus, and sat back in her chair. She had spent the last few hours transcribing her mother's diary, and she drooped with fatigue. Everyone was in bed, and the only sounds she could hear were the ticking of the clock and the muted hiss of the gas lamp.

The substance of her mother's message answered many of the questions that had troubled James and her. She ached for the senseless waste of a life. But there was more to Faith's grief than this. Disappointment mixed with resentment shimmered through her. Her mother's words drummed inside her head. *A clean break. A bargain. No regrets.* What kind of parents would do that to their child? Her mother had not even mentioned her by name. Faith was more forgiving to her father. He, at least, had tried to make a home for her, but it was all built on lies.

She got up and stretched her cramped limbs. Madeline showed no guilt at deserting her daughter. All she'd done was follow her star. She'd chosen her own destiny. Faith had known that Madeline was no ordinary woman, but she'd secretly hoped that there were extenuating circumstances to account for her mother's exit from her life: an unhappy marriage or a love affair gone wrong. Something. But this cool and hurtful vindication of the choices she had made touched something inside Faith that shriveled and died.

Madeline had never once watched her daughter from afar. That she had never corresponded with her was certainly true. If her parents had communicated at all, it would have been through the solicitor.

She felt disoriented, as though her whole world had been turned upside down. Her life as a teacher at St. Winnifred's now tasted like ashes in her mouth. She'd been proud of those girls and had tried to instill in them a desire to excel in their chosen fields, but not to the detriment of every finer feeling that made them human. Had she ever told them that?

It was fatigue, she told herself, that was making her fractious. She knew that the few references to herself were no more than footnotes. It was the substance that mattered, not a mother's indifference to her only child. She was a grown woman. She would get over it. What she couldn't understand was why it hurt so much.

It would have been harder for her father to get over Madeline. Her intuition told her that he had never stopped loving her mother. Whether he could live with her was a different matter. Single-minded people who were totally focused on following their own destiny thought nothing of breaking a few hearts.

She got up and squared her shoulders. One good thing had come from her mother's diary. She'd learned that she didn't want to be like her. In time, perhaps, she would come to admire her again, but she would not be willfully blind to her faults.

She was on her way to bed when her eye fell on the book she had treasured for as long as she could remember, her father's commentary. On a sudden impulse, she picked it up and flicked through the pages. In many of the margins, he had penciled in notes to draw her attention to items of interest. Blinking back tears, clutching her most precious possession to her bosom, she went to bed and fell asleep almost at once.

"Well," said James, *"your mother's diary certainly fills in many* of the blanks." He carefully placed the pages Faith had given him on the sofa table.

Two days had passed since Sophie Hughes's death, two

days in which James was confined to his bed. It was now late evening, and he and Faith had shut themselves up in the yellow parlor so that they could talk freely without interruption. James was lounging on a sofa, propped up with cushions. Faith had taken one of the upholstered chairs and seemed lost in her own thoughts.

"What did you say?"

He leaned forward and studied her pale face. "Try to put Sophie Hughes out of your mind, Faith. She can't hurt you now."

"I wasn't thinking of Sophie. I was thinking of my mother. That coded message took me hours to work out. I don't know how she managed to get all that down in the short time she had left."

"Practice. She knew the code inside out. Though she makes light of it, I think she must have been very frightened." When Faith's face lost the little color it had, he steered the conversation onto a different path. "I saw the photograph of Arthur Toombs, you know. It's still there on the mantelpiece of the house on Greek Street. I read the name after I'd decoded the first few lines of your mother's diary, and it seemed familiar. The name came up in one of the replies to your advertisement. The woman who wrote to you said that she thought her aunt, Bertha Toombs, had once known your mother."

His words arrested her. "Then why didn't I reply to it?"

He shrugged. "It didn't seem genuine. She was only interested in any money that might have been left to her aunt. As it turns out, the only thing she knew was that a woman named Madeline Maynard had once boarded with her. It was the photograph that mattered, because I knew it was Hughes. He has changed in the intervening years, of course, but he is still recognizable as the man in the photograph. 'Oily,' your mother called him, and he had that look about him even then. 'Ingratiating,' I would call it. No wonder he was shy of the camera."

She said musingly, "I'm surprised he wasn't terrified that his face would be recognized in London."

"No one from his old life moved in his new circles. He took chances, there's no doubt about that. But he was not a murderer."

She swallowed hard. "That was who Madeline feared—Basil Hughes, not Sophie. So much killing, and for what? Basil Hughes was a confidence trickster and a humbug. Sophie knew it, and she did not care." She looked up. "They're all touched by the same brush, aren't they? I mean Sophie, Dora Winslet, and the steward, John Arden? They were willing to do almost anything for the one they loved. I should say 'the one they worshipped.' Sickening, isn't it?"

"Sickening," he agreed. "Even though he's facing the hangman's noose, Arden won't say a word against his mistress."

She looked at him curiously. "Where are you getting your information?"

"From my father. He has made it his business to keep abreast of the case. I've never known him expend so much energy in, well, anything that doesn't involve Drumore. It's not as though one of his sons is facing the hangman's noose."

"Your father? I'm not surprised. When we brought you home looking as if you were at death's door, he went to pieces; they all did." She edged forward in her chair and looked intently into his eyes. "Your family loves you dearly, James. I hope you know how lucky you are."

She could see that she had surprised him, so she pressed on. "Do you know what I think, James? I think your father has too much time on his hands. He's bored.

When there is something worthwhile to do, he rises to the occasion."

He shook his head and smiled indulgently. "My father is never bored when he is in the company of good Scotch whiskey and a pack of cards."

Noting the prim set of her lips, he changed the subject. "He did find out something of interest, though. Your other abductor, the one you so handily disabled in the house that was being demolished—" He paused as he remembered how panicked he'd been when he could not get into her mind to discover where she was, and he clenched his good hand to suppress a tremor.

"What about him?"

"He's singing like a bird. Trouble is, he doesn't know very much. He played only a minor part in things. But he did tell the police that he and John Arden waylaid us after we left Lady Cowdray's place. He was only following orders, he said, and no one was supposed to get hurt."

She snorted. "And what about abducting me? What did he have to say about that?"

"Same thing. He did, however, tell the police how they knew how to find you. It seems that at Danvers's funeral my aunt told Sophie Hughes that you had an appointment with your dressmaker on the day in question to select materials for your trousseau."

Faith sat back in her chair. "I didn't have an appointment with Madame Digby. It was the exhibition that we were going to take in, and yes, do a little window shopping."

"I know. I believe my aunt wanted to surprise you. Something to do with making you a present of your wedding gown."

Faith looked down at her clasped hands.

James shifted his position and winced when pain shot through his shoulder and down his arm. "No, I'm fine," he said quickly when she started to her feet. "The doctor warned me that any sudden movement would hurt like the devil."

She sank back in her chair. After thinking things over, she said, "Does this mean that there is going to be a big trial?"

"I can't say for sure. Arden is pleading guilty to Danvers's murder. That's about all they can prove against him anyway. But we may be called upon to testify. In fact, I'm sure we will."

"I was afraid of that." She shook her head. "All this because Basil Hughes committed one small criminal act. My father used to say that our choices have consequences, but this became a tragedy worthy of Shakespeare." She looked up. "What will happen to Hughes?"

"It's possible that he will be charged with bigamy, but with Sophie dead, the authorities may decide it's not worth the effort. No, the real punishment will come in his pocket. Since he is not married to her, he can't claim a penny from the estate. Everything will go to the nephew."

She said slowly, "You mean to Alastair?"

"Yes, Alastair Dobbin."

Her eyes went wide, and her face was suffused with pleasure. "I'm happy for him. I know how he'll spend it. He'll head up the next expedition to Egypt. He said I should join it."

"The next expedition." He checked himself. It was the name Alastair Dobbin that annoyed him. "Will you join it?"

Their eyes met and held. A moment of silence went by. If a pin had fallen on the carpeted floor, they would have heard it. Finally, Faith cleared her throat. "Perhaps I shall," she said.

"Oh?" Another heartbeat of silence went by. "And what about us?"

"Is there an 'us'?"

"You know damn well there is." His features looked as though they were carved in granite. "We are lovers, Faith. We share dreams—"

"What we share are nightmares," she cut in. "The only reason you're here is because you had a premonition about me."

"A premonition that came true."

"Yes, I know. I shall never forget that I owe my life to you. But you told me yourself that saving me was your mission in life. Well, mission accomplished. You're free to do what you want, as am I."

She felt as though her fate was hanging in the balance, and her breath caught as she waited for his response.

He struggled to his feet. "Stop spouting rubbish," he said, not angry, not amused, more in the tone that one would use with a tiresome child. "I know what you want better than you do."

Stung, she shot back, "You don't know what I want."

"Oh, yes, I do." His lips were turning up. "I'm a wizard, remember?"

Before she could think of a cutting reply, the door burst open, and Roderick came in. He was waving a piece of paper over his head, and words spilled out of him. "This telegram just arrived. James, we're in. Daimler has accepted our, well, *your* investment, and I'm to go to Paris just as soon as I pack my bags."

Faith forgot her quarrel with James. The difference in Roderick startled her. Gone was the mask of the world-weary man of the world and in its place was something far more appealing. "Who is Daimler?" she asked.

"Hasn't James told you? He has developed a self-propelled vehicle that runs on petrol, and I've been accepted by the French firm that he has licensed to make his machines. I'll be working on the technical side of things. This is a dream come true for me."

She looked from one to the other. "A—what kind of vehicle?"

"He means automobiles," said James.

Roderick added, "Automobiles are the thing of the future, Faith, just as trains were in their day. The Americans and French are streets ahead of us here in Britain."

"Really?" She smiled at Roderick and ignored James. "I'm truly pleased for you, Roderick."

James said, "You told me to take an interest in Roderick, and I followed your advice."

Her eyes fairly bored into his. "So your new focus is to be automobiles now, hmmm?"

"Nothing of the sort. Well," James amended, "it would be impossible not to be interested, but I'm not going to get involved."

"Oh, I'll just bet you're not. Just make sure you don't turn Roderick into a replica of yourself. Excuse me, it's time for bed."

When the door closed behind her, Roderick said, "Was it something I said?"

Chapter 25

✴

Her eyelashes lifted, and she came slowly awake. *"Who is* there?" she called out. There was no reply. She rose onto her elbows. "James?" she whispered. She was sure some-one had called her name.

Silence.

Her lids grew heavy, and she sank back against the pillows.

She was in a grove of trees. It was dark, and a fine mist was rising from the warm earth. James was there, running ahead of her. She saw a terrace and light streaming through the French doors.

They were outside the parlor where she had confronted Sophie Hughes.

Get ready to run, Faith. I'm going to distract her. When I do, run like hell.

She knew, then, that James was reliving the night he had saved her. His heart was pumping hard and fast as he raised his revolver and fired into the air. He didn't bother to try the door handle but kicked in the door and charged into the room.

She could feel his panic when he came into the hall and thought he had lost her. When he heard the first shot, he started to run. Two more shots made him as fleet-footed as a deer. He was on the servants' staircase, pounding up the stairs, hoping to get between her and Sophie Hughes. She could hear his breath coming loud and harsh as he pushed himself to the limit, sensed his stark terror at the thought of losing her.

Faith, where are you?

He sagged with relief when she answered. He heard the fourth shot go off then the fifth, and he gritted his teeth. Only one bullet left in the chamber.

Why was he counting shots?

He was in a dark corridor. Ahead of him was the gallery. He could see Faith, but between Faith and him was Mrs. Hughes. She had one shot left. He was afraid to use his own gun in case he hit Faith. Sophie Hughes was raising her revolver. She couldn't miss Faith at that distance. He had to do something. Only one bullet left. He started to run.

Come on, woman, aim your gun at me. "Mrs. Hughes, you're under arrest for the murder of Madeline Maynard."

"No . . . !" Faith's scream came out a moan.

The bullet hit him with the force of an exploding artillery shell. His revolver skittered away, and he sank to the floor. He heard the click of the hammer on the empty chamber. Sophie Hughes had wasted her last shot on him. Faith was safe.

A new terror confronted him. The Hughes woman was trying to force Faith over the banister. In a haze of pain and sheer animal ferocity, he dragged himself to his feet and started forward. The only thing that made him move was the fierceness of his emotions. If he stopped now, he would be utterly helpless, and Faith would die. He knew what he had to do. As he came on, he roared the ancient Burnett battle cry.

A battle cry? Faith was frozen. This was something new. This was not how the dream should end. What did James think he was doing? A wave of panic swept through her.

She had to stop him.

"Wake up, James! Wake up!" She said the words over and over. "Wake up!"

The scene on the gallery faded, and she came awake on a cry. Pushing out of bed, she grabbed for her robe and went tearing out of her room, along the corridor to James's room.

The lamp was lit, and he was sitting on the edge of his bed, his head cupped in his hands. He looked up at her entrance.

"I'm all right," he said. "Faith, it was only a dream."

When she crossed to him, he got to his feet. Still disoriented, she spread her fingers over his chest. Beneath the fine lawn nightshirt, his flesh was warm. She could feel the steady beat of his heart.

She closed her eyes and let out a shivery breath.

Then she pinched him, hard, on his good shoulder.

"Hell and damnation, woman!" He groaned and rubbed his shoulder. "That hurts!"

"How do you think I feel?" Her voice was rising with every word. "You did that deliberately."

He looked faintly guilty. "Did what?"

"The battle cry. I saw what was in your mind. You were going to rush Mrs. Hughes and let your momentum carry you both over the banister."

He didn't deny it. "I wouldn't have hit the marble floor. That's the nature of dreams. We always waken before something really bad happens."

She spoke through her teeth. "That's not what you once

told me. You said that many people die in their sleep, and there was no accounting for it."

He scratched his head. "Did I?"

He captured her in his arms and pulled her down to sit beside him on the bed. "Why are you so angry? When you rushed in here, you looked as though you were ready to fall into my arms. Now you want to beat me. Why?"

She saw the laughter in his eyes, and that made her tip up her chin. "You're the seer," she said, "you tell me."

He dropped a kiss on her jutting chin. "Fine, I will. I think you're in love with me. That's why you're so angry."

"What?" she choked out.

"You're in love with me."

She almost scowled. She almost fell into the familiar pattern of taking refuge in an air of injury. For so many years, she'd thought that he had abandoned her. Though she'd come to know it wasn't true, the old hurt had become second nature to her. But no longer. The dream tonight had been an awakening. She was no seer, but she had experienced every emotion as he experienced it, and just remembering how he'd felt made her catch her breath. If that was not love, she did not know what love was.

It came to her in a flash: James and her mother. She'd told him that he and Madeline had much in common. It wasn't true. Madeline did not know what love was. She'd read her diary. There had been plenty of lovers, but no one had ever touched her heart. She and her father could attest to that. Poor Madeline. She never knew what she had lost.

James wasn't going to go the way of Madeline, not if she had anything to do with it. He had her, he had his family and his cousins. She didn't expect him to dote on them, but a little interest and encouragement wouldn't come amiss. He might be surprised at the result.

"Cat got your tongue, Faith?" he teased.

"I used to think," she said, "that Penelope was pitiful, spinning and weaving all those years while her husband was off adventuring. I used to think that when he came through the door, she should have seized the nearest bow and shot an arrow through his black heart."

He looked baffled. "Penelope?"

"And Odysseus."

"Ah. The Greek legend. But now you think—what?"

"I feel sorry for Odysseus. All those years adventuring—for what? He never knew what he had lost." She looked directly into his eyes. "When we are married," she said, and almost laughed at the way his jaw sagged, "I'm not going to be like stay-at-home Penelope. I don't mean I'm going to follow you from pillar to post like a piece of lost luggage. It works both ways. Where you go, I go, and where I go, you follow."

He was laughing when he draped an arm around her shoulders. "Is this a proposal, Miss McBride?"

"That depends on how much adventuring you intend to do."

"Very little. In fact, I don't want to go anywhere. My business seems to run itself. I'm ready for something different." He frowned. "What are you thinking? And don't try to look innocent. A look comes into your eyes when you're plotting something."

"I don't plot! I make plans. If you must know, I was thinking of your father. He doesn't have enough to do. You have your trains, Roderick has those motorized thingies, and Margaret would be content if your father was content. She loves him very much, you know. You should do something for him, James."

"Such as, for instance?"

"Such as help him to restore Drumore Castle to its former glory. That's his main interest in life, isn't it?"

James was aghast. "Do you know how much money it would take to restore a crumbling castle?"

She answered him coolly. "You're the financier. You know how to make things happen. I'm sure if you put your mind to it, you'll find a solution."

His stare was almost a glare. By degrees, it melted. He leaned toward her and nipped her shoulder. "What about me? I told you that I'm ready for something different."

"Such as?" She was smiling, because she knew well enough what he was ready for. His mouth was warm as it brushed over her cheeks and hovered just above hers.

"A sorceress would do," he said. "You know, someone like you who can share my dreams. It would save us a lot of misunderstanding. I've never been good with words. That wouldn't matter to a sorceress. You'd always know what I was thinking and feeling and vice versa."

She made a face. "Oh, no, you're not going to cheat me of the words. And you're not going to read my thoughts whenever the fancy takes you. I forbid it! Everyone is entitled to a little privacy." She framed his face with both hands. "We'll use words. It's easy. Trust me. Repeat after me," she looked earnestly into his eyes, "I . . . love . . . you."

He kissed her throat. "I love you, love you, love you," he whispered fiercely, then his lips found hers.

THE *ABERDEEN JOURNAL*, AUGUST 29, 1885

James Burnett, heir to the Laird of Drumore, was married at Drumore Parish Church on Friday to Miss Faith McBride with the Reverend Peter McEcheran officiating. The bride wore white satin with a Burnett tartan sash, and in her hair, the traditional sprig of Burnett holly leaves. Miss McBride is the daughter of the late Professor McBride of Oxford and his wife, Madeline Maynard.

The guests represented many of the leading families of Grampian and the east coast of Scotland, among them the Burnetts of Crathes, the McEwans of Banff, the Hepburns of Feughside, and the Gordons of Aberdeen. Also present were the locals for miles around who had come to witness the marriage of their favorite son.

The happy couple will spend the next few months on an extended honeymoon, touring Egypt and Greece before taking up temporary residence in Paris, where the groom's younger brother is employed designing and testing the Daimler motorized automobile.

The laird intimated that his own traveling days are over, and he intends to renovate and refurbish the castle with a view to letting it to interested parties, most likely Americans, who have strong ties to Scotland. His own family will continue to live in the castle in their private apartments. He also graciously intimated that visitors to the castle will always be welcome and may call on him to show them around this historic building that played such a significant part in Scottish history.

The reception was held in the castle. When it came to the groom's speech, he ended it by asking everyone to rise and toast his maternal grandmother, the late Lady Valeria McEcheran, who, he avowed, was the matchmaker who had brought him and his bride together. This confidence was met by thunderous applause from the inhabitants of the local village. Shouts of "To the Witch of Drumore" made those ancient stone walls reverberate like thunder. The question that was on everyone's lips when the shouting had died away was, "Who is Lady Valeria's successor?"

So far, no one has come forward to claim the title.

ABOUT THE AUTHOR

Elizabeth Thornton was born and educated in Scotland and now lives in Canada. Ms. Thornton has been nominated for and received numerous awards and is a seven-time Romance Writers of America RITA finalist. When not writing, her hobbies include reading, watching old movies, traveling to the United Kingdom for research, and enjoying her family and grandchildren. For photographs of the settings of *The Runaway McBride*, and for information on the McBride contest, visit Elizabeth on her website at www.elizabeththornton.com.

*Enter the rich world of
historical romance
with Berkley Books.*

Lynn Kurland

Patricia Potter

Betina Krahn

Jodi Thomas

Anne Gracie

Love is timeless.
penguin.com